The Major's Faux Fiancée

ERICA RIDLEY

Four left for war…
Only three made it home.

Chapter One

February 1816
London, England

Despite the icy wind pelting the windows with snow, hot rivulets of sweat dripped from Major Bartholomew Blackpool's skin.

He was facedown in the center of his town house parlor, the muscles of his upper arms trembling as he pushed his prone body up from the faded Oriental rug again and again. As he did every morning. Balancing on the toes of just one foot.

Not that Bartholomew had much choice. Half his right leg was missing.

He'd lost the limb—and everything else he'd ever cared about—seven long months ago, at the Battle of Waterloo. His pride. His twin brother. His very identity. All gone, in the space of a few seconds.

Bartholomew gritted his teeth and increased his pace. He couldn't replace his brother or his missing leg, but he wasn't going to sit around weeping about it. He'd lived through the pain thus far. He could survive a great deal more.

A loose floorboard squeaked in the corridor. Someone was approaching the parlor.

With a muttered curse, Bartholomew flung himself off the rug and behind the pianoforte. He snatched up his discarded prosthesis and barely got the wretched thing secured before the parlor door slowly creaked open.

The fury in Bartholomew's tone could have melted iron as he hoisted himself up from the floor to scowl at his butler.

"What the devil is so important that you would disrupt me when I have expressly forbidden all interruptions?"

Only the slightest twitch of his nose betrayed Crabtree's affront at this rebuke. Impassive, he strode into the parlor bearing the morning missives on a burnished silver platter, just as he'd done every single day of his seven years in Bartholomew's employ.

Every day until his master left for war, that was. Upon returning home, Bartholomew had requested all incoming correspondence be delivered directly to the closest fireplace.

"Who put you up to this?" he demanded, although there could really only be one culprit. "Fitz, don't you dare hide around the corner like a coward. If you've stones enough to order Crabtree about, you've stones enough to bring me your complaints in person."

Silence reigned for a few moments before Bartholomew's thin, excitable valet appeared in the doorway, wringing his pale hands and casting beseeching looks at the ever-stoic Crabtree.

Bartholomew let out a slow breath. This was his own folly. If he had been less vain and self-important when he left for war, he would not continue to pay his sought-after valet's exorbitant fees, just to keep Fitz out of the clutches of the two-legged dandies.

And if Bartholomew hadn't been the most shameless braggadocio, the most infamous rake, the most imitated Corinthian—Fitz might not still be here, hoping against hope that someday, he might once again fluff and pluck and adorn his master back into his rightful place as the most celebrated pink of the *ton*.

Foolishness, of course. Without two legs, a man couldn't ride, box, waltz, or whisk pretty young ladies into shadowy corners. Nor did he wish to. Not anymore. Without his twin, Bartholomew couldn't even smile, much less face the judgmental countenances of his peers.

What was life now, but solitude and phantom pains and locking himself in his chambers whilst he attended to his own toilette? He could no longer stand for his valet to glimpse what had become of the once-perfect body he had been so arrogantly proud of. It was nothing, that's what it was. 'Twas pride that kept him from allowing any help. And it was pride that kept him from letting Fitz go.

Or allowing anyone to see him, now that he was less than perfect.

"Whatever those missives are, you know what you can do with them." Bartholomew wiped the sweat from his face with his towel. When he glanced back up, neither of his servants had moved. "If you need suggestions on where to put those letters, you might start with your—"

"'Tis the Season," Fitz blurted.

Bartholomew shook his head. "Twelfth night is long past. It's February."

"Not *that* season, sir." Fitz looked horrified. "The Season that matters. The *London* Season. It's here. You're here. All we have to do is—"

"I said no."

"You should be out in Society. You were *made* for Society."

Bartholomew snorted and gestured at the awkward wooden prosthesis strapped to his right knee. "With this leg, Fitz? What would be the point?"

"Not every moment must be spent dancing."

"Or sparring in Gentleman Jackson's, I suppose, or riding hell for leather through St. James Square, or hiking to remote follies, or sweeping ladies off their feet?" Bartholomew tossed his towel over his shoulder.

"You don't have to *literally* sweep them off their feet," Fitz said earnestly, his thin hands wringing without cease. "You could use your... your *charm*, sir. Surely you didn't lose that in the war."

"My charm? What I had was good looks, two legs, and plenty of arrogance." Bartholomew crossed his arms. "That was then. This is now. If wooden pegs haven't suddenly become an aphrodisiac to gently bred ladies, I fail to see—"

"You *do* fail to see, sir! Your apparatus is scarcely an eyesore. It's got moving ankle joints and five cunning little toes—"

"*Wooden* toes..."

"—and one cannot even discern it beneath your breeches and stockings and boots. Truly." Fitz took a deep breath and rushed forward, his fingers stretching toward his master's chest. "If you would just let me do something about this *hideous* waistcoat—"

Bartholomew batted away his valet's hands. He glared over Fitz's shoulder at the butler, who hadn't changed position or expression since entering the room. "Crabtree, if you've nothing to say for yourself, could you at least brain Fitz with that silver platter until he recovers a modicum of sense?"

"What about *your* brain?" Fitz put in before Crabtree could respond. "If your charm is rusty, surely your mind is not. Do not discount yourself so easily, sir. You went to Eton and Cambridge, and you were a major in the King's Army. If you would use—"

Bartholomew scoffed. "My brain is irrelevant. The *ton* has never held the least interest in intellectuals. My conversations with men centered on sport, horseflesh, and women, and my conversations with ladies were limited to ballroom gallantry and bedroom whispers. Attempting to force a crippled, but intellectual version of myself upon Society would be a nightmare for all involved. No, thank you."

"But sir—"

"I've no wish to be part of that world anymore, Fitz. Not from a distance, and not as an object of pity." He lifted his chin toward Crabtree's silver tray. "Why do you think I receive so much correspondence? Because no one wishes to *visit*. No one wishes to see me in person. Not with this crippled leg. The *ton* sends letters to make themselves feel better, not because they long for the presence of a broken soldier."

"You did so have an invitation," Fitz stammered. "Last month, for the annual Sheffield Christmastide ball. I saved it."

Bartholomew sighed. "The sister of one of my best friends sent me that invitation."

"You receive many invitations, sir," came Crabtree's

bored voice. "It's simply difficult to respond to them once they've burned to ash. Are you certain you wish the same fate for these?"

"I do." Bartholomew smiled tightly. "'Twould be embarrassing for all parties to have me show up and clomp about their lymewashed floors as they try desperately to think of something to say that doesn't involve my missing leg or my missing brother. Coping with my own grief is hard enough. I bloody sure won't waste my time scribbling platitudes to people I hope never to see again. And I'll be damned if my name pops up in the scandal sheets for stumbling on my prosthesis and falling on my arse in front of all and sundry." He gestured toward the fireplace. "Go on. Toss them in."

"Only once you've verified they're all rubbish." Crabtree lifted the first missive from the pile. "Addington? It certainly *looks* like an invitation."

Bartholomew cut him a flat look.

Crabtree tossed the folded parchment into the flames and squinted at the next. "Grenville? I'm told that family still has unwed daughters."

Bartholomew crossed his arms and turned toward the windows. Snow clung to the panes and whirled past in clouds of white, blocking his view, but anything was better than enduring the ritual of his unwanted correspondence. He refused to read any of it, and his butler refused to destroy a single word without first ensuring he wasn't tossing anything of importance.

"Montgomery... Blaylock... Kingsley..."

Seven months. Bartholomew closed his eyes and let the names fade to silence.

His closest friends had visited when he'd first returned from war. The Duke of Ravenwood. Lord Carlisle. Captain Grey.

Bartholomew hadn't been fitted for a false leg yet, so he'd refused to let them in. He wouldn't let them see him as a bedridden invalid.

Even once he got his expensive prosthesis—a fully articulated contraption designed by James Potts, a true craftsman and a visionary—it had taken months for Bartholomew to accustom himself to the strangeness of its weight, to its lack of feeling and sluggish behavior. But he'd never stopped exercising. Never stopped trying.

His arms, chest, and stomach were in the best shape of his life from all the strengthening exercises. He did his damnedest to ensure there was no muscle loss in his good leg or what was left of the other. But he couldn't run. Couldn't ride. Would have to carry a cane if he ventured out-of-doors in the winter because his articulated wooden miracle couldn't be trusted on snow or ice, even when ensconced in a boot.

Not that he'd be going anywhere. He had alienated all his friends. He wouldn't even be visiting his parents. His mother was too distraught to leave her bedchamber, and the one time Bartholomew's father had visited, he'd barely muttered a single word. Not that it had been necessary. The accusation in his father's eyes had spoken volumes in the brief second he'd gazed down at his one remaining son before turning around and walking away.

Bartholomew had rid the house of all the mirrors the next day. His father couldn't bear to look at him and he couldn't bear to look at himself. He was no longer a whole man.

Worse, he'd let Edmund die.

"Jersey…" Crabtree droned on. "Vaughan…"

Bartholomew spun around, his good leg catching him in time. "What did you say?"

The butler's fingers paused, mere inches from the flames. He lifted the missive from harm's way. "Vaughan, sir. Would you care to peruse this one?"

Bartholomew hesitated, then shook his head. "Hamish Vaughan was our parish vicar when I was a child. He was a kind man, but even the good Lord cannot return what I have lost. Burn it."

Crabtree didn't move. "It says Miss *Daphne* Vaughan, sir. Not Hamish."

Daphne? Red-gold plaits and a sunny smile sprang to Bartholomew's mind. How old was the chit now? Twelve? He hadn't laid eyes on her since he'd left for Eton back in…

His eyes widened as he did the maths. She had to be twenty-one, or near enough. A grown woman. If she'd had a Season, it had been while he was at war. And if her name was still Miss Daphne Vaughan, it must not have been a successful one, although he couldn't imagine why. She'd been too clever for her own good. A pretty child with a heart as big as the sea.

"Give me that." He stalked over and snatched the missive from his butler's fingers.

He ought to toss the letter into the fire with all the others, but... *Daphne*. He smiled at the memories. Laughy Daffy. The girl next door.

She'd been a few years too young to be part of his immediate circle of friends, but that hadn't stopped her from following them around and trying to rope them into charity missions and knitting brigades. Why on earth would she be writing him now?

His smile faded. If this was just another *rotten luck about your amputated leg and dead brother* letter, he would never again stop Crabtree from tossing anything into the fire. He unfolded the parchment and began to read.

> *Dearest Bartholomew,*
>
> *I'm sorry to write you while you've so many troubles of your own, but I don't know to whom else I could turn. My father passed unexpectedly some months back, and my new guardian has no desire for a ward. In fact, he will commit me to an asylum if I do not take a husband forthwith, and has given me a sennight to decide which fate it shall be.*
>
> *He has arranged for the single men of his acquaintance to visit the vicarage and press their suits. I've no doubt that they are just as disreputable as my guardian and I have no wish to become anyone's property. Yet my guardian intends to sign a marriage contract by Saturday. If I do not choose a name, he will do so for me.*
>
> *Do not fear I'm asking you to marry me. I merely hope you might feign an attachment. Once I*

come into my majority, we may quietly cancel the engagement. I shall come into a small bit of money on my next birthday, and will be no burden to anyone from that day forward... if I can avoid asylums and forced marriages until then.

Please, Tolly. Come at once. I am begging you.

I trust no one else.

Daphne

"Sir?" came Fitz's anxious voice.

Bartholomew glanced up from the letter with a frown. "What day is it today? Tuesday?"

"Thursday," Crabtree corrected impassively.

Fitz clapped his hands in excitement. "Why, sir! Do you realize that's the first time you've cared about the day of the week since—"

"Crabtree, summon the landau. Fitz, find a trunk and stuff it with a few days' worth of clothing." Bartholomew tucked the letter into his waistcoat pocket and turned toward the door. "We leave at once."

Chapter Two

Maidstone, Kent

Later that night, a heavy fist crashed against the surprisingly sturdy door to Daphne Vaughan's bedchamber. Her stomach tightened. That fist could only belong to her second cousin and new guardian, Captain Gregory Steele.

He didn't enjoy being called "cousin" or "guardian" or even "captain," however. Since returning from war, the epithet he most frequently responded to was *Blackheart*. Rogue. Renegade. Pirate for hire.

The door rattled in its hinges as Captain Steele's fist rained hell upon it. He was big enough and strong enough to shatter it with one square kick. That he refrained from doing so was even more unsettling.

His boots clipped against the floorboards, indicating his departure from the corridor, but Daphne knew better than to believe he'd decided to give in. Not a pirate. Anyone who spent months at a time at sea had mastered the art of waiting for the right opportunity.

Before becoming a full-blown pirate, he had started his career as a ruthless barrister, then a Royal Navy captain, and then a merciless privateer. His familiarity with the courts meant he knew he couldn't legally force her into a betrothal—but his experience in skirting the law meant he'd have no problem finding a way to make her acquiesce on her own.

Hands trembling, Daphne adjusted her reading spectacles and tried to focus her attention on her correspondence.

There were a dozen loose threads of even more importance than Captain Steele's desire to rid himself of his ward by end of week. There were the miners to think of, and hundreds of weavers, and the squalid conditions in various London rookeries. She couldn't abandon them.

She hoped the choice wasn't taken from her, but she wasn't one to waste tears fretting about things she could not change. Her time was better spent focusing on the things she could.

This was what she'd been born to do. Fight for the less fortunate. It would be easier to accomplish had she been born wealthy, male, and titled, but one did what one could with what one had been given. In her case, the power of words. No one knew who stood on the other end of a quill pen.

Yes, very well, perhaps the daughter of a vicar shouldn't falsely imply she was a reclusive landowner of middle age and deep pockets, but if a wee misrepresentation here and there reduced the occurrence of disease or circumvented injury or saved the lives of innocent children, then it was *precisely* what she should be doing. What anyone with a brain or a heart ought to do.

She dipped her quill in the standish and began to write.

Moments later, another knock sounded upon her door. Not the hamfisted pounding of Captain Steele—he'd stormed off some minutes earlier. This knock belonged to a lighter hand. A *friendly* hand.

"Come in, Esther. 'Tis unlocked."

Which might be proof that Captain Steele wasn't one hundred percent irredeemable. Or that he'd decided to grant Daphne's privacy now, because in another few days she wouldn't have any. Her shoulders tightened. Either she'd become betrothed to a man who refused to let his wife dedicate her life to something so vulgar as charity work… or she'd find herself on an extensive holiday in Bedlam.

Unless—

"You've a visitor," came Esther's rushed whisper from the open doorway. "It's Major Blackpool."

The quill tumbled from Daphne's limp fingers, splattering her careful script with specks of ink. Her breath caught as her pulse galloped wildly. Major Blackpool. She splayed her trembling hands atop her escritoire and pushed to her feet. He'd come. He'd truly come! Her heart sang. For the first time, she dared to let herself feel… *hope*.

"Where is he?"

"In the entranceway. He says he won't take another step until he sees your face."

She tossed her spectacles onto her correspondence. "Then I mustn't leave him waiting."

Daphne slipped from her bedchamber and glanced both ways. No sign of her guardian. The corridor was empty. Captain Steele was undoubtedly interrogating the new arrival.

She ran a hand through her hair and hurried toward the front door.

Chapter Three

Daphne pulled up short the moment she saw Major Blackpool. She couldn't help it. Her limbs had frozen in place. For a moment, she even forgot how to breathe. Her heart was the only part of her that still moved, and it was clamoring loud enough to tumble right out of her chest.

Ten years. That was how long it had been. *Ten years*.

The last time he'd seen her, she'd sported a pinafore and pigtails. And the last time she'd seen him…

There had been two of them.

He and Edmund had been inseparable. Indistinguishable. Always playing tricks and trading places with the other. She'd been one of the few who could tell them apart, although it didn't matter anymore.

Now there was only one.

"Tolly," she breathed.

The corner of his mouth quirked. "Laughy Daffy."

Her heart thundered. His voice was so deep. So… manly. Like the rest of him. She tried not to blush. She couldn't help but drink him in.

He was taller than she remembered. Her heart beat faster. Of course he was taller. She'd been ten or eleven years of age, and he'd been, what? A lad of fifteen, perhaps? Of course he was taller. And older.

The years had been more than kind. His brown hair was longer. Wilder. His crystalline blue eyes now had laugh lines at the edges, although she doubted he'd found much humor recently. His face was more chiseled, more defined. A faint hint of stubble darkened the line of his jaw.

That brief little quirk was already gone from his lips. She missed it.

He didn't look like Tolly, puller of pigtails. He looked like Major Bartholomew Blackpool. Soldier. Survivor.

Everything about him was more than she'd expected. His youthful reediness was gone. Broad shoulders and thick muscles filled out a coat that looked as though it had been tailored for someone less powerful.

She'd heard he'd become a rake and a dandy. His more passionate exploits had graced every scandal sheet in the country. As for his sense of fashion... He could not have appeared more handsome if this were his wedding day.

Despite what must have been an entire day's journey, his cravat was starched perfection. His greatcoat was similarly pristine and devoid of wrinkles. The buckskin of his breeches looked buttery soft and clung to every muscle of his thighs. His Hessians gleamed, as though they had been freshly polished moments before he walked through the door.

She blinked. Hessians. Plural. She'd heard he'd lost a leg in the war trying to save the life of his fallen twin, but as far as she could tell, the boy next door looked nothing short of perfect. No wonder he'd cut a swath through the *ton* as a dashing rake before setting off for war. She doubted a single bosom failed to tremble in his presence.

Heavens. Daphne wouldn't have the slightest trouble feigning a betrothal with him. The difficulty would be pretending she wasn't truly interested. No doubt her flushed cheeks and racing pulse had already given her away.

She forced herself to meet his gaze.

His clear blue eyes were staring at her with a mixture of shock and wonder. As if he, too, was having difficulty reconciling the Daphne in his memory with the Daphne standing before him.

She wished they had weeks, or even a few hours, to sit and discuss everything that had happened since last they'd met. But for this ruse to work, she needed her guardian to believe Bartholomew's suit was sincere. She glanced over her shoulder.

If Captain Steele uncovered her deception, Daphne had no doubt his reaction would be swift and merciless. Instead of a false betrothal with Bartholomew, she'd find herself leg-shackled to one of the would-be suitors in the parlor.

She rushed forward to close the distance between them. She could take no chances. Not with her future, or Bartholomew's. They mustn't look like the strangers they now were.

He took her hand in his and lifted it to his lips as if to kiss it, but paused inches before his mouth touched her fingers.

"Daphne." This time, the corners of his eyes finally crinkled, rendering him devastatingly handsome. "You're…"

Her hand remained in his. He didn't kiss it. Nor did he let her go. He looked… mystified. As if he wasn't certain whether to treat her like a girl or a woman.

Her heart thudded in dismay. What if Captain Steele found them like this? He would never believe they'd had any sort of courtship.

Panic began to crowd out her burgeoning sense of hope. "Stop that. You can't look at me like you've never seen me before."

"I feel like I haven't." As his eyes traveled over her body, every inch of her felt bared to his gaze. "The last time I saw you…"

"—was mere months ago, if anyone asks," she whispered desperately. "You received my letter. You'll play the part?"

He nodded. "If it comes to that."

Her blood ran cold. "What do you mean, if it comes to that? It's *come* to that."

He shook his head. "I'd like to have a chat with the man first. Perhaps all he needs is for a voice of reason to talk some sense into him—"

"He would garrote the voice of reason. He's a *pirate*. It's his way or no way at all."

Bartholomew dropped her hand. "He's a *what?*"

"A pirate. My father's cousin. He was a privateer until abiding by law and ethics became too much for him." She failed to keep the sarcasm from her tone. "During the war, he was known as Captain Gregory Steele, but now he mostly goes by—"

"Blackheart?"

Her mouth fell open. "You *know* him?"

"I know *of* him. A friend of mine hired him to abduct his wife's—it's a long story, really, and not relevant at the moment." He ran a hand through his hair. "Captain Steele has a significant reputation for being ruthless to his enemies and loyal only to the highest bidder. And he's your *guardian?"*

She pursed her lips. "He doesn't wish to be. That's why he wants me married off at the earliest opportunity."

His eyebrows rose. "We should be thankful he didn't throw you over his shoulder and haul you onto his ship."

"He said women are too much bother." She lifted a shoulder. "His misogyny is my saving grace. He wants me gone. To rid himself of me legally, his options are limited. Marriage is the least distasteful."

"To him or to you?" He pinned her with his gaze. "Why *not* get married? Weren't you planning to eventually?"

"I categorically refuse to," Daphne answered flatly. "I've an endless list of goals I mean to accomplish, none of which will be possible if I'm to act like an arm bauble the rest of my life. I cannot be both a wife and a crusader—"

"A *what?"* he choked out.

"—and so spinsterhood it shall be." She stiffened her spine. "I'm simply awaiting the month of March. I'll inherit a small portion on my twenty-first birthday, and will no longer need to be anyone's ward—or wife."

He rubbed his forehead. "Provided you can put off Captain Steele until then."

"Provided I can put off *marriage* until then." She hesitated. "He wants the first banns read this Sunday. As soon as the contract is finalized."

Bartholomew recoiled. "I'm expected to sign a *contract?"*

"You're expected *not* to honor it," she reminded him in a low voice. "It's a lie. Nobody has to know. I certainly won't hold you to it. In five short weeks, I'll be out of your hair and out from under my guardian's thumb. It's distasteful, but my only chance for independence." She lifted her chin. "Will you help me?"

Chapter Four

Would he help her? Bartholomew swallowed. He wasn't at all certain what he'd got himself into. Yet he inclined his head in assent. "Why else would I have come?"

Why else, indeed. He'd hurried to play hero because... Well, because it seemed like it might be his last opportunity to do so. He was no longer in demand. As a rake, as a soldier, as anything.

For a toff with a fake leg, a faux fiancée was the best he could do.

He massaged his temple. When he'd been whole, he hadn't been concerned with being heroic. He'd only wanted to be better than all the other men. Thief of every woman's heart. Perhaps if he hadn't been so damn successful at everything he did, he wouldn't have believed himself invincible.

Believed his twin equally invincible.

Bartholomew could no more have stopped that bullet from entering his brother's chest than he could have redirected the cannon-fire that had pulverized his own leg. He had tried, but he hadn't been able to staunch Edmund's wound or carry him from the battleground. If criminally kindhearted Oliver York hadn't risked his skin to drag Bartholomew to safety, he would have died on the bloody soil right next to his twin.

Every day, he'd wished that was exactly what had happened.

Until today.

"Why else would I have come?" he repeated, more softly this time.

Her answering smile was weak. He wasn't surprised.

The look in Daphne's wide green eyes was one he well recognized: Desperation.

She was fighting her own war. With Captain Steele and the world at large. She'd lost her mother as a child, but her father had always seemed like the young, ruddy-cheeked, sparkly-eyed sort who would live forever.

He knew better now. There was no such thing as forever.

Even Daphne had changed. He could hardly believe she was twice as old as the last time he'd seen her. Twice as beautiful. She might not want a husband, but he was frankly surprised she didn't already have one. She was young and smart. Whole. Happy.

Any man would be lucky to have her.

It was Bartholomew's duty to keep her safe until she found that man. The *right* man. Not some degenerate her privateer guardian had flung up from the sea. She needed to marry a husband she desired. A man who deserved her. But until then...

"Now that I'm here, I'd like a word with your new guardian." He smiled at Daphne and proffered his arm. "Shall we?"

She placed her fingers in the crook of his elbow without the slightest hesitation.

His bravado cracked. If only she knew what a piss-poor hero he made. He'd ruined his life. Broken his parents' hearts. Failed to save his brother.

The people in Bartholomew's orbit never escaped unscathed. If the pirate wanted to fight, it would lead to his own destruction. Bartholomew's expression hardened. So be it.

As long as nothing happened to Daphne. He glanced down at her and smiled.

Her hair was the same red-gold he remembered, but longer and thicker. Despite being coiled to her head in some sort of no-nonsense coif, stray ringlets framed her face like little curls of sunshine.

Most of the freckles had faded from her once-plump apple cheeks, leaving high cheekbones and a roses-and-cream complexion... save for a smudge of ink across the bridge of her nose. Her hair and skin smelled of lilacs. He liked the scent.

He supposed she'd grown taller, but so had he. The top of her head barely crested his shoulders. She'd always been petite, but the scant width of her waist and slenderness of her arms made him wonder if she was getting enough to eat. Was Captain Steele too tightfisted or too ignorant to properly care for a ward?

Or was Daphne still getting lost in her own worlds and forgetting to eat?

His eyes kept straying back to her. Her air and mannerisms were no longer that of a child, but of a grown woman. Her voice was huskier, her stride accented by the swing of the hips.

Ten years could do that. He couldn't believe he'd missed the transformation.

His jaw clenched. If he'd come home once in a while, he might have noticed sooner. *Should* have noticed sooner.

He couldn't even count all the things he wished he'd done differently.

Perhaps, if he'd been less self-centered—if he'd been the *good* twin instead of trying so hard to be the *best*—he'd have a woman like this on his arm for a reason other than a faux betrothal.

He'd have been selected because he was a worthy suitor, not because he was so laughable a choice that it hadn't even crossed her mind to wonder if he already had a paramour.

Perhaps Daphne had assumed he was unattached simply because he'd never *been* attached. Lord knew he'd never tried to cultivate a lasting relationship. The beauty of being a rake was that one wasn't required to call with flowers the next day. After the night was through, he was never expected to do anything at all. That was how he liked it.

At least, that's what gentlemen of a certain background were expected to like.

If being a Corinthian and a rake were half as fulfilling as he'd always pretended they were, maybe he wouldn't have run off to war in search of something more. He'd still have his brother. The love of his family. And his leg.

Daphne hadn't said a word, but she wasn't blind or deaf. Bartholomew couldn't help wincing at the clapping sound his hand-carved foot made every time it snapped back into place. It shamed him. Everything about his misshapen body shamed him. There was no way to hide it.

Daphne paused a few feet from a familiar doorway.

He swung his head to face her. "Your father's office? Captain Steele has taken over your father's study?"

"It is a small home," she replied quietly, shoulders stiff. "There is nowhere else for him to be. The other gentlemen are in the main parlor."

Bartholomew clenched his jaw to keep from responding. There might not be much space, but what there was had belonged to her father. The vicar had only passed recently. Daphne was still in mourning clothes.

"What happened?" he asked, then immediately wished to kick himself. Using his false foot, so it would hurt more. He'd promised himself he wouldn't ask questions, that he would let her grieve and decide whether or not she wished to discuss her loss at her own pace, without any bullish interrogations from—

"Apoplexy," she said softly. "At least, that's what we think. He was upright one minute and prone the next. He never got back up." She shuddered. "'Twas over in moments."

Bartholomew nodded. It sounded dreadful. His heart ached for her.

He wished he had the right words. He knew from experience there weren't any. There was nothing a friend could say, nothing anyone could do. Not when you were praying for an impossible miracle. Time could not be turned back. "I'm sorry."

"I know." She squeezed his arm. "I'm sorry, too. I didn't want to mention…"

"Edmund." Bartholomew's throat dried. She'd been doing the same thing he was. Trying to leave painful subjects alone. Yet they were impossible to ignore. Captain Steele didn't belong in her father's study any more than this blank empty space belonged at Bartholomew's side. Was it as strange for her to see him like this? He wasn't certain Daphne had ever glimpsed either twin without the other. "We're easy to tell apart now. I'm the one with the wooden leg. He's the one who's dead."

Her face jerked up at him, her eyes wide with shock.

"Forgive me," he muttered and glanced away.

He was always saying the wrong thing these days. He couldn't stifle his words, although they weren't funny to him, either. They burst out of his mouth on their own. His jokes were awful because they were true. They were all he had left. A nervous tic, he supposed. Or a subconscious attempt to poke fun at himself before anyone else could beat him to it.

"Well, Miss Vaughan?" came a languid drawl from somewhere within the vicar's study. "Are you going to whisper in the corridor all evening, or are you going to introduce me to our newest guest?"

Bartholomew raised his brows at Daphne. When she nodded, they walked into the study side by side.

A tall, slender man with a scar across his left temple and slight salt-and-pepper in his stubble leaned against the vicar's old desk.

The infamous Captain Steele.

He was more compact than Bartholomew had expected. More lithe. The captain's sleekly muscled frame and all-black ensemble gave the man more an air of a panther than that of a pirate. Yet there could be no doubt as to his identity.

"Blackheart."

The blackguard smiled winningly. "That's 'Captain' to you, I'm afraid. My darling ward refuses to allow 'savage' nicknames in her father's home."

Daphne's fingers tightened around Bartholomew's elbow. She flashed him a tense smile. "This is my guardian, Captain Gregory Steele. Captain Steele, this is the first and only man who ever stole my heart—Major Bartholomew Blackpool."

Captain Steele smiled like a shark that tasted blood. "Well, damn me."

Daphne flinched, but held her tongue… and held fast to Bartholomew's arm.

He didn't take his eyes from the captain.

Steele leaned back against the desk. "Major Bartholomew Blackpool. The King's Army, I presume?"

Bartholomew inclined his head in silence. He had no interest in engaging in idle chitchat.

"I've nothing but respect for men who fought on the front lines," the captain continued. "Me, I did all my fighting from my ship. Took care of things with some well-aimed cannon fire." Another shark smile curved his lips. "Run into any cannon fire abroad?"

Daphne jerked up straight. "Of all the inconsiderate—"

"Shh." Bartholomew hauled her to his side and curled his arm about her waist. Her muscles were tense with anxiety. He raised his cold gaze to the pirate. "Mock my injury all you like. You can't hurt me and you *won't* hurt Daphne."

Steele's eyes widened in injured innocence. "I've no wish to hurt our darling girl. Only to see her happily married. Isn't that what guardians do?"

"*Happily* married," Bartholomew ground out, "means you cannot force her."

"Who's forcing her? I'm just... recommending strongly." Steele shrugged. "As you said, one cannot force a chit into wedlock."

"She said you threatened her with an asylum."

"Oh, yes. I can certainly follow through on that." Captain Steele bared his teeth. "If the lady wishes."

Bartholomew ground his jaw. "You'd commit her on what grounds?"

"On the grounds that she's a raving lunatic."

Daphne stiffened. "I'm nothing of the sort!"

The pirate chuckled. "You believe yourself to be multiple people. Last I checked, that's called 'madness.'"

"I'm Daphne Vaughan and no one else," she said hotly, her hands curling into fists.

Captain Steele leaned back and brandished a handful of letters. "Then explain these."

Her mouth fell open. "You stole my correspondence?"

"I waylaid it temporarily." He flipped through the pile.

"Either you believe yourself to be Mr. Caldwell, Mr. Baker, and Mr. Smith, or you're purposely and fraudulently attempting to bamboozle... Parliament, is it? What do you think, Major Blackpool? Is our girl bound for Bedlam or the Fleet Prison?"

Good Lord. Bartholomew sent her a sharp look.

She flushed and reached for the letters.

Captain Steele held them out of reach. "Right fortunate she is to have me for a guardian and not some upstanding, moral sort of chap who gives a fig about fraud. I've no intention to turn her in. I intend to marry her off."

Bartholomew considered him carefully. "Why bother?"

"Pirates mind ships. They don't chase after wards. I set sail a week from Sunday, and I expect to have the matter settled before I go. The contract will be signed by Saturday night, and the first banns read Sunday morning."

Bartholomew frowned. "You're not staying for the wedding?"

"Yes, yes, it won't be the same without me present. She'll just have to make do. I've an extremely lucrative... project that I cannot reschedule. I'll return in a month's time." Captain Steele smiled cheerfully. "If she's not married when I do, it's off to Bedlam for her."

"You are *heartless*." Daphne's voice shook with rage.

"I am more than fair. I've given you a choice in the matter. If you or your future fiancé make the wrong decision, how are the consequences my fault? You will have chosen your fates."

Bartholomew narrowed his eyes. Although he couldn't deny Steele's ruthlessness, the pirate was no doubt exaggerating his reach. "I suppose you're powerful enough to send the fiancé to Bedlam as well?"

"Newgate," Captain Steele corrected, flashing his teeth. "Sanitarium for her, prison for him."

Daphne sucked in a breath. "You said you wouldn't turn anyone in to the courts!"

"I said I wouldn't do that to *you*, love. Any so-called gentleman who breaks a solemn vow with Blackheart, however, gets prison rot in Newgate or impaled upon my sword. His choice."

Her face went ashen. "You're a monster!"

Steele tipped his hat. "At your service. Until Saturday, that is. Unless you've already chosen? Is your gentleman friend here to make me an offer?"

"We..." The look in her eyes wasn't as confident as before. Bartholomew didn't blame her. The threat of institutionalization was credible. So was the threat of prison. "I'm not certain."

Captain Steele tapped Daphne on the nose. "As your guardian, *I* will exert final approval. Choose wisely, or I shall choose for you."

"I need a moment alone with Major Blackpool," she said tightly.

"Like that, is it? You can have a moment alone with all the gentlemen you wish. Try before you buy, as they say. You're a clever one, all right." He rose from behind the desk and swaggered from the room.

Daphne turned to Bartholomew with tears in her eyes. "This is a disaster."

"That's why I'm here," he said simply.

She shook her head. "I can't let him send you to Newgate for breach of contract."

Nor would he. Bartholomew made his decision. "If I go, he goes, too. Fraud is illegal, but so is coercion into an unwanted marriage. It must be bluster."

"Are you willing to risk the point of his sword on it?"

"I'd like to see him try." He belatedly recalled he was no longer light on his feet. Even a child could beat him at fencing now. "What did he mean about final approval?"

"He doesn't trust my judgment." Her cheeks flushed, but she lifted her chin. "It's my charity work. He says a young lady like me is meant for ballrooms and ices, not playing nursemaid in the rookeries, and he intends to pair me with a man who can keep me in line."

To his chagrin, Bartholomew didn't completely disagree. But it was not his decision. "There is a chance Captain Steele won't *let* me sign a marriage contract?"

She gazed up at him in wonder. "You still wish to?"

Save her from an unwanted betrothal? Yes. Help her to ruin her life? No. "I won't let him send you to prison or Bedlam, but I need to understand what I'm getting myself into."

"Then you'll need to see what I'm fighting for. Why it is of utmost importance that I remain unwed." She scooped up her letters. "Come with me."

Chapter Five

Daphne's heart thumped as she led Bartholomew Blackpool to her bedchamber.

The last time she'd been anywhere near him, she'd been too young to think of boys as anything more than vexing playmates. Ten years later, they were both older and wiser—but there could still be nothing between them. No matter how handsome and heroic he might be.

She needed to continue her charity work. It was all she had left.

When she was a child, she'd thrown herself into charity work to gain her father's approval. It hadn't worked. She never managed to hold his attention at all.

The parishioners, however, appreciated her little kindnesses. They might forget the incident—and her—in a fortnight or two. But first, for a few scant hours, she was important to their lives.

That was the moment that had changed everything. The moment she realized if she couldn't be wanted, she could be *needed*. If not by her father, then by the hundreds of thousands of people throughout England who didn't have food to eat or clothes to wear.

Fear twisted her stomach as they approached her bedchamber door.

What if Bartholomew didn't understand her need to help others? To *matter?* What if he refused to take part in her charade after all?

Now that she'd built her life around charity work, she couldn't imagine doing anything else. Not only would it be selfish to choose marriage over the masses, she wouldn't be able to live with the shame of abandoning so many worthy causes. Men. Women. *Families*.

Dedicating her life to the common good and dedicating her life to the will of a husband were mutually exclusive and irreconcilable. She'd chosen the path that would help the most people. For Bartholomew to risk Newgate to help her, however, she'd have to prove to him it was the *right* path.

Which meant inviting him into her bedchamber. Yet she was terrified to do so.

The wheezing rattle in her too-tight lungs, the appalling tremble in her ice-cold fingers, the fear that flooded her whirling brain until she couldn't even think—*that* was because she dreaded letting him see that her bedchamber was actually her office. Her center of operations. Her biggest, deepest secret. There would be no going back.

She hesitated with her hand on the doorknob.

The documents, correspondence, and figures piled upon her escritoire and papering her walls were how she tracked the many worthy causes lacking a champion, lacking a focus, or lacking results. She applied herself to every one of them. Sending letters. Rifling through ledgers. Recruiting help. Marking progress.

She never threw anything away. One never knew when it might be the key to saving a life. Sometimes it took days to find this precise figure or that specific newspaper reference, but they were all right here within her grasp. Somewhere.

She took a deep breath and opened the door.

To the untrained eye, well... Captain Steele was right. She no doubt looked positively mad.

To his credit, Bartholomew refrained from pointing out the similarity.

"Interesting," was all he said aloud. "And here I thought debutantes preferred decorating with pastels and flowers. I burned some letters this very morning that I could've brought to add to your collection."

She cuffed his arm. Some of the tension finally seeped from her shoulders. This was Bartholomew. He would help her, not judge her. Nothing would have to change. Her work could continue.

Her life would matter.

She stepped into the center of the room. "I said I was a crusader. These are my causes. I'm married to every one of them." She traced her fingers along the clippings covering her walls. "Wheat farmers. Weavers. Miners. Workhouses. Orphans. Apothecaries."

"Apothecaries?" His brow creased. "If you're referring to the act prohibiting unlicensed medical practitioners, wasn't that passed last year?"

"Formal qualifications and compulsory apprenticeship are a wonderful first step, but training and methodology is still wildly unpredictable and, in far too many cases, deadly." She paused and tilted her head to study him more closely. "I'm surprised you've heard about it."

"Because I'd been at war, or because you doubted I knew how to read?" he asked dryly. "Something about spending months in bed waiting to see if an amputated leg will heal gives one a new appreciation for passing time with the written word."

She frowned but didn't look away.

A hint of belligerence in his stance indicated he'd expected his words to shock her. Why should they? Did he think she'd cringe at the forthright way he'd said "amputated leg?" She arched a brow. If he had any concept of the atrocities that crossed her escritoire daily, he wouldn't think her as missish as that.

Or did he fear that his reputation as a rake and a dandy had given her the idea that there was nothing between his ears but waistcoats and women? Daphne would be the last woman to make assumptions about another person based solely on the persona they portrayed to the public. She was a vicar's daughter... and perhaps England's most clandestine political agitator on behalf of the poor.

She placed her correspondence onto her desk next to her reading spectacles. "This is why I must remain unwed. Every minute attending routs or planning dinner parties is a wasted minute these desperate people can ill afford to lose."

"Perhaps it's not as bleak as that. There must be *some* gentleman out there who wouldn't expect you to plan or attend society functions."

"Must there?" She couldn't help but scoff. "Some gothic recluse who lives in a rundown castle in the moors? Some palsied invalid who wants me to hold his hand until he leaves this earth?"

His eyebrows rose. "Are invalids and recluses any less worthy than other people?"

"Of course not," she said softly. "But a husband is *fewer* than 'other people.' I cannot devote myself to one individual, no matter how worthy, if it means abandoning ten thousand more. No one voice or single letter causes change. It needs many voices. Many letters. By remaining unencumbered, I can help make a difference." She tilted her head and studied him. "You're the last person I would have expected to make a case for marriage."

A startled laugh escaped his throat. "God's teeth, have I? 'Twas not my intention. I have never wished to wed, nor shall I, so it would be the height of hypocrisy to demand anyone else get leg-shackled. Your vehemence surprised me, that's all. I wanted to make certain you've thought this through."

She turned away so he wouldn't see her clench her jaw. She did nothing *but* think things through. Why did he imagine she was choosing charity work over marriage and family?

Of course *he* couldn't imagine abandoning the world of routs and soirées willingly. He'd been king of the ballrooms and the prince of every young lady's fantasies.

In fact, that was the primary reason she'd chosen him for this farce. He would make her a terrible husband, and she would make him a terrible wife. Hades would freeze over before Bartholomew Blackpool would limit himself to any one woman. Much less give up the glittering world where he'd reigned supreme.

Therefore he could be counted upon to dissolve the contract willingly and promptly.

"I *have* thought this through," she said quietly. "My future—England's future—is the only thing I think about. Improving the world we all share is the worthiest goal there is. 'Tis all I do, from the moment I rise to the moment I tumble into bed, exhausted. It's what I *want* to do. Become a housewife is not." Her mouth tightened. "Your 'competition' out in the front parlor? Trust me, they're better off without me. I have no time for anyone if I'm worrying about everyone."

Those were most of her reasons. There was one more. One she was unwilling to admit aloud. The true reason she would never marry.

Fighting for thousands of faceless individuals was so much easier, so much *safer* than allowing someone into her heart.

Everyone she'd ever cared about left her. In the worst ways possible.

Her mother had died in childbirth. An accident, of course, but the catalyst for Daphne's fervor to help others, to improve medical conditions. Her father's father had also been a vicar. Daphne adored her grandparents. They died. Scarlet Fever. Then it was just her and papa, on their own.

She'd thought, *At least I have Papa. At least I'm not alone.*

She was wrong.

Papa had focused on his "sheep." His parish. He'd believed the only virtue came from helping his flock. He'd had little time for his daughter.

Daphne had done her best to do the same, to live up to his standard, but she was young. She'd longed for friends. The closest neighbors were twin boys, too old to be proper playmates. Soon, they too had gone away. It hadn't taken her long to realize her life was fated to be lived alone.

Even her new guardian didn't want her.

She had no doubt she would never have seen Bartholomew again had her circumstances not been so dire. If her father hadn't died. If her guardian hadn't threatened her with an asylum.

If rakish, fashionable Bartholomew Blackpool hadn't got his leg shot off and found himself so bored with his long recovery that he was reduced to reading something so mundane as a newspaper.

For him, this visit was nothing more than a diversion.

For her, it would define the rest of her life.

She turned toward the door. "Come on, then. It's time to meet the others."

Chapter Six

At first, Bartholomew couldn't identify the unsettled edge to his gut, or how the deuce his palms could be clammy during a British winter.

And then it hit him. The most improbable, unlikely, unfathomable of all circumstances had actually come to pass. He was nervous.

Nervous. Him!

He didn't have to wonder if he'd ever felt such a sensation before. He well knew he hadn't. From the mindlessness of youth to the bravado of university days to the swagger of the *haut ton* to the zeal of fighting enemy soldiers—no. Not once had he been nervous.

How could he have? He was always the best. Of course he could climb that tree. Trounce that prefect. Win that game. Race that horse. Steal that kiss. Live through anything.

Even war.

And yet here he was, in the cottage of a deceased vicar of all places, about to be paraded like livestock before a degenerate pirate and a handful of "competition."

'Twas ludicrous that such an insignificant word should bring about uncertainty in a man who had once been a total stranger to fear. He'd never *had* competition; he'd always *been* the competition. And won.

Until he didn't. Until he lost everything that mattered to him, including hope for his own future. Until he was here, in Kent, feigning so much more than a faux betrothal. He was armed with his rakish smile. Had his rapier charm at the ready. His hallmark self-confidence exuding from every pore. His goddamn knee itching like the devil because he wasn't used to so much walking, and... He clenched his jaw in frustration.

Curse his arrogance and curse his pride. Why bother pretending to be whole? Everyone knew what had happened to him. Even if he managed to hide his limp and muffle the clapping noise of the vanguard technology powering his very expensive, very clever, very obviously false leg, they all knew he was no longer the better man. This wouldn't be an easy battle.

Even *with* the young lady's pretend consent as a given, he still had to convince that scoundrel Blackheart. Captain Steele. Their entire charade could be moot even before it began. No doubt Captain Steele had handpicked the other men for a reason.

And Daphne—what was he to do with sweet, big-hearted Daphne?

She couldn't be trusted to remember to eat when she was in her father's home, surrounded by servants who'd known her since birth. Imagine her all alone, in some dismal-but-economical shack, with naught but a maid-of-all-work and mountains of ink and paper. Impossible.

He couldn't fault her the desire to plan her life as she pleased. He certainly had no say in the matter. Nonetheless, the right man *must* exist…

Someone wealthy enough to keep her in style, but not so lofty as to dismiss her concerns for the common people. Someone compassionate enough to help her wage her campaigns, and wise enough not to suggest she end them. Someone whole and handsome whom she would be proud to have at her side. Who could toss their daughter in the air or teach their sons to ride and waltz a scandalous number of sets with his wife at high-flown dinner parties.

Bartholomew had no idea who that paragon might be— *he* certainly held few of the required characteristics—but he had no doubt that someone, somewhere, would make the perfect partner for Daphne. He liked her too much to wish her an unhappy marriage.

If she would not open her eyes, he would have to keep a look out for her. And keep her safe from her guardian's suitors in the meantime.

"Ready?" Daphne whispered as they approached the front parlor. Her guardian was nowhere to be found, but her maid stayed close behind her. Candlelight and male voices spilled from the open door.

The game was afoot. Bartholomew rolled his shoulders back and walked into the fray.

"Blackpool?" came a droll voice from the side of the room. "Do my eyes deceive?"

"Lambley?" he blurted back, as he whirled to greet an old acquaintance.

How the devil had Captain Steele got a *duke* to court a vicar's daughter? More to the point, why on earth should Lambley wish to court anyone?

By all accounts, he'd taken over Bartholomew's role as charming-rake-of-the-*ton* within seconds of his leaving England's shore. And worse. Lambley was the last suitor for an idealistic innocent like Daphne. The duke's masquerade parties were high society's worst-kept secret. She'd end up accompanying him to every soirée in Christendom and having to put up with her husband slipping away behind every curtain.

If Lambley even came up to scratch. He was far more likely in search of an amusing dalliance, not a wife. Bartholomew flexed his fingers. Lambley wasn't a choice. Daphne deserved better.

"Blackpool?" came a disbelieving voice from the other side of the room. "Bartholomew Blackpool?"

He whirled again, and this time came face to face with a nattily dressed gentleman more famous for his predilection for gaming hells than for attending Society events. Bartholomew lifted his brows. The parlor was beginning to feel like a circus, with he and Daphne in the center ring.

"Anthony Fairfax." His smile troubled, Bartholomew inclined his head at the young man.

Fairfax's presence was both more and less surprising than Lambley's. Unlike the duke, Fairfax had grown up near the vicarage. His sister Sarah was about Bartholomew's age, and he'd always considered her a good friend.

She had also been in love with Bartholomew's brother.

She and Edmund had expected to marry the moment he returned from the war Bartholomew had talked him into fighting. The war he hadn't survived.

Edmund hadn't left behind a widow, but rather something even worse.

Sarah was seven months pregnant.

Bartholomew's throat grew tight. Once Society found out, neither she nor her bastard child would be welcome anywhere again. He wished there was something he could do to protect her. And his unborn niece or nephew.

Sarah's brother likely felt the same. Anthony Fairfax's roguish smile and good-natured charm still opened many doors, but his gambling debts grew ever deeper. Despite his good blood and well-connected family, soon he wouldn't be able to show his face anywhere near King Street without a pocketful of banknotes or a loaded pistol in hand.

Or an heiress.

Bartholomew cast a considering glance toward Daphne. He'd taken her at her word when she'd mentioned inheriting a "small portion." Was it possible the sum was more significant than she'd implied? Or had devil-may-care Fairfax sunk to such lows, he was desperate enough to swindle the dowry of a vicar's daughter just to pay a few vowels?

He frowned. Did she even *have* a dowry? Captain Steele certainly hadn't mentioned one.

An insidious thought made Bartholomew rethink the situation. He'd known Lamely and Fairfax for years. Despite their faults, they were good sorts. Couldn't it be true that a well-liked duke and the brother of a good friend might make perfectly acceptable suitors, and it was Bartholomew's bitterness over his less-than-ideal new reality that was causing him to overstate their faults?

"I see you know His Grace, the Duke of Lambley, as well as Mr. Fairfax. Have you met Mr. Whitfield?" Daphne motioned over Bartholomew's shoulder. "Mr. Whitfield, this is Major Blackpool."

"Chauncey Whitfield?" Bartholomew's smile froze as he turned around.

Impossible. Yet there he was. Bartholomew fought a spike of jealousy.

Chauncey Whitfield, the darling of the caricaturists. Tall, handsome, and larger than life, with his twice-broken nose and bashful, bedimpled smile.

After Bartholomew had left for war, Whitfield had become the reigning king of the sparring rings—both legal and illegal. He had endless admirers. He even had a slogan. *Take a chance on Chaunce* could be heard everywhere from underground fighting dens to London ballrooms. Two places Bartholomew could no longer navigate with ease.

He swallowed and inclined his head. "How do you do."

Dimples creased Whitfield's boyish cheeks as he grinned back at Bartholomew. "Never thought I'd meet the legend in the flesh, sir. I'd probably never have beaten your sparring record if you hadn't gone off to war and lost your leg. Lucky break for me."

Anthony Fairfax spun on Whitfield in horror. "How can you *say* that?"

"I'd never be champion otherwise." Whitfield gave a pretend punch to Fairfax's shoulder. "You're a gambler, mate. Think like one. The only reason why a man like you would put money on me instead of Blackpool is because he's no longer fighting. Dem shame, if you ask me. If he still had both legs, I've no doubt the major could—"

"I'm standing right here," Bartholomew gritted out. "I lost my leg, not my ears."

"A gambler, am I?" A slight flush crept up Fairfax's cheeks as he glared at the fighter. "Never you mind what I do with my blunt. I won't be 'taking a chance on Chaunce.' I'd put a monkey on Blackpool drawing your cork any day of the week, even *if* the war left him nothing more than a—"

"I am *right here*," Bartholomew repeated through clenched teeth. "Missing half a limb doesn't make me less of a man."

Except of course it did.

The room fell silent. He waved away their awkward apologies and regretted agreeing to this farce. He'd meant to help Daphne, not parade his new weakness in front of others.

He didn't need four sets of pitying gazes to recognize the truth. He *wasn't* getting invitations to fencing clubs or races or sparring matches. Even his Almack's voucher had been revoked for failure to comply with the dress code.

Bartholomew curled his fingers into fists. He'd like to knock the bleeding heart pity right off of Fairfax's face.

And Lambley's. And Whitfield's.

As for Daphne… his throat stung. Her kindheartedness made her even worse than the others.

In her chambers, she'd looked scared, but determined. In this moment, she also looked infuriatingly compassionate. As if he was worse off than her. He could no longer fool himself for why she'd invited him here. It wasn't just because a man without two feet was unlikely to already have a romantical entanglement.

It was because she, too, considered him less than a man. Devoid of options. Easily managed. No more a captain of his own fate than a lapdog would be.

He *hated* the poor-old-Tolly look in her eyes. Despised the pitying glances the other men weren't even trying to hide. Look at them. The true farce was him believing he'd ever had a chance.

Daphne had called these blighters his "competition." If they would have heard her say so, all three of them would laugh until they hiccupped. Bartholomew wasn't competition to anyone. He curled his fingers into fists and set his jaw.

There was nothing to do about it except prove them wrong. He was still Bartholomew Blackpool. Still a person. Still a man. He didn't need to impress anyone in the ring or before an orchestra to know that his iron will was still intact. He just needed a new goal. To excel at something else. Something that didn't require… feet. Or the crushing weight of sympathetic stares.

He affected his haughtiest posture. "I suggest we move on to other topics." He turned his gaze to the duke. "Lambley, what brings you to Maidstone?"

"Why, the lady, of course." The duke lifted Daphne's fingers to his lips. "Does a man require any other reason to bask in the presence of such beauty?"

"Daphne isn't just beautiful. She's resourceful and clever." The words were out of Bartholomew's mouth before he could pull them back. Devil take it. He'd meant to illustrate the shallow nature of Lambley's compliments, not lower Daphne's worth in the marriage mart. Most gentlemen didn't consider working brains a desirable characteristic in a female.

Not that Daphne should settle for an imbecile who didn't value her for more than her looks. She was different than other women. Passionate. She wasn't afraid to be interesting in her own right. It made her irresistible in a completely different way. He wished they had hours to sit and talk. He wished they were alone.

"Of course she's clever," Lambley said soothingly, casting Daphne soulful glances as he held her fingers to his lips a beat longer than was necessary. "Aren't bluestockings always the most breathtaking?"

A slight blush touched her cheeks.

Bartholomew's smile tightened. Weren't bluestockings always the most... He shook his head. There was no way to respond to blatant flummery like that without inadvertently insulting Daphne.

She *was* beautiful. But there was no possible way that Lambley found bluestockings remotely breathtaking. At least, not any more so than the countless other women that passed through his arms in and out of Society ballrooms and secret masquerades. Lambley would never make an offer.

Then again... Bartholomew's brow creased.

Lambley was in Kent, not London. Why would he be, if he *weren't* interested in Daphne? Why would any of them be there? Daphne was young, pretty, compassionate, and wise enough to keep her more questionable charitable projects a secret. In short: marriageable. Bartholomew had been intrigued from the moment he walked through the door. Which could only mean one thing.

Bloody hell. These men were real beaux. If he turned around and went home without another word, Daphne could be a duchess by springtime. The envy of her peers. Would he truly do her any favors by standing in the way of such a match?

Whitfield glanced at the clock upon the mantle. "I suppose we ought to summon our carriages if we're to make the assembly."

Bartholomew stared at him blankly. "The what?"

Daphne's shoulders slumped. "There's dancing tonight in the Maidstone assembly hall. It's unnecessary and uninteresting, and not remotely a priority. I can't imagine why Cousin Steele even thought—"

"It's more than interesting," Fairfax interjected, reaching for her hand. "I've no greater priority than being the first name on your dance card."

That was likely a true statement. Bartholomew curled his lip. He was surprised Fairfax had any priorities at all. He ought to be home with his sister, not here courting Daphne.

"As do I," said Whitfield quickly. "It's also *my* priority to be the first name on your dance card."

Fairfax cut him an exasperated look. "We can't *both* be the first name."

"Of course not," Whitfield responded cheerily. He bounced on his toes, flexing his muscles. "I'd fight you for it, but I believe the victor is a foregone conclusion."

Fairfax burst out laughing. "I'd wager a—"

"Gentlemen," Bartholomew interrupted. He tried not to feel smug when Daphne edged a little closer to his side. He liked having her there. "If the lady doesn't wish to attend the assembly—"

"Of course we'll *attend*." Fairfax stared at Bartholomew as if he'd grown an extra leg, rather than the opposite. "Miss Vaughan's dance card will be the envy of Kent."

"I should doubt that." Daphne gestured toward her dark attire. "I can't stand up with any of you. I won't be out of mourning until the end of the week."

Ah. Bartholomew rubbed his jaw. That explained Captain Steele's sudden rush to get his ward betrothed by Sunday. It would be the blackguard's first opportunity to marry her off.

"Just so." Whitfield puffed up his chest. "Although you can't dance, you shan't lack for company a single moment. I, for one, will never leave your side."

"I, on the other hand," Lambley said with a glance at his pocket watch, "am afraid I must. Parliament opens session tomorrow, and I must hurry if I'm to arrive on time. Miss Vaughan, forgive me. If you're... available in a fortnight, my cousin is hosting one of her soirées, and I know she'd be delighted if you were to attend." He sketched a bow. "As would I."

Fairfax sniffed in gentlemanly offense. "From the way that was worded, I'm assuming only Miss Vaughan is invited?"

Lambley smiled. "You're ever so astute."

Daphne pressed his hand. "Katherine did invite me to London, but I'm afraid my place is here in Kent. I do thank you for the kind invitation. And for your visit."

"Your servant." He bowed. "Until next we meet, do take care."

"I shall do what I can." She dropped his hand to dip in curtsey. "Safe travels, Your Grace."

Bartholomew shouldn't have been quite so pleased to see the last of Lambley, but he couldn't help a small rush of relief at one less competitor.

Daphne might believe a faux fiancé solved all her troubles, but that was only if Captain Steele approved the match. No guardian would choose a one-legged soldier over a rich, eligible duke. Particularly not someone as opportunistic as a pirate.

He tensed. No one in his right mind would choose a one-legged soldier over *anyone*.

Not that it mattered. He straightened his shoulders. He had no intention of paying suit to right-minded people. He just had to make a positive impression on Captain Steele, sign a sham contract, and then return to his life of endless solitude as if this interlude had never happened.

As if being the recipient of feigned interest hadn't made him yearn for the real thing.

He gazed at Daphne. What might it be like if she felt a fraction as passionately for him as she did for her charity work? She was not completely immune to him. The expression on her face when she'd first laid eyes on him indicated she found his appearance more than pleasing.

Of course, that was because his false leg was disguised beneath layers of clothing. His flesh turned cold. No matter what sparks might fly between them, nothing could come of it. He had no wish to sink his fingers into her hair and cover her mouth with his own, only for her to feel revulsion when she saw him naked.

They'd been friends before. They would simply have to remain so. No matter how a part of him might wish there was a chance for something more.

Captain Steele swept into the room with a smile on his face and a sword at his side. "Miss Vaughan. Gentlemen. I've just taken possession of the delivery I was waiting for. If tomorrow is as clear a day as today, who would like to take my new horses for a run?"

Bartholomew groaned inwardly. The devil only knew how a pirate had managed to purchase horseflesh at half ten on a Thursday night, but that was the least of Bartholomew's concerns. Fairfax and Whitfield were already arguing over which path would allow them to race the fastest, and even Daphne had clapped her hands together in delight. Bartholomew's shoulders sank.

He had no competition. He couldn't even play the game.

Chapter Seven

Unfortunately for Bartholomew, the following day was bright and sunny, with nary a snow cloud in the uncharacteristically blue sky. The ground was still frozen and the frigid air would slice painfully across the wind-chapped face of any rider foolish enough to race an unfamiliar steed across frost-ruined terrain.

In other words, everyone except him.

The other gentlemen were already astride their horses, laughing and prancing and bickering over which path would be the fastest route around the lake. He stared wistfully at the rolling hill dipping below the horizon. Lord, how he wished he could join the fun.

Instead, he hung back near the doorway. Which meant he was the first to see Daphne step outside to join them. His breath caught at the sight.

She wore a simple day dress and spencer, rather than a riding habit. Perhaps she did not own one. Her red-gold curls were pinned beneath a wide-brimmed bonnet. Her eyes were bright, her cheeks flushed.

"Did they leave us the slowest nags?" She grinned up at him from beneath her bonnet as she took his arm. "Or give us the feistiest steeds?"

He cleared his throat. "You'll have your pick of the remaining horses. I won't be riding."

Her smile fell. Her eyes lost some of their sparkle. "You don't want to join me?"

Bartholomew's jaw locked. Her obvious disappointment curled about his heart like a fist. How he longed to join her. To see her smiling at him with her eyes bright and her cheeks flushed as they raced side by side over the frozen hills.

Enjoying the moment together.

But the mood was already broken.

"I'm afraid I cannot," he said. "I'm on my last leg, as it were."

Her eyes widened in sudden sympathy. "Oh, I didn't think... Of course we don't have to ride. 'Tis too cold for such rubbish anyway. Let me talk to my guardian, and I'll—"

"Balderdash." His neck heated in embarrassment. He didn't need or want her concern. "The horses are here and ready, as is everyone else. I won't be spoiling anyone's fun. Now tell me which of these fine animals you'd like to ride and I'll fetch the mounting block."

Her lips tightened as if she were biting back a protest. Something in his eyes must have convinced her of his intractability on this point. Nodding, she pulled an apple from her spencer pocket and gestured toward the closest mare. "This one. Thank you for assisting me."

He left her stroking the mare and turned to fetch the mounting block.

Once upon a time, he would not have needed such a thing. He would have handed her up himself without thinking twice. Lingered a moment too long with his hands cupping her curves.

He no longer could do such things.

His fingers clenched. He had thought the ridicule of his peers would be the worst part of returning to Society, however briefly.

Now he suspected the worst would be the thousand little deaths every time he wished to do something and could not. His hands wouldn't know the feel of her waist as he lifted her onto a horse. His arms wouldn't know the warmth of her embrace as he pulled her into a waltz. His mouth wouldn't know the feel of her lips, the sweetness of a stolen kiss.

He was here to be a faux fiancé, nothing more. He should be satisfied with that much. If it weren't for her, he wouldn't have left his town house. Even that 'twas more than expected, after the accident.

Once his leg had healed—as much as it ever would—an all-consuming depression had kept him bedridden for several

weeks as he came to grips with his new reality. He was
crippled. It was never going to get any better. Life as he
knew it was over.

In despair, he'd dragged himself from the bed to the
bottle, and might've whiled away the next forty years with
whisky and laudanum his only companions, had his
insufferable pride not snapped him out of it at last. Others
might see his ruined body as useless, but he wouldn't be
worthless. Not in his own home. That had been the end of the
whisky and the laudanum.

From that day forward, he spent every waking hour
stretching and exercising. Pushing his limits. Becoming
stronger.

His atrophied muscles had screamed with agony.
Mottled bruises had covered every inch of his skin from a
series of endless tumbles as he'd taught himself to sit and
rise without aid, to walk without a cane, to climb ropes and
increase endurance.

But he never expected he'd have to endure a challenge
like this.

He hefted the mounting block and carried it back over to
Daphne. One of the footmen was already fitting the horse
with a sidesaddle.

Bartholomew could have sent a servant after the
mounting block as well, but he'd wanted to do *something*
helpful. Given he couldn't lift her up himself without risk of
falling. He shuddered at the thought. Embarrassing them both
would be a fate even worse than embarrassing himself. He
couldn't bear to have her look at him in pity. Or contempt.

"Thank you," she said softly as he placed the block next
to her horse. She laid her hand in his for balance as she
mounted the mare.

He gave her fingers a light kiss before releasing them.
"Enjoy the ride."

She tucked a stray tendril behind her ear and blushed. "I
would enjoy it more if you joined me."

An entirely different image of her riding him rose
unbidden to his mind and his stomach tightened with desire.
He pivoted away before the hunger in his eyes could betray

him.

There would be no riding of any kind. Not today. Not ever.

He saluted Captain Steele and turned back toward the house. He would watch Daphne ride away from a distance. Out of her way. Away from temptation.

"Are you certain you won't join us?" Whitfield, bless his soul, still seemed to believe Bartholomew the unstoppable juggernaut he'd once been, back when Bartholomew's legendary antics were fodder for amazement and envy.

"I'd rather keep my feet on the ground." He gestured at his legs. "Or foot, as the case may be."

Captain Steele grinned down at him from atop a rearing stallion. "I've a pony tied up behind the house, if these horses are too much for you."

Bartholomew flashed his teeth. A pony wasn't quite as insulting as an ancient broodmare would have been—any pony of Captain Steele's was bound to have a little devil in him—but the meaning was clear all the same.

Frowning, Daphne tossed her reins aside and moved as if to dismount. "I'm staying with him."

"No." He dashed forward to rescue the reins and placed them back into her gloved hands. When was the last time she'd ridden a horse? He couldn't deny the sparkle in her eyes or the flush to her cheeks. Riding might be a rare treat. He couldn't take that away from her. "Have a little fun. You deserve it. I'll still be here when you get back."

The expression in her eyes was unreadable, but she accepted the reins and joined the others.

Captain Steele raised his arm, his fingers cocked like a pistol as if about to fire the opening charge.

Without warning or waiting, Fairfax launched off with a whoop, flying down the hill with reckless abandon and infectious laughter. Bartholomew couldn't hold back a wistful smile. *Everything* Fairfax did was with reckless abandon and infectious laughter.

The others instantly gave chase.

Captain Steele was ahead of the pack in no time, his stallion impossibly swift despite its impressive size.

Whitfield and Daphne raced neck-and-neck, just behind, until they split ranks to belt along opposite paths around a frozen pond.

Bartholomew stood stiff and tall, watching her retreating form until he could no longer hear the horse hooves. Only then did he close his eyes and turn his back to the wind, to the things he could no longer do. To the man he could no longer be.

He'd seen more than enough to know what he was missing.

Everything.

How he wished he could be racing across the hills at Daphne's side. He wished he could treat her to the sort of courtship he'd always imagined undertaking, when the day came that someone finally stole his heart. Surprise flowers, dancing too close, moonlit kisses.

Instead, he would be a faux fiancé in name only. Their "relationship" would never even leave these grounds. They weren't even together *on* these grounds. She and her horse had torn off with the same buoyant joy as any of the others.

To his surprise, she was an excellent horsewoman. He doubted she'd had much practice in the art. On the other hand, even as a young girl she'd been a quick study and curious about everything. He didn't doubt she had a thousand hidden talents, with riding sidesaddle being the least of them.

Nonetheless, the sight of her dashing off down the slope, every bit the equal to Fairfax or Whitfield, made him wonder anew if spoiling their suit was truly the right thing to do. With her passion and big heart and exuberance for life, she would make any man a splendid wife.

Anthony Fairfax might frequent gaming hells more than a gentleman ought, but Bartholomew had known him his entire life, and could easily vouch for Fairfax's good heart and integrity.

Chauncey Whitfield was the current champ in London's pugilistic underworld, but that didn't mean he had rocks in his head or that a gentle young lady oughtn't to take a chance on Chaunce. He was good-natured and easy to please, and could be counted upon to keep those he cared about safe and cared for.

Bartholomew sighed. 'Twas precisely this sort of thinking—his tendency to analyze outcomes far into the future—that made him such an effective Army major and such a terrible knight in shining armor.

Daphne didn't want to wed. Blocking her guardian's stratagems was the easiest way to win that battle. But what was the war?

He furrowed his brow. The consequences of winning the current skirmish might be that she never got such an opportunity again. Daphne was a vicar's daughter. She was unlikely to catch the eye of another duke. Even title-less men like Fairfax and Whitfield were more plentiful in London than Maidstone.

Not only that, these easygoing gentlemen were apt to appreciate and encourage activities like hell-for-leather racing and all night waltzing than the humdrum suitors she was more likely to attract in the countryside. He let out a deep breath. Daphne needed someone to share her interests, not stifle them. What if his intervention spoiled her best chance to make that happen?

Just as he turned to go back inside, horse hooves sounded from the opposite side of the cottage.

Bartholomew frowned. He didn't expect the others back for at least a couple of hours, and yet the incoming rider wasn't coming from the direction of the public road. He paused on the threshold to see who it might be.

Daphne. Cheeks pink, lips rosy, her hair a golden cloud of windblown curls beneath a cockeyed bonnet.

She'd never looked more beautiful.

"Why did you come back?" he demanded. The answer couldn't be more obvious. His neck heated in embarrassment. She hadn't wanted to abandon the poor, crippled soldier, so she'd raced down an alternate path in order to double back and make sure he was still well. "I don't need your pity."

"That's fortunate." She arched her brows. "You don't *have* my pity."

Clearly. He lifted his chin toward the trail. "You wanted

to ride a horse. Go ride. You may not get another opportunity for some time."

"So be it." She dropped her reins, then hesitated. "You're right. I did feel awful, leaving you standing in our dust. Quite literally. It wasn't well done of me. I shouldn't have gone."

See? Pity. He lifted his hands to her hips. "Don't do me any special favors. I'm not your real fiancé. I'm not even your fake fiancé."

"Not yet." She slid into his arms. "Am I allowed to do favors when I'm your faux fiancée?"

"No." He set her down. Slowly. Letting her body slide against his.

She didn't back away. "Why not? You're doing quite a large one for me."

"Am I? I'm not sacrificing more than a few days." And his pride. "This is the first time I *have* been out since I returned from war. Perhaps you're the one doing me a favor. In which case, we're even."

She reached behind him and handed him the reins. "If that's all the bonding we're to do, mind this horse while I slip off to attend to some correspondence."

He gave her a grudging smile. Cheeky chit. And one of the most selfless, focused people he'd ever met. "Which nonexistent gentleman are you going to impersonate today?"

The corners of her lips quirked. "Perhaps I'll pretend to be you."

"Don't spite yourself just to spite me." He tied the horse and leaned against the post. "My opinions carry little weight."

She tilted her head. "What *are* your opinions?"

He straightened. Did he even have any? Who would care? No one had ever asked him before. Perhaps because they thought he wouldn't have any. Or perhaps because he had surrounded himself with the wrong kind of people. "My opinions on matters such as…?"

She bit her lip. "Do you remember what I showed you in my chambers?"

How could he not? A mere year ago, an invitation into a

lady's chambers would have ended quite differently. Perhaps even an invitation into Daphne's arms. A woman who didn't want a husband might still want a man. Her room had been more than adequate for a rendezvous. "One four-poster bed, sturdy, three pillows. An open wardrobe containing—"

"Not *that*." She gave his shoulder a teasing push.

He caught her hand. His heart was beating far too fiercely. She must feel its pulse beneath her palm, racing faster than any stallion.

He hadn't spoken to any young ladies since returning from war. Hadn't teased or been teased. Hadn't been shoved playfully without a thought to whether his sensibilities—or his balance—could withstand physical interplay.

In seven long months, it was the first time he'd been treated like he was... *normal*.

Of course he knew how deeply he'd missed it. But he hadn't realized until right this moment that he could have that feeling again. Of belonging, of bantering, of being himself.

Even if he would never truly be himself again.

He dropped her hand. "Yes, I remember your room. Wheat farmers. Weavers. Miners. Workhouses. Orphans. Apothecaries. Particularly in the areas of training and methodology."

Her beautiful mouth fell open. "You listened to what I said? And memorized my causes?"

"I recalled, not memorized. Soldiers are trained to remember things." He gave her a devilish smile. "Shall I tell you more about the contents of your wardrobe?"

Her cheeks flushed. "I already know what's in my wardrobe. I don't know what's in your mind. *Those* are the things I most care about. What are your opinions on the topics you recall?"

He dipped his head. "Honestly?"

She leaned forward, nodding as if eager to hear his insights and hidden depths.

He gave her the truth. "I don't have any opinions."

Not in the way she meant. He had plenty of opinions, one of which was: you can't save everyone, no matter how hard you try. He'd sacrificed enough. 'Twould be foolish to add hopeless causes to the mix.

She stepped back, disappointed. "You said you read the newspapers!"

He shrugged, knowing it would vex her. She shouldn't have illusions about him. He was here to help her escape her guardian, not become a white knight. "Reading newspapers doesn't mean I'm a 'crusader.' It means I'm bored. And literate."

Her eyes flashed. "If you're bored, it's your own fault. Interesting people are never bored."

"I wasn't always a wretched bore." He had barely had time to sleep. Wine. Women. Waltzing. Gaming. Pugilism. Adventure. The army was only more intense. Troops. Weapons. Enemy soldiers. Stratagems. "My days were far too busy for boredom to set in. Or to develop strong opinions about weavers and wheat farmers."

Her lips pursed as she considered him. "What fills your days now?"

"Nothing," he said simply. Although he found her idealism endearing, he did not share it. The war had taught him that some fights just couldn't be won. "After what I've been through, I quite prefer it."

"But the farmers—"

"You may keep your causes, my dear." He brandished his wooden leg with a self-mocking smile. "I'm done crusading."

Chapter Eight

The following morning, Daphne's eyes flung open in a panic. Sun trickled in around the shutters. She closed her eyes as quickly and as tightly as she could, but it was too late. Saturday was here. The changes would begin.

Today she was officially out of mourning. She could wear colors again. Dance at assemblies. Wed the suitor of her guardian's choosing. Dread made her fingers shake and her limbs leaden.

She rolled over and buried her face in her pillow. Lucky her. She didn't *want* to do any of those things. There was no one she wished to wed. And she would mourn the loss of her father the rest of her life. No matter what color she happened to be wearing.

Her cheeks heated as she thought back to the previous day. She certainly hadn't *felt* like she was in mourning when Bartholomew was around.

When he was near, his presence muddled her brain. Made her think of foolish things, like the width of his shoulders or the strong line of his jaw.

When he kissed her hand, heat spread through her. When he'd lifted her from the horse, letting her body slide down his in a most shocking and brazen manner... her bones had nearly melted. If he had let go of her just then, she would surely have crumpled to his feet. And wrapped her arms about him.

She had never doubted his reputation as a rake. She now wondered if all he had to do was stand still and let the women throw themselves at him. Her inability to control her body's reaction to his touch was infuriating. And more than a little intriguing.

What might it be like to be the sort of woman who gave in to such desires? A woman unafraid to throw her reputation to the wind in exchange for a night of passion in his muscular arms? She clutched a pillow to her chest.

Making love with Bartholomew would be incredible, she had no doubt. He would be the sort of lover who would give a woman his complete attention. Make her feel wanted. *Needed*.

And then he would leave before morning, never to be heard from again.

With a sigh, she shoved Bartholomew and certain heartbreak out of her mind and pushed herself out of bed. There was no time to be maudlin. She had to focus.

She washed her face and her teeth, then settled down before her escritoire. Today was full of risk. Tomorrow, even more uncertain. She had best attend to as much charity work as possible while she still could.

It might be her last chance to leave a mark before she faded into obscurity. Into a loveless marriage. Or Bedlam.

She pushed aside a tall stack of correspondence and perched at the edge of her chair. After luncheon, she'd begged off from playing Charades (Mr. Fairfax's idea) or battledore and shuttlecock (Mr. Whitfield's) with the excuse of a megrim. Instead, she'd stayed up until the wee hours of the morning, penning every last outstanding letter until her eyes and fingers ached.

Now all that was left was forming a plan.

Her gaze wandered over the clippings covering her walls. She wasn't nearly as efficient solving problems as she was finding them. Some days she wished she were a dozen Daphnes, so that she could divvy up her endless chores amongst her many selves and finally be able to cross some things off her lists.

Papa, she knew, would have scolded her much the same way she'd scolded Bartholomew for being bored. Daphne could never do the right thing. If she felt overwhelmed and overworked, 'twas her own fault.

He saw no need to save the world. 'Twas an impossible task. If she focused on her parish, on her neighbors and the other inhabitants of Maidstone, she could make a direct and appreciable difference in the lives of those around her. Just as Papa had done for thirty years.

But she didn't want to limit herself to Maidstone. Maidstone was *fine*. They didn't need her.

Was there truly that much honor in polishing the windows at All Saints Church or helping a happy, well-adjusted parishioner become even happier? Here, she was forgettable. Outside of Kent, she could make a difference. She could be remembered.

The people who needed the most help were the people she couldn't reach out and touch. The people *no one* reached out to. The ones whose livelihoods had been ripped away by drought or disease or dangerous working conditions. The people for whom the slightest act of kindness might be the balm that let them live another day.

Only if she was free to do so.

Which meant she could never marry. Not when there were so many worthier subjects to command her attention. Who might give her theirs. And definitely not any gentleman Captain Steele had chosen as a potential suitor.

As for Bartholomew… Handsome, roguish, unforgettable Bartholomew. He was the worst of all possible choices. Now more than ever.

He had no hobbies. No activities. Nothing with which to pass the time.

A *bored* husband would be the worst kind of all. He'd expect a wife to cleave to him day and night, mutually doing nothing at all, seated side by side in boring marital harmony. While England's poor struggled and died.

Heaven save her. She could not let that happen. Thank God their betrothal was only make-believe.

Presuming they could convince Captain Steele to sign the contract.

Daphne dipped her quill into the inkwell and wrote *Priorities* across a sheet of parchment. She bent her head over the sheet of parchment and began organizing her projects by level of urgency.

In the event that her time became severely limited due to

some mishap or another, she could devote what little she had to whichever cause was the most important at that moment.

She rose from her escritoire only when her maid entered the chamber with buckets of steaming water and all but forced Daphne to ready herself to face the day.

Esther refused to even consider allowing her mistress to don yet another gray and black ensemble, and fairly crowed with glee when she managed to talk Daphne into pale blue instead. A few ringlets later, Daphne was pronounced fit for joining the others at breakfast.

If they were still at the table. A glance at the clock indicated the hour was later than she realized. An unsurprising circumstance that transpired more often than not these days. Sometimes, she worked straight through lunch and only recognized the grumble of her stomach when she was too lightheaded to hold her pen properly.

Rather like now.

She slipped from her chamber and headed toward the dining room. The low rumble of conversation indicated the men had not yet quit the table. Her footsteps slowed.

What if Cousin Steele had already promised her to someone other than Bartholomew? Her hunger pangs vanished. She would not be able to eat until she was confident she would not wake up to find herself the new Mrs. Whitfield or Mrs. Fairfax in a few weeks' time.

She paused to listen just out of sight from the open doorway.

"—wonder when the weather will be warm enough to take a dip in the river. I do miss swimming."

Daphne's shoulders relaxed slightly. That voice belonged to Mr. Whitfield, and the subject was certainly safe enough.

"I wager it won't be properly warm until May or June, but why wait? They say the Russians go straight from the sauna to the snow. What's a cold river compared to snow?"

And that was Mr. Fairfax. Always primed to race pell-mell into one reckless scrape or another. Daphne narrowed her eyes. When he was younger, Bartholomew used to do the same. It was no surprise at all when he ran off to join the army. She half expected him to disappear again the next time adventure knocked.

"What's a cold river?" came Mr. Whitfield's incredulous voice. "It's ague, is what it is, and I've a match next week. Got to be in top form if I'm to best Quinton. Ever spar with that one, Blackpool?"

"My brother did," came Bartholomew's low, smooth voice.

"Your brother! Win or lose?"

"You have to ask?"

Mr. Whitfield's warm chuckle drifted out into the corridor. "I should say not. One glance tells me you're in better form than anyone at Jackson's, so I can quite imagine the damage a brother of yours might have done."

As could Daphne. Bartholomew and Edmund had been more than twins. Their own parents had difficulty telling their lads apart. Perhaps it was for that very reason that the brothers became so competitive, each of them fighting to be stronger, faster, *distinguishable* from the other. She sighed. That struggle was finally over.

Daphne lay the back of her head against the wallpaper and closed her eyes. Poor Tolly. He'd never intended to win like this.

A strong hand clamped down on her shoulder.

Her eyes flew open. She immediately closed them again. And pretended she was invisible. Perhaps if she didn't acknowledge her guardian had just caught her eavesdropping on guests in her own dining room, she could melt through the wainscoting and disappear.

"Not in the mood for kippers, are we?" Captain Steele didn't bother to hide the amusement in his voice. "Table too crowded for you, love?"

Chapter Nine

Breakfast had been excruciating. Bartholomew struggled to keep his mask in place.

He'd managed to exchange a few light words about his brother without his face or voice betraying just how completely his world had shattered when he'd lost his twin, but the memories were flooding back and it was becoming hard to breathe.

He pushed to his feet, careful not to upset his dining chair with his false leg. "If you'll excuse me, gentlemen."

Before he could do more than stand, voices sounded in the corridor. Daphne all but stumbled into the dining room, propelled forward by none other than her guardian, Captain Steele.

She looked tired and furious. And absolutely beautiful. Red-gold ringlets framed her ivory face. Her cheeks were a light pink. Her slender frame was all the more becoming draped in light blue linen instead of charcoal gray.

Then again, now that he'd had his hands at her waist and felt her body slide against his, it wouldn't matter if she wrapped herself in brown paper. Her curves had been burned into his mind. He couldn't look at her without wanting to draw her back into his embrace.

Whitfield and Fairfax nearly crashed into each other as they scrambled to their feet. "Miss Vaughan! Good morning!"

Bartholomew's jaw set. There was no point in bouncing about like a puppy. His leg would likely crumple if he tried.

"You look lovely," Whitfield stammered, gazing at her as if he'd just noticed her beauty. "Powder blue is quite a departure from…"

Daphne's eyes darkened, rather than brightened. Bartholomew understood perfectly. Being *out* of mourning didn't mean one had *stopped* mourning. But it did mean one had ceased being treated that way.

She smiled tightly and followed the footman to the empty chair at Bartholomew's side. "Please. Sit. Enjoy your breakfast."

"Happily." Fairfax's eyes twinkled as he arched a brow at Bartholomew. "I'm afraid Blackpool was just leaving, though. Isn't that what you said, Major?"

Bartholomew slanted him a flat look and sat back down. All of them had finished breakfast an hour ago. Their plates had been long cleared, and only their tea or coffee cups remained.

Fairfax doubtlessly wished Bartholomew out of the picture. Today was the day the marriage contract was to be signed. Only one of them would win Daphne's hand.

It had better be Bartholomew.

Captain Steele slid into a chair at the head of the table. Within seconds, the footman reappeared with a fresh tray from which he began to serve the new arrivals.

Steele ate with gusto. Daphne did not.

After watching her flick her toast about her plate a few times, Bartholomew murmured under his breath, "Your heart is your own, no matter what color you're wearing."

She shot him a quick, grateful glance and nodded firmly. "You're right."

He smiled. "That doesn't mean you ought—"

"What's that?" Fairfax lifted his brows, his eyes mischievous. "I can't quite hear you all the way across this not-particularly-wide table. 'Tis almost as if you're whispering on purpose, just to keep—"

The footman interrupted this sally with another tray. Delivered straight to Mr. Fairfax. Instead of more foodstuffs, however, the otherwise empty tray bore only a folded missive.

Frowning, Fairfax broke the seal and scanned the letter's contents. His face was pale when he faced the others. "I'm afraid I've been called away. I must leave at once."

Frowning, Bartholomew felt no pleasure at this sudden departure. Fairfax's sister was expecting Bartholomew's niece or nephew, but the baby wasn't due for another month and a half. His fingers turned to ice at the thought of Sarah or the baby in danger. "Is it…?"

"No," Fairfax said quickly. He rose on shaking legs. "Not yet. But I must be off. My apologies, all. Until next time."

He rushed from the dining room before anyone could so much as bid him farewell.

The remaining four looked perhaps less baffled than the situation warranted. Daphne was still toying with a crust of toast as if she hadn't registered Fairfax's departure at all. Captain Steele was singlehandedly demolishing every other edible item on the table. And Whitfield kept vacillating between long, mooning gazes in Daphne's direction and more surreptitious glances toward Captain Steele.

Bartholomew's eyes narrowed. From the looks of it, Whitfield might offer for Daphne right here at the breakfast table, without any eye to propriety or common sense. Or was that the wiser move? Now that both Lambley and Fairfax were out of the way, 'twas simply a question of which would-be suitor stated his case first.

Whitfield opened his mouth.

Bartholomew leapt to his feet. "Steele, may I speak with you privately?"

The pirate arched a thick black eyebrow as he chewed a mouthful of food. "At this precise moment?"

"If you'd be so kind." Bartholomew's fingers brushed against Daphne's shoulder to indicate it was time. He had promised to help, and he intended to keep his word. Whitfield was a good lad, but he wasn't the right man for Daphne. She deserved a better partner. A love match.

Captain Steele set down his fork. "Very well, then. Come to my office. Shall we meet alone, or should Miss Vaughan join us?"

The fire in Daphne's eyes at the reference to "his office" indicated there was no chance she'd stay away. She rose to her feet. "I'll join you in Father's study."

The pirate led the way, his swagger and amused grin indicating he enjoyed having others dangle upon his strings.

When they reached the vicar's study, Captain Steele settled himself behind the desk and stroked the salt-and-pepper stubble along his scarred jaw. "Now, then. How may I be of service?"

"Enough with the games." Bartholomew wished he had a sword. Captain Steele was a hard man. He would respect decisiveness, not sycophancy. Bartholomew drew himself to his full height and glared down at the pirate. "You want Daphne off your hands. I wish to oblige. Let's settle this and move on."

Steele's eyes danced merrily. "Well, that's certainly romantic. Minus the compliments and flowers and avowals of love, of course, but since my own entanglements tend more toward wrapping an arm around the closest tavern wench, I must and do commend your efforts. I also award you special consideration for making the trek all the way from London to Kent to press your case."

"I don't want special consideration," Bartholomew bit out. "I want—"

"You want Miss Vaughan. Yes. So you've mentioned. With all the eloquence of a stampeding bull." Captain Steele rolled his eyes toward Daphne. "I suppose you find yourself so overcome with emotion by this heartfelt proposal that you'll quite literally die if I don't accept his suit in favor of a better candidate?"

"One of us will." Daphne crossed her arms and scowled at him. "I shouldn't sleep with my door unlocked if I were you."

"Now, now. Is that any way for a vicar's daughter to speak to her elder? I'm shocked. *Shocked*. And not at all certain the two of you are remotely suited for matrimony."

Bartholomew smiled tightly. "Your experience in the matter being..."

"True. You make a fine point, Major. So here are mine." Steele ticked them off on his fingers. "We will sign not one, but two copies of the marriage contract. Miss Vaughan, you get neither. I don't trust vicars or their daughters. The first copy is mine, and the second copy goes to the major so that he does not forget his duties. Which are: having the first banns read tomorrow morning, concluding the marriage ceremony by the end of February—"

"But it *is* February," Daphne interrupted. "Today is the third, which gives us less than four weeks to—"

"—accomplish what only requires a fortnight to do," Captain Steele concluded. He held up his last finger without missing a beat. "Finally, you're to take the lass from my sight as soon as possible. She's mouthy and opinionated. Two of the worst possible traits a female can have."

Bartholomew allowed the outrage to show on his countenance, but nudged Daphne's toe with his own. *They'd done it!*

All they had to do was stall the wedding until Daphne came into her portion and then break the false betrothal. Bartholomew couldn't cry off without damaging her reputation, so she would have to be the one to do the jilting. His reputation was of no consequence. He would return to his life of solitude just as soon as the ink dried, and never think of it again.

Oh, very well. He would think of it. Think of *her*. Every night, most likely.

He'd wonder where she was and what she was doing. If she'd found a husband and gotten married. If she ever thought of him, and what it might have been like if their betrothal had been in truth. If they would have indulged in a torrid affair.

Or if she had found someone else. Someone she could love.

Captain Steele pulled two identical contracts from a drawer in the desk. He filled in Bartholomew's information in the blank area reserved for the suitor's name, then pushed both documents across the desk along with two plumes and an inkwell. "Sign."

Bartholomew scanned the tiny print for hidden surprises, then signed his name at the bottom. For better or worse, the deed was done. He switched copies with Daphne and repeated the process. He then walked both sheets over to the fire to encourage the ink to dry as quickly as possible.

When the script no longer shimmered, he handed one of the sheets of parchment back to the pirate. He rolled the other into a narrow tube and slid it into his waistcoat. "Are we through?"

"You and I, perhaps." Captain Steele tossed his copy of the contract into the wall safe behind the desk. "Your life with Miss Vaughan, however, is just beginning."

"And you are no longer part of it." With a gentle touch of his fingers to the small of Daphne's back, Bartholomew angled her out the door. Thank God that was over. He lowered his mouth to her ear. "This could have been solved so much easier with dueling pistols."

"Or just pistols," she muttered back. "No sense waiting until dawn. I've no idea how that man is still alive. Everyone he meets becomes his enemy."

They reached the corridor just as the footman hurried straight toward them.

"Visitors, miss." He glanced about nervously. "Shall I send them away?"

Daphne rubbed her temples. "Pray, do. I'm through with company for the day."

"I'm certainly not." Captain Steele slipped from the vicar's study and widened his arms in welcome. "Who's come to see me?"

"No one. They've come for Major Blackpool." Flushing, the footman wrung his hands at Bartholomew. "Sir, your parents are here."

Chapter Ten

Parents. Daphne's breath whooshed out of her at the word.

It was impossible not to feel sorry for herself. Not to be jealous. How could she? Bartholomew's parents were still alive. They showed up even when he wasn't expecting them. They loved him. They certainly weren't forcing him to marry against his will, just because they didn't wish to deal with him.

No. She swallowed hard. That wasn't fair. Just because Bartholomew's parents were still alive didn't mean all three of them hadn't suffered a loss just as powerful as hers.

And here she was, forcing Bartholomew into a faux betrothal.

How would they possibly keep his parents from finding out? She looped her arm through Bartholomew's and dragged him forward. This was dreadful. They had to send his parents home immediately, before they ran into—

Captain Steele's hand fell upon Daphne's shoulder before she finished taking her next step. "What's the hurry, love? Of course we'll invite Mr. and Mrs. Blackpool in for a nice spot of tea. It'd be right churlish to turn them away in this sort of weather."

Rooted in place, she slowly turned her head up toward Bartholomew, expecting to see writ upon his countenance the same panic jolting through her veins. That, or fury at Captain Steele's obvious glee from meddling with their lives.

Instead, she saw abject sorrow flit across his face, followed by a wince of pain. Frowning, she held fast to the crook of his arm. He let out a slow breath.

"They're going to be so disappointed in me." He rubbed

the back of his neck, his face pale. "I've no idea how they learned I was here, of all places, but to discover me a half mile from their door when I haven't left London since returning from war…"

"You haven't *seen* them?" she whispered in disbelief.

"I saw my father. Once." He nodded to the footman. "Show them into the parlor, please."

The footman glanced at Daphne, then behind her at Captain Steele.

Her guardian lifted his hand. "By all means, the parlor. We're not animals. I'll fetch the port."

She glared at him. "It's ten o'clock in the morning!"

"I'll fetch two bottles." He winked and disappeared back into the study.

Daphne shook her head. Only a pirate. She kept her fingers curved around Bartholomew's arm as they headed toward the parlor. Her head, however, was still spinning from his casual admission of little to no contact with his parents. What in the world could cause such a thing?

She frowned. During the first few months of recovery, he wouldn't have been able to leave his bedchamber, much less take a carriage ride to Kent. Yet his father had visited his sole surviving child only once? She narrowed her eyes. Something was amiss. If anything, the Blackpools had always struck her as *overly* doting on their twin sons.

Surely they didn't blame Bartholomew for Edmund's death! That blame lay with Bonaparte's army, not with the honorable soldiers dedicated to defending against it.

Then again, she, too, had felt abandoned when the twins left for Eton and then to war, leaving her adrift in the countryside with an absent father and nothing to keep her company but her own loneliness. She had dreamt of them coming home. Of having friends. Of mattering to someone.

No doubt Bartholomew's parents had been even more desperate for the safe return of their sons.

And now this.

She bit her lip. With such an obvious rift in their family, the worst thing to do was to spring a surprise betrothal on them, but there was no way to avoid it now that they were here. Her stomach churned. Bartholomew's parents were bound to think the reason they knew nothing of their relationship was because their estranged son hadn't deigned to inform them.

The only thing she could do was smooth their ruffled feathers as quickly as possible. But was that even a help, when they'd be crying off the engagement in a few weeks' time? Her stomach soured. No matter what, hopes would be dashed. What was the best plan?

She didn't want to make *too* good of an impression. She might never speak to his parents after today. Bartholomew, on the other hand, was going to have to go through a heart-rending dust-up with them all over again when the wedding fell through.

Presuming they were still speaking to him.

Daphne would instruct him to blame everything on her, of course. She would never forgive herself if his relationship with his parents worsened because of her involvement.

Familial relationships were to be cherished. One never knew how much time one had left.

She settled onto a wingback chair to await the inevitable disaster.

Bartholomew took the wingback chair opposite. His posture was stiff, his eyes glassy.

She frowned. They didn't look like a besotted couple. They looked like strangers. Awaiting sentencing.

Hollowness seeped inside her chest. Of course that's how they looked. Why should she have expected anything else?

From childhood, she had been taught that her needs were of secondary importance. That she herself was of little importance, forgotten by her flock-minded father and their entire little town.

A part of her had always hoped that someday, someone would look at her selfless life, her years of devoting herself to the welfare of others, and think, *Miss Vaughn has made a difference*. Or *Miss Vaughn matters*.

A deeper part of her once hoped that someday, someone would actually want her in his life. Not because he was in search of a wife or in want of companionship. But because he wanted *Daphne*. Someone who wanted to chase her dreams *with* her instead of force her to abandon them completely. Someone who loved her. Who couldn't imagine life without her.

Today… was not that day. Even her faux fiancé could not look less interested.

She curled her fingers into fists. Next month, the ruse would be over. Bartholomew would be gone. But here today, beneath her guardian's watchful eye, they needed to look like a couple that intended to marry. Now that they'd signed the contracts, they could not risk him making good on his threats of Bedlam and Newgate. She glanced around the room.

Closer to the fire, two wingback chairs sat opposite a chaise longue. Perfect. They could sit next to each other, with nary an armrest between them. She could force her cracked lips into a smile and at least pretend her handsome, rakish neighbor really had returned to Maidstone to beg for her hand.

She dashed to the chaise longue and motioned for Bartholomew to join her.

He tilted his head quizzically, his mind obviously elsewhere.

Urgently, she thumped her hand on the cushion. "Come *here*."

"What am I, your lapdog?" he groused. But he smiled as he joined her on the chaise longue, his attention focused on her once more. "You're fortunate this is a counterfeit betrothal."

"*Shh.*" She rapped the back of her knuckles against the side of his thigh. "Or what? You'd toss me over your shoulder like a heathen and lock me in some gothic attic on the moors?"

"If I could do so without my fake leg giving out on me, absolutely." His blue eyes twinkled as he gave her a chastising look. "If we did make it to the altar, you'd be the one who should carry *me* over the threshold."

"Me!" she exclaimed, clutching a hand to her bosom in mock affront. "Just what might you be implying about my ladylike figure, sir?"

He blinked back at her innocently. "Was it too subtle? As clever as you are, I assumed wordplay wouldn't be too far above you. I can think of other things I'd prefer to have above—or beneath—you, however you like it. May I offer my..." He coughed into his gloved fist and sprang to his feet.

Flushing, Daphne did the same. Bartholomew might not have lain eyes on his mother in three years, but Daphne had run into her now and then at All Saints Church while he'd been gone. Until they'd got the news about their children, of course. There'd been no sign of any Blackpool since. Without Edmund's body, there hadn't even been a funeral to attend.

Her breath caught as they walked into the room. In the interim seven months, 'twas safe to say that Bartholomew's parents had... deteriorated. She could scarcely believe her eyes.

Mr. Blackpool—once as wide and tall and arrogant as his sons—hovered in the doorway like a leaf caught in the wind, neither rising up nor falling down. Despite his height, he seemed fragile. Ephemeral. His expression was vacant, as if his body were an empty shell and his mind no longer present.

Mrs. Blackpool, on the other hand... everything about her was *very* present. She'd gained at least two stone in the past few months, and her entire body quivered like a volcano about to burst. Her red-rimmed eyes watered. Her handkerchief trembled from shaking fingers. The gasping sounds escaping her throat were somewhere between weeping and outright hysteria.

Daphne's throat convulsed. She had felt exactly like this when her father first died. Some days, she forgot to eat. On others, her eyes wouldn't stop watering. Her father might have always been busy tending his flock, but he was the only person who loved her. And now he was gone.

She curtseyed awkwardly, unsure of how to proceed. Bartholomew took a hesitant step forward, his face ashen.

With a sob, Mrs. Blackpool threw herself directly into her son's arms.

Bartholomew's false leg crumpled, sending both mother and son barreling right over Daphne. All three landed on the floor in a tangled heap of skirts and limbs, with Daphne underneath. The wind rushed out of her lungs.

As the footman rushed over to pull Mrs. Blackpool from the top of the pile, Bartholomew's mouth brushed the shell of Daphne's ear as he whispered, "You needn't worry about my sense of balance. I know better than to sign my name to any dance cards."

She was prevented from shaking him for flippantly undermining his self-worth at a time like this, due to her arms being trapped beneath her body.

During all of this, the elder Mr. Blackpool hadn't moved a muscle. He remained in the doorway, neither in nor out, eyes focused on nothing.

Captain Steele edged around him, entering the room just as the footman was steadying Mrs. Blackpool on her feet. With neither merriment nor any particular hint of surprise in his eyes, the pirate crossed the parlor in two long strides and held a hand out to Bartholomew.

Bartholomew ignored it.

He rolled off of Daphne and into a sitting position. He quickly swung both knees up to his chest, falling backward as he did so as if gathering momentum. Then he rocketed forward, his false leg outstretched before him, and sprang upright on the force and strength of his good leg alone.

Daphne gaped at him in disbelief. She couldn't rise from the floor that fast using both arms and both legs, much less do so gracefully. She was absolutely going to let the footman help her to her feet.

Bartholomew held his hand out first. He was neither winded nor perspiring. He looked magnificent.

If she wouldn't have seen him crumple like a marionette, if she hadn't been trapped beneath him and his mother just a few seconds earlier, she might have believed he'd never fallen at all. She, however, was trying to catch her breath.

He mistook her awe for distrust in his ability to help and lowered his proffered hand. Lips tight, he glanced over his shoulder toward the others. "Footman? If you'd—"

"No." She reached up, her arm and gaze steady. After a beat, he took her hand and pulled her smoothly to her feet. Too smoothly. She had to fake a small stumble in order to press against his chest long enough to whisper, "Pure laziness is the only reason you wouldn't carry me over a threshold."

The corner of his lip quirked. "You didn't see me fall?"

"I saw you get *up*." She stepped back to shake out her skirts, then turned to face his parents. "Pardon my clumsiness. I get lightheaded when I fail to break my fast properly, and I—"

"She's scarcely to blame," Bartholomew interrupted. "My pride prevents me from carrying my walking stick as I ought, and the last thing I expected was..."

Daphne glanced around as he trailed off. Neither of his parents was listening. His father had retreated back into himself. And his mother was moaning to the room at large about how it was too much, just too much, to have one son dead and the other as helpless as a babe.

"Twenty-six years old," she wailed, hurling herself into her husband's cravat. "We'll have to hire help to watch over him, like a nanny. He cannot even *stand* reliably. Whatever will I do?"

From the flat expression on Bartholomew's face, the reunion was going about as well as he'd expected. He made no further attempt to hug his mother. She would likely either cosset him like a newborn baby, or throw herself back into his arms and tumble the entire party to the floor all over again.

"Well, then," Captain Steele boomed from behind the desk. "Port?"

Why not? Daphne accepted a glass from the pirate, then handed it directly to Bartholomew.

He handed the port to the footman and pulled her over to the chaise longue. "Mother. Father. *Sit*."

Mrs. Blackpool pulled her tear-streaked face away from Mr. Blackpool's cravat and staggered into the wingback chair closest to Daphne and Bartholomew. Mr. Blackpool did nothing.

Bartholomew didn't breathe. His fingers clenched and unclenched, his posture stiff, his cheekbones touched with pink.

This was killing him, Daphne realized. How could it not? His mother wasn't thinking of him as a survivor. She thought of him as a baby, a burden. A disappointment. All her grief was due to her own pain. She hadn't yet spared a thought for how her son must feel. What he might need. Daphne brushed the back of her fingers against Bartholomew's fist.

After a long, tense moment in which the only sounds that could be heard were the halting sniffles of Mrs. Blackpool and the clink of Captain Steele's glass of port against the desk, Mr. Blackpool nodded slowly. He crossed the room with the jerky gracelessness of an automaton and folded himself into the wingback chair nearest his wife.

"Why didn't you visit?" Mrs. Blackpool burst out sobbingly, wringing her handkerchief and casting huge, beseeching eyes at her son. "Three and a half *years* since last I've seen you, and when you finally come home, it's to visit… the vicarage?"

"Oh, that," Captain Steele put in pleasantly. "'Twasn't to visit the *vicarage*. He and Miss Vaughan are to wed later this month."

Mrs. Blackpool sucked in a shocked breath, her pallid face a mixture of hurt and despair. "You couldn't have *mentioned* this?"

Bartholomew gazed back at her stoically, his spine straight, his shoulders rigid, his tongue as silent as that of his father's. The poor man. Daphne doubted he wished his first words after all this time to be lies. This was her fault.

She took a deep breath and faced his parents. Before discussing a fake wedding, they needed to address the more important issue. His mother. She directed her gaze at Mrs. Blackpool. The woman needed to acknowledge that she was not the only one who had suffered a loss. Families needed to support each other.

"Three and a half years since you've seen your son?" She edged closer to Bartholomew's side and faced his mother squarely. "Why didn't you visit him in London, when he was recuperating from having his *leg* blown off?"

"And leave *Edmund?*" Mrs. Blackpool gasped. "Never!"

"He's not there," her husband said dully, his eyes focused somewhere above his wife's head. "'Tis an empty grave, so there's no sense you sobbing upon it, all hours of every day."

"He will be there," Mrs. Blackpool countered staunchly, "just as soon as the army returns his body. We shall have a fine ceremony. You shall return home where you belong, Bartholomew. It would ease the emptiness in my heart to have both my sons back."

"Even if one of our lads is in his grave?" her husband asked dryly. "You must know it cannot be the same. Edmund is *dead*."

"Then Bartholomew's presence alone will have to fill the void." Mrs. Blackpool's lip trembled as she turned to her son. "Stay by my side and keep me company whilst we await your brother's remains. Will you not do that for your mother?"

Bartholomew's voice was strained. "They're not going to find a body. Even if they did, how would they know who it was or where to send him? He's not coming home. If it makes you feel any better, I never found the rest of my leg. That doesn't mean it's not *gone*."

"I know he's gone," Mrs. Blackpool snapped. "Why do you think I haunt his gravestone? I'm trying to spend all the time with him now that I failed to do back then."

"And ignore the son that survived?" Daphne blurted indignantly. Dear heavens. Was the woman blind to Bartholomew's pain?

"He's the one who got Edmund to join." Mr. Blackpool's gaze sharpened and focused directly on his son. "He promised they would both be fine."

Bartholomew nodded slowly, accepting the blame. "I only brought half of us home." He lifted his false leg and let it thump to the floor. "Less than half."

Daphne entwined her fingers with Bartholomew's. He stiffened, but did not pull away. It might well have been the most support he'd received since returning home.

Mrs. Blackpool's voice rose in pitch. "What did you do with Edmund's things? His town house? His paintings?"

Only the slight tightening of Bartholomew's hand in Daphne's betrayed his emotion. His grief-stricken mother was more concerned about the son who'd died than the one who'd lived.

"I've done nothing," he answered. "I haven't visited Edmund's town house."

Mrs. Blackpool gasped in horror. "What if his possessions have been stolen?"

"They have not," Bartholomew bit out crisply. "I continue to pay the rent on his town house and the salaries of his staff."

Daphne slanted a surprised look at him. Not only was that a shocking waste of money, it was inadvertently cruel to his mother. If there were personal effects in the town house that might bring some peace to the obviously hysterical Mrs. Blackpool, then those items were better off in Kent than in some living mausoleum. Surely he saw that.

Then again, Bartholomew was far from heartless. He must have some reason for refusing to dismantle his brother's house.

She lowered her voice. "Why don't you—"

"I *can't*." His gaze jerked away from her. After a moment, he cleared his throat. "My mother cannot stay away from his memory, and I can't bear to face my grief or my failure. I'd rather let the town house sit empty than to organize and dispose of all the things my brother believed he'd come home to."

She squeezed his hand and desperately wished there were something she could do to ease his pain. There were no words to convey her horror at his plight or the depths of her sympathy. How much worse would the past months have been if she'd felt responsible for her father's passing? If the people she most cherished, the people whose love and acceptance she most craved, *blamed* her for his death?

"It's not his fault," she said suddenly. Her tone came out stronger than she'd intended, but she did nothing to temper it. She glared at his parents. "Edmund's death is not

Bartholomew's fault."

"Of course it isn't," cried Mrs. Blackpool, casting a self-righteous glance toward her husband. "I *told* Mr. Blackpool the lads were too weak to face something like war, and when Bartholomew came home a cripple, I sent my husband straight to London to bring him right back to Kent, where he could stay safe in my home for the rest of his life."

Bartholomew's grip on Daphne's fingers was tight enough to bruise. She didn't blame him one bit. He didn't need his mother to keep him safe. He needed her to love him.

"Your son is scarcely weak."

"He collapsed when I *hugged* him!" Mrs. Blackpool dissolved into tears. "Come home, Bartholomew. The house is so lonely. Stay with me. With us. We'll employ so many servants, you'll never have to lift a finger again. You won't even have to get out of bed."

Good Lord. Daphne slid a startled glance in Bartholomew's direction. His smile was brittle and failed to reach his eyes. His mother didn't want him home because she missed him. She wanted him home because she believed him no longer capable of being his own man. And because she thought his presence would erase her own grief.

Daphne's shoulders stiffened. No wonder the man hadn't stopped by for a quick visit. His mother would never have let him leave.

Captain Steele drained his port. "May *I* move in? I quite adore fawning attention and the thought of having untold chambermaids at my disposal."

Bartholomew sent him a dark look and returned his focus to his parents. "How did you know I was here?"

His father blinked as if awakening from slumber. "'Twas the note."

Bartholomew's gaze sharpened. "The what?"

"A message arrived for you by special courier. Carlisle. Once I saw the seal, I rushed outside to try and catch the earl's man, but the carriage was already gone." Mr. Blackpool shook his head. "That's when young Fairfax rumbled by. He knew nothing about Carlisle, but had seen you at the vicarage. So I went to fetch your mother."

Mrs. Blackpool smiled tremulously. "And here we are."

Silence reigned.

Bartholomew loosened his hold on Daphne's fingers and leaned forward. "May I see the note?"

Mr. Blackpool fished it out of his coat pocket and handed it to his son.

Bartholomew read it in silence.

Mrs. Blackpool aimed her trembling smile toward Daphne. "I always did like you, dear. I'm so thankful you were the one to win Bartholomew's heart, and not some horrid Londoner with a penchant for city life. Now that he's crippled, Bartholomew can't endure such frivolity. He's better off at home, and of course, there is plenty of room for you, too. There will be no reason to leave. I'm assuming this gentleman inherited your father's house?"

"I'm no gentleman," Captain Steele corrected, his grin roguish. "But yes. This shack is mine now. Want to buy it?"

"Whatever for?" Mrs. Blackpool glared down her nose at him. "Bartholomew and my daughter-by-law have a home with us. It will be like having two children all over again." She turned back toward her son, her expression determined. "You *must* apply for special license, so we can have the ceremony in the garden."

Mr. Blackpool raised an eyebrow. "Next to Edmund's empty grave?"

"I couldn't if I wished to," Bartholomew cut in. "The Archbishop favors those with a coronet, and you'll notice I have none."

"Not *always*," his mother insisted. "One or two times he's made an exception, and if the Earl of Carlisle would put in a word for you..."

"Oliver has his own matters to deal with." Bartholomew folded the missive and slid it into a waistcoat pocket. "He's getting married on the morrow, and he'd like me to bear witness."

"Darling, you can't!" His mother sprang from her chair to clasp her son's hands in hers. "You mustn't even think such nonsense. No more London! Not in your condition. No more trips anywhere at all. I've already lost Edmund, and I'll die if I lose you, too. I need you at home."

Bartholomew extricated his fingers from his mother's grasp. "I'm afraid I'll have to disappoint you yet again, Mother. As I mentioned, the Earl of Carlisle wishes me to be a witness at his wedding, and I'm certain you realize that I cannot refuse. I owe him my life. If he hadn't carried me from the battlefield at risk of his own life, you would have lost both of your children the same day."

Daphne glanced at Bartholomew in admiration. Even the most cloying of mothers—and there could be no doubt that Mrs. Blackpool deeply loved her son and truly wished no harm to befall him—could scarcely deny such a simple request from the friend who had saved her child's life.

Mrs. Blackpool grasped Daphne's hands instead. "You'll stay with me, then. Starting this very night. You wouldn't leave me alone, would you, with my son all the way in London? Not when you'll be living with us from now on anyway. Besides, Bartholomew will come back sooner if you're with me. And we can plan the wedding. The garden would have been ideal, but All Saints Church is lovely and full of history. If only your father were still alive to perform the ceremony! I haven't met the new vicar yet because I can't bear to leave Edmund, even on Sundays, but with the two of us together, I might—"

"Daphne is also going to London to visit a friend." Bartholomew cut her a speaking glance. "Didn't you say someone was expecting you?"

Daphne's eyes widened at the reminder. Panic clawed at her insides. To get even halfway through her list of priorities, she'd need to spend every waking hour between now and her birthday locked in her chamber with her escritoire and an extra pot of ink. London was completely out of the question. As was moving in with Mrs. Blackpool.

"Right you are," her guardian put in, fixing Daphne with his crocodile smile. "Miss Vaughan said the Duke of Lambley's cousin had sent her an invitation. One oughtn't to offend the cousin of a duke. Of course she'll be going to London." He stood up from the desk. "I'll see to it personally. I've decided to cancel my upcoming venture in order to ensure no unfortunate delays befall our darling lovebirds."

Daphne's dream of making huge strides on her charity projects vanished. If Captain Steele intended to send her to London, there would be no stopping him. Now that he'd canceled his pirating venture, it would become even harder to stop her faux betrothal from becoming alarmingly real. She would have to go and put his mind at ease.

She forced a smile at the Blackpools. "I'm very sorry. Miss Ross is a very good friend of mine. She's been planning this visit for ages."

Mrs. Blackpool clasped her hands even tighter, her voice trembling. "Oh, I do wish you wouldn't go. I would love to have a reminder of my son. But go, if you must. Take care of my boy. Promise me you'll keep him safe until he returns home to Kent. And that when you do, you'll stay with us forever."

Chapter Eleven

Bartholomew allowed his valet to clothe him in the finest items in his wardrobe. Fitz adorned his neck with a starched white cravat of monumental proportions. Its careful white folds soared so high that Bartholomew doubted he'd even be able to see the ceremony.

All of which was fine with Bartholomew, for he didn't want to watch other people staring at him. Pitying him. Especially not people who loved him. Watching his mother fall apart had been worse than watching his leg explode. He could not bear to see the same dismay and pity on the faces of his closest friends. He dreaded the ceremony.

Yet he could not ignore the Earl of Carlisle's summons. Oliver had carried Bartholomew's mangled body to safety. The least he could do in return was attend the man's wedding.

Heart thudding, Bartholomew allowed Fitz to spritz him with perfume and adjust the painstakingly mussed curls on his head one last time before heading toward the stairs.

He thought again of his mother. Of her disappointment. His throat tightened. He missed his family and had no wish to deprive them of their living son, but he couldn't be himself and Edmund, too. Bartholomew had enough guilt of his own without also shouldering his parents'.

Or his friends. His breath grew shallow. London suddenly seemed terrifying. What if his friends blamed him for the death of his brother? What if they, too, expected him to be more, not less? To somehow take the place of both twins?

He rubbed his face. After he put down the whisky and picked up his spirits, he had been too busy strengthening what was left of his body to correspond with his friends. He should have paid more attention. The world had gone on without him.

Oliver. *Married*.

Bartholomew had seen the infamous compromise alluded to in the scandal sheets, but he hadn't expected to be invited to the wedding. Much less to have duplicate invitations show up at every address he'd ever frequented. He no longer wondered why his parents had received the note, but rather why he'd been invited in the first place.

The first—and last—time Oliver had dropped by Bartholomew's sickbed, Bartholomew had thanked the earl bitterly for saving his life and then ordered him to quit the premises and never return. Bartholomew hadn't wanted *anyone's* eyes on him or his infirmity. And yet, here he was. Making his first public appearance.

Well, semi-public. Weddings were traditionally small, but Oliver was taking it a step further for all their sakes. Modest church, no bystanders, invitation only. He was aware that Bartholomew had no wish to be seen by the general population. The risk of curious eyes was even more critical for Sarah Fairfax.

Who would have been his sister-in-law. If Bartholomew hadn't failed to bring Edmund back alive.

Bartholomew's throat convulsed as he shrugged into his greatcoat. Was he *really* going to present himself to her after being unable to return her intended to her arms? Sarah was not only facing a future without Edmund, but a lifetime of being shunned by her ex-peers, as soon as they discovered she'd birthed a bastard child.

It was Bartholomew's fault. And there was no way to stop it. The only way to avoid that fate would be to marry as soon as possible. But who would wed a pregnant bride?

He squeezed the back of his neck. What would Edmund want him to do? Surely not marry his bride. To rescue Sarah from ruin would be to consign her to an even greater hell: a lifetime wed to the crippled failure who'd let her true love die.

If Bartholomew's mother had any inkling of her

impending grandchild, she would approve the match in a heartbeat. To hell with anyone's wishes—Daphne's, Bartholomew's, or Sarah herself. One hint that Sarah was increasing, and Bartholomew's mother would happily hide her and the child away in Kent for the rest of their natural lives.

Would that be a better or worse fate for Sarah and the baby?

He turned toward the door.

Crabtree was there waiting.

Bartholomew straightened his shoulders. "Landau?"

"Ready for you, sir. With a warming brick inside."

Bartholomew nodded and reached for the door.

"Wait!" Fitz careened around the corner bearing an armful of sundry accessories. "You cannot go to a wedding in those ancient gloves, sir. What can you be thinking?"

He snatched Bartholomew's trusty linen gloves from his fingers and replaced them with a more starched, less comfortable version of the same.

Bartholomew smiled dryly. "Thank you, Fitz. You have saved me from certain embarrassment. Do I now meet your high standards?"

Fitz eyed him critically, the edges of his thin lips turning down with displeasure. "Something is missing. Something important." His eyes lit up as he clasped his hands together in delight. "Of course. A walking stick!"

Ah, yes. Bartholomew's wry humor faded. No matter how one dresses a cripple, he remains a cripple. No amount of starch in his gloves would change that. "I don't think—"

"But you must! Oh, it's not because of..." Fitz flicked pale fingers in the direction of his master's vexing prosthesis and fixed him with beseeching eyes. "It's a vital accessory, sir. You must take it. A natty walking stick is the crown jewel to a princely appearance."

He dashed from the room and returned in a trice, this time bearing a freshly buffed walking stick. Beaming, Fitz presented it with both hands. 'Twas the walking stick with the claw handle and the hidden sword.

Bartholomew's stomach twisted. He used to love that

walking stick.

Now? He hated it. Hated that he needed it, rather than carried it for show. Hated that everyone knew he needed it. That without it, he risked going down like a rock, just like he'd done in front of his parents and Daphne. And Captain Steele. And a footman.

His muscles tensed as he snatched the walking stick from his valet. Steady. He was *not* going to fall. He would *not* humiliate himself. No one was going to laugh at him.

He'd survived war. Surely he could survive a marriage ceremony.

Particularly since it wasn't his.

He pushed out the front door and clapped a hand over his hat when an icy burst of wind threatened to whisk it away.

The tiger leapt from the coach and rushed forward. The arm he held out was tentative, as if he wasn't certain whether the major was more likely to require his assistance or crack him on the head with his walking stick for trying.

Bartholomew refrained from both courses of action. He'd had enough of violence. But he would go to the devil before his damnable pride permitted him to clutch a schoolboy's arm like a feeble old woman.

He kept his head back, rather than gaze out the window at the London streets as they rolled along. Not because he didn't care, but because he missed it terribly. London wasn't his world anymore. His reign had ended.

For the hundredth time, he found himself thinking about Daphne. He supposed her guardian had packed her off to London by now. Was she enjoying her stay with the duke's cousin?

A smile flitted on his lips. She must be having a fine time. How could anyone fail to be impressed by London's breadth and opportunities? Especially Daphne. Whatever charity work she could accomplish from Kent, she could do here sevenfold. Perhaps she would fall in love with the city and wish to stay. His heart warmed.

The landau pulled up at the church a half an hour early. As much as Bartholomew had dreaded these few hours, arriving early was the lesser evil to arriving late and making a further spectacle of himself.

If he was lucky, perhaps he could find an unobtrusive seat in the back before any other guests arrived and enquired about his prosthesis or its quaint little clacking sound.

As luck would have it, he was not the first inside the church. He cringed. No matter how softly he tried to walk, he could not hide the telltale clicking. He rolled his shoulders back and pretended not to care.

Oliver, the groom, was pacing beneath a stained-glass window. Another friend, Xavier Grey, was the sole occupant of the furthest pew. No sign of the bride or the clergyman.

Bartholomew made his way to Oliver first.

Delight lit the earl's warm brown eyes. "You came!"

"Of course I came," Bartholomew grumbled. "That'll teach you to invite me. Congratulations on your new countess."

Oliver beamed at him. "I can't wait for you to meet Grace. You'll love her."

"I'm sure I will." Bartholomew lifted his chin toward the rear of the church where Xavier sat. "Is he…"

"Xavier again?" Oliver's grin faltered. "He's mobile. And verbal. But I don't know if we'll ever truly get him back. Some days are better than others."

Bartholomew nodded his understanding. The war had changed Xavier. Had marked them all. He clapped Oliver on the shoulder. "I'll leave you to your pacing."

Oliver flashed an embarrassed smile. "Thank you. This section of the floor was far too clean. I was… giving it some character."

Bartholomew's lips quirked. Oliver looked positively terrified. The poor sod. Marriage must be terrifying. Thank God Bartholomew's betrothal was a sham. And a secret. His friends would never let him live down the infamy.

He made his way to the back of the church and slid into the pew next to Xavier.

Once seated, he arranged his false leg with stiff precision. Just because everyone knew it was fake didn't mean he wanted it sticking out at all angles. He hated that Xavier was witnessing even this much of his endless, fruitless struggle to appear normal.

Captain Xavier Grey had returned from war whole… in body only. The rest of him had been trapped deep inside his mind, somewhere even his best friends couldn't rescue him. Slowly, he'd become more aware of the world around him. Bartholomew hoped he'd stay.

He didn't share this thought with Xavier, of course. It wasn't done. The same way Oliver hadn't asked after Bartholomew's missing leg, or whether the grieving process was coming along. The same way Bartholomew had refrained from enquiring what the devil Oliver had been thinking to kiss a young lady in a library that was not his own.

Oliver was usually the hero, not the villain. For him to succumb to passion in such a way meant the lady was very important indeed. And for him to be so charmingly nervous at his own wedding meant he had fallen in love at last.

Good for Oliver. He deserved to find happiness.

Bartholomew ignored a pang of envy. He was pleased to see Xavier alert and present. He, too, deserved happiness. Xavier might not be ready for courting, but Bartholomew could at least give him friendship.

He used his walking stick to gesture toward Xavier's midsection. "Hideous waistcoat."

Xavier nodded. "What happened to your neck? Get tangled in a bed sheet?"

"Mm. Wouldn't you like to know."

"Going to show off your distinctive fashion sense at the Grenville musicale tomorrow?"

"I wasn't asked." Bartholomew paused. "Or perhaps I burned the invitation."

"I'll send you mine. I get invited to everything." Xavier consulted his pocket watch. "I'm retiring to Chelmsford."

"For a while?"

"Permanently."

Bartholomew's gut hollowed. Now that he was finally out of the house, he realized how badly he had missed his friends. And they were all moving on with their lives. "When?"

"Soon as I can. Oliver's forcing me to attend an opera with him first. Wife's orders." Xavier rolled his eyes toward the pacing groom. "Not surprised he was the first to fall."

"We're too smart for that," he agreed. Or too damaged. Bartholomew had lost part of his leg on the battlefield, but Xavier had lost part of his soul.

The door eased open and a round woman in a thick black coat slipped into the church.

"*Sarah*." Xavier sprang up and stared. "She looks so…"

"Pregnant?" Bartholomew finished wryly. He, too, could scarcely believe the transformation. "That cloak might disguise her face, but it's doing nothing to hide her belly."

"Even the bed sheet around your neck couldn't hide that belly."

"Could strangle you, though." Bartholomew watched from the back of the church as Sarah waddled over to hug Oliver. "Could probably *cut* you, given its current cloth-to-starch ratio."

"And mop up spilled blood all in one go," Xavier said approvingly. "Well done. That much fabric could even double as a sail, should you need to escape by sea."

"Your waistcoat could double as fool's treasure," Bartholomew shot back. He tugged a quizzing glass from his pocket and peered at Xavier's tailoring. "What are the shiny flecks? Glass?"

"Paste. The very finest. I'll sell it to you for ten quid."

"For that monstrosity?" Bartholomew choked. "Not even if the ugly bits were diamonds. I'm hemorrhaging self-respect just by standing next to you. Do you *have* a valet?"

"Don't require one. I'm retiring to Chelmsford, remember?"

Before Bartholomew could respond, Sarah turned from Oliver and plodded down the aisle toward Xavier and Bartholomew.

His good humor vanished as she approached, leaving his gut filled with guilt and pain. He hadn't seen his brother's fiancée since returning from battle. By the time the surgeon had pronounced Bartholomew well enough to receive visitors, she had already confined herself in her parents' house for fear of being seen.

That she was here today either meant she was confident her disguise would protect her long enough to attend a friend's wedding… or that she no longer cared what the *ton* thought and had resigned herself to a life on the margins.

"Sarah…" He swallowed. He'd meant to say more than just her name, meant to tell her he would've happily traded his own life if it could have saved Edmund's. But his voice had broken on the very first word, and now Bartholomew could say nothing at all.

"I wish I could say it was good to see you." Her voice was low, her eyes tired and red. "But you look exactly like Edmund. You always did. And it's…" She jerked her face toward the vaulted ceiling and blinked far too rapidly for several seconds before returning her gaze to Bartholomew. "It's *hard*. Terribly hard. You're the only one who knows how I feel."

He nodded, but of course it wasn't the same at all. He hadn't simply lost his twin brother, the mirror image of his soul. He'd failed to *save* him, which was altogether worse. He'd ruined his parents' lives, and Sarah's, and the unborn babe's.

He was the twin who should have died. But he didn't. And here they were.

Sarah leaned around him to buss Xavier on the cheek, then sat down on the pew. She bunched up her cloak several different ways before finding the perfect width of cloth between the small of her back and the hard wood of the pew. Then she turned back to Bartholomew. "Well? Out with it."

He blinked back at her in confusion.

Out with what? That he'd drown in guilt and sorrow the rest of his life because of his mistakes? That he could have killed Oliver for rescuing him, and then very nearly killed himself with whisky and laudanum? That it still took all his strength, every day, to find a reason to get out of bed, much less keep pushing himself to stretch and exercise a lopsided body that would never be perfect again?

Until he'd received Daphne's entreaty, he'd *had* no such reason, other than his own stubbornness. Now, at least, he could say he'd done one good thing since returning from war. No one would know about it, but that was fine. He was no hero. He wasn't even a whole man.

His gaze lowered to Sarah's belly. He was going to be one hell of an uncle, though. He had to make up for everything the baby had lost.

His lips curved. "Have you picked a name?"

She stared at him as if he'd lost his mind. "I don't want to talk about *me*. I want to talk about you. When on earth did you get betrothed to little Daphne Vaughan?"

His throat went dry. The news was out? How? When? He tried to calm his racing heart. The first banns had been read in Maidstone, not London. For obvious reasons they hadn't wanted to announce their faux engagement to the whole city, so Maidstone was the only choice. Which left what?

"How did you find out?" he demanded hoarsely.

Her brow creased. "The newspaper, of course. I've nothing better to do than read such things from front to back. Bit of luck, since your announcement was last."

Announcement. He covered his face with his hands. Of course a *pirate* would never take a man at his word. That rat! Wasn't a marriage contract enough? Steele must have put that notice in the paper for the same reason he canceled his trip. He trusted no one. Not even a war hero and a vicar's daughter.

Not that he was wrong.

"Don't tell anyone," Bartholomew managed, then turned to face Xavier. "You either. Understand?"

Xavier blinked back at him slowly. "Hmm?"

"What on earth?" Sarah laughed and shook her head. "Why shouldn't we speak of a union that's already been printed in the newspaper?"

He took a deep breath. Sarah was part of his family and would never betray a secret. "Because it's a lie. Daph and I are pretending to be betrothed so her guardian doesn't force her to marry someone else. We need him to believe it for another month. Just until Daphne reaches her majority."

Sarah's smile faded. "If a signed contract isn't proof of

intent, a mere announcement won't prove anything either. What are you two doing to convince him that you're a couple in love?"

Doing? Absolutely nothing. Bartholomew's mind raced. They weren't in love. They were strangers.

"Bloody hell." His fingers tightened their grip on his walking stick. "I have to find her."

Find her and court her. Publicly, at least. Until her birthday. He hadn't come this far just to let her down now.

"After the wedding," Sarah whispered, and patted him on the leg. "Here comes the bride."

Bartholomew grimaced. For his rescue to work, they needed to convince Captain Steele their matrimony was imminent. For that to happen, *London* would have to believe it. Whatever the gossips believed, the world believed. His stomach bottomed. Such a feat would take a lot more than just declaring it publicly.

For the next few weeks, he and Daphne would have to be the most besotted couple in England.

Chapter Twelve

Daphne gazed at her sumptuous guest chamber in dismay. It looked like a museum. Knowing Katherine, its contents had likely come from one.

Every horizontal surface was glossy and dust-free… and covered with dozens of priceless antiquities from all over the world. Even the escritoire in the corner had more decorations than writing space. There would be no room for Daphne's towers of documentation here.

Not even on the walls. The wallpaper was pristine and colorful, the wainscoting spotless and shiny. Blast. She couldn't possibly affix clippings to such beautiful paper. She turned in a slow circle, frustrated.

Centered in the furthest wall of the chamber, there was even a little balcony overlooking the park.

But there was nowhere for Daphne's *things*.

Her fingers clenched. She wouldn't have come to London at all, if her guardian hadn't forced her. But now that she was here, how was she supposed to work? She'd brought the smallest trunk of correspondence she could, and still there was nowhere to put it, other than a dark little corner of the dressing room.

Untenable.

"What splendid living quarters," her lady's maid breathed in awe. Until today, the finest rooms Esther had seen were in the vicarage. Katherine's town house looked like a palace. Esther clapped her hands in delight. "I feel like I'm in a dream."

Daphne wrinkled her upper lip. "Quite."

"Thank you!" Katherine beamed at them both. "It took years to collect just the right pieces to create the effect I wanted. The other guest chamber is rather rococo, but I much prefer this look, don't you? Early baroque was so much richer."

"Indeed." Daphne tried for a smile. Katherine had received her at a moment's notice, had been inviting her for years, and the last thing she deserved was a churlish friend with her nose put out because the accommodations were *grand*. "Thank you for everything."

"'Tis my pleasure." Katherine glanced down the corridor. "Why, look. Here comes Aunt Havens. How do you do, Aunt?"

This time, Daphne's smile was genuine. Katherine's great-aunt was marvelous. Daphne stood a little straighter and motioned for Esther to do the same.

A sprightly older lady with bright blue eyes and powdered hair poked her head about the corner. "Guests! I adore guests! Who's come to visit, Kate?"

Katherine led her great-aunt forward gently. "Come and meet my dear friend Daphne Vaughan. She lives in Maidstone. Do you remember Maidstone?"

"All Saints Church! I was there just the other day. Darling people." She lowered her voice conspiratorially. "That's where I met my husband, you know."

Daphne did know. That was how they had met. Katherine's great-aunt had been the wife of the previous vicar. Daphne's father had taken over when he got too old, and had later presided over his funeral. Sadness filled her chest. They had both lost the most important man in their lives.

The year after her husband passed, Mrs. Havens had gone to London to chaperone Katherine during her come-out. Katherine lost her parents shortly after, and she and her great-aunt decided to stay on as each other's companions. Katherine was too young to respectably live alone, and her great-aunt's memory problems were becoming too frequent to ignore.

Not that Mrs. Havens noticed a lapse. Senility was both a blessing and a curse.

Daphne dipped a curtsey. "Pleased to meet you, ma'am.

Next time you're in Maidstone, you must stop for tea."

"I would love that, child." Mrs. Havens frowned and glanced over both of her shoulders. "Where did the dog go?"

Katherine's eyes widened. "I don't know, Aunt. Shall I look for him?"

"Of course not," Mrs. Havens chided her. "You *must* chat with your friend. The dog is no doubt hiding under my bed again. I'll coax him out."

"As you please, Aunt." Katherine shook her head as her great-aunt hurried away. She lowered her voice. "If she finds him, I'm hiding 'neath the closest bed. This house hasn't had a dog in ten years."

Daphne grinned back at her. "If a phantom canine appears, I'll join you under the bed."

Katherine laughed. "Thank you so much for letting her introduce herself again. She remembers the past better than I remember what I ate for breakfast, but the day-to-day is far more slippery."

"I adore your aunt," Daphne assured her. She would give anything to have an aunt half as sweet-natured. To have any family at all.

Mrs. Havens was one of the kindest women Daphne had ever met. 'Twas no hardship at all to repay that kindness however she could.

The Havens family had been legendary in Maidstone for their warmth and dedication to the community. Daphne's father had often said his greatest challenge was living up to the previous vicar's example, and that he hoped Daphne would do the same. She had spent her life trying to fulfill that promise. To earn his love. To be important to someone.

Katherine touched her fingers to Daphne's arm. "Are you certain you shouldn't like something to eat? If you're too weary for the dining room, 'tis of no trouble to have a tray brought here to your chambers."

"No, thank you." Daphne had dined at a posting house during her journey, and wanted nothing more than to get back to her projects. Somehow. "May I use that escritoire?"

"Absolutely. Please, make yourself at home. Adjust the room to your needs. I have some correspondence to attend to, so I shan't be bothering you. A benefactress's work is never done." Katherine rolled her eyes, as if she found correspondence a chore. "Don't hesitate to ring for service if you need anything at all."

Adjust the room to her needs? Daphne smiled. "I will."

The moment Katherine disappeared down the hallway, Daphne shut the door behind her. Esther was already unpacking Daphne's clothes from the first trunk and arranging them in the wardrobe.

Daphne's eyes narrowed as she considered her options. "Esther, stop."

Her lady's maid froze in place. "I oughtn't to hang your gowns?"

"The large items, yes." Daphne glanced about the room. "The smaller things—stockings and underskirts—let's use them to wrap up these artifacts."

"I'm to put Miss Ross's antiquities in… your underthings?" Esther repeated doubtfully.

"That's the only way they won't break when we store them all in my trunks."

Esther's eyes widened. "The other trunk isn't empty. It's got all your papers."

"Precisely." Daphne gave a brisk nod. "Documents out, antiquities in. I won't be able to cover the walls, but at least I'll have my most important items at hand."

Who needed excess underskirts anyway? Other than taking occasional meals with Katherine, Daphne intended to spend every other waking moment making good use of that escritoire. She'd already given her most important contacts her new direction, and wouldn't be surprised if post started arriving for her nom de plumes first thing in the morning.

Until then, there was plenty to do. She'd already lost nearly a full day to travel. She couldn't afford to waste another moment.

People needed her. The weavers' situation was deteriorating rapidly and the revolutionary Davy lamp was causing miners more harm than good. A Luddite disturbance had taken away the livelihoods of dozens of families. The collapse of a cave in South Tyneside had left desperate wives without their husbands.

She picked up her reading spectacles. Correspondence was not a chore. These were *families*. Fathers, mothers, children. People who had no one else. People who were grateful for the aid and sympathy of a little-known country miss named Daphne.

Er, perhaps better known as Mr. Caldwell. Or Mr. Baker. And Mr. Smith.

An hour later, when a knock sounded upon the door, she jerked her gaze up from the pile of letters on her lap with a frown. She'd assumed Katherine would be unlikely to intrude once she'd shown Daphne the guest chambers, but perhaps something had come up with Mrs. Havens and Katherine needed Daphne's help. If so, Katherine was about to find out how literally Daphne had taken her suggestion to make herself at home.

With a sheepish glance at the twine-bound stacks of papers where the antiquities used to rest, Daphne swallowed her guilt and opened the door.

A footman stood in the corridor.

Daphne raised her eyebrows in surprise. "Yes?"

"Forgive me for bothering you, ma'am. There is a gentleman here to see you. Miss Ross is talking to him in the parlor."

She blinked. A gentleman? Yes, she'd forwarded her temporary direction to several key parties, but they all knew her under one of her false names. The only person besides Katherine with any inkling Daphne might be in town was... Bartholomew?

She accepted the card from the footman. *Major Bartholomew Blackpool* was embossed in gold script. She pressed the card to her rapidly beating heart. *He was here.* How? Why?

Warmth infused her. She hadn't expected to see him again. He'd done his part. Above and beyond. It hadn't occurred to her to send him Katherine's direction or to beg him to come visit. It hadn't occurred to her that he might *wish* to.

She stared at the card again. Despite the interruption, she

couldn't hold back a rush of pleasure. For the first time, part of her wished she hadn't committed herself to aiding so many families, so that this sort of unexpected visit wouldn't have to *feel* like an interruption.

Was he just stopping by to see if she was settled? To make certain the accommodations were comfortable and her hostess far more considerate than her guardian? Daphne's heart warmed at the idea of Bartholomew checking after her the same way Daphne checked after her destitute families. She did so because she *cared*.

Of course, it was foolish to assume—or even hope—that Bartholomew could come to truly care about her, after all this time. Yet she was possessed of a very foolish heart indeed, for she could not help but hope that might be the case. To hope he had *missed* her, as she had missed him.

Breathless, Daphne handed the calling card to her maid and followed the footman down the stairs.

Bartholomew was speaking to Katherine in the parlor, his body angled away from the open door. Daphne's heart fluttered at the sight. He'd been sharply dressed when he'd called upon her in Maidstone, but in black breeches, a frothy white cravat, and a crisp black greatcoat, he was positively resplendent.

He was also holding her fur-lined winter spencer.

As soon as he caught sight of her, his smile widened and he held her coat open for her. "Put this on. We're going to be late. My carriage is out front."

She slipped her arms into the sleeves without thinking, then paused. "Wait. Where are we going?"

He shivered with mock horror. "To a musicale. My heartfelt apologies."

"A what?" She blinked up at him in confusion. "Why?"

He handed her an invitation. It failed to clear up the mystery.

She stared at the crinkled parchment. "This says, 'Grenville Musicale: Captain Xavier Grey.' Your name isn't even on it."

"I burnt mine." He glanced over her shoulder. "Where is your chaperone?"

"I don't have a chaperone." She bit her lip, conflicted. She'd dreamed of seeing him again. But her first duty was to the desperate women and children counting on Daphne's support. They *needed* her. "I don't need a duenna, I'm afraid. I cannot go anywhere."

Katherine chose that moment to interrupt. "Of course you can. You shall borrow my chaperone. Aunt Havens adores musicales."

Bartholomew inclined his head. "Wonderful. Thank you. Please ensure Mrs. Havens is properly bundled against the weather." He turned back to Daphne and frowned. "Where is your bonnet? Have you no muff for your fingers?"

Her head spun at the idea of being swept away. By *Bartholomew*. His demeanor implied that musicales were the seventh level of hell, but Daphne had never been to one and wouldn't know.

She'd always assumed society musicales were just another venue for the idle rich to applaud themselves for having nothing better to do than spend thousands of pounds to show off their children playing a Stradivarius. She'd never imagined being invited to one.

Much less escorted thither on the arm of a man who could melt her insides with little more than the press of his wide, firm lips against her gloved fingers. Of course she wished to join him.

If only she could.

Life was about choices. She'd already lost so much time. She would not compound that folly with choosing to attend a musicale over choosing to save lives. She was simply not a woman who could pursue pleasure for pleasure's sake. No matter how tempting the offer.

Daphne swallowed her disappointment. "I apologize. I cannot go. I've too much work to do, and—"

"You can and you will, if you've any care for your freedom." Bartholomew pressed her hands, his tone urgent. "Your guardian thinks he's being quizzed. He put a wedding announcement in the newspapers."

Daphne's stomach dropped. "He put a *what?*"

Bartholomew's low voice was full of portent. "He's

trying to ensure we dance to his strings. We have to make him think his plan is working. How much longer until your birthday?"

"Three weeks," she stammered, her mind dizzy. What if they didn't make it? What if her guardian forced her into marriage after all? Or locked her in a sanitarium?

Bartholomew's mouth tightened. "We can put him off until then. Provided we give every impression of a happy couple fully intending to comply with his wishes."

She nodded jerkily. He was right. They couldn't risk her guardian making good on his threats. If she thought Mayfair was ill-suited for charity work, Bedlam would be far less pleasant. They had to ease Captain Steele's mind before he took matters into his own hands.

She looped her hand about Bartholomew's arm and forced a smile. "A musicale sounds brilliant. I cannot wait for the wedding."

Katherine's mouth fell open. "You two are getting *married?*"

"Yes," Bartholomew said firmly. "Unless we should unexpectedly suffer a shocking breakup just prior to the as-yet-unplanned ceremony. Which would be extremely unlikely because we are completely in love. Isn't that so, Daphne… poppet… dear?"

Daphne Poppet Dear was singularly unimpressed by her new appellation, but terrified at the specter of her plan to escape her guardian's schemes unraveling so quickly. What had made him doubt her? How was she meant to act like a young lady in love?

Her heart raced in panic. It wasn't going to work. She had no invitations. The one Bartholomew possessed didn't even have his name on it. What if they were denied entry? What if they failed to prove to anyone, least of all her guardian, that their betrothal was in truth? What if it was already too late?

No. Captain Steele *had* to believe she and Bartholomew intended to wed. Daphne's future depended on it.

She spun toward Katherine. "You have to join us."

Katherine recoiled in horror. "What? Why?"

"Bartholomew's invitation says 'Captain Grey.'" Daphne reminded her. "We are not invited. But you're a cousin to the Duke of Lambley. No one would dare cut you. Or, by extension, us. Please, Katherine. We need your help."

"But I hate musicales." Katherine reached for a silver platter on the mantle. "Here, I'll give you my invitation. I'll write your name on top."

Daphne stilled her arm. "You can't just write extra names in the margin. They'll think we pickpocketed both of you. Over a musicale."

"You could be famous in a completely different way," Katherine agreed in delight. "A couple in love... and unafraid of the law. Two lovers joining forces against Society in the mad, mad search for musical entertainment. There's no captain too menacing, no duke's cousin too hoydenish, whom they wouldn't assault in their own front parlors to steal invitations to a good—"

"Katherine." Daphne valiantly refrained from doing bodily harm. "Get your spencer. Then get in the carriage."

"You could *try* to be romantic about it," Katherine grumbled in good humor. She motioned for a footman to fetch her things. "I can't believe you didn't tell me you were betrothed. I'm invited to the wedding, aren't I?"

Chapter Thirteen

By the time they reached the Grenville estate, Daphne's nerves were frayed beyond all hope.

Everything she'd worked for, everything she hoped for, hinged upon her deceptively simple plan not falling completely apart. Step one: Trump unwanted betrothal with false betrothal. Step two: Break fake betrothal as soon as her inheritance materialized. Step three: Be financially independent and free from male guardianship for the rest of her life.

She smoothed her gown with trembling fingers and stepped out of the carriage. If they didn't sell step one well enough, she wouldn't even make it to step two.

Katherine, for her part, was brilliant from the moment they knocked upon the door. The Grenville butler did not even blink to see the ebullient Miss Ross flanked by two unexpected guests.

As Katherine dragged them through the entryway, she murmured into several key ears that it would make her quite happy indeed if her dear friend Miss Vaughan and her fiancé Major Blackpool would trouble themselves to be seen more in Society.

Although none of them had seen Daphne before in their lives, all of Katherine's acquaintances professed to be delighted to include the happy couple in any upcoming events. Such was the power of being first cousin to a duke. Daphne expected to have a half-dozen invitations by morning, all from Katherine's good-humored intervention.

The surprising part was that it might not have been necessary.

From the moment they entered the main salon,

Bartholomew was surrounded by well-wishers jostling to be the first to greet him.

"Blackpool!" crowed a tall, well-dressed gentleman. "Jolly good to see you back in society!"

"And with your cravat as exquisite as ever," said another. "Never say that valet of yours has spent the last year perfecting his art, just so you could show us all up. How do you do it?"

The waves of eager faces were overwhelming. The noise, deafening. In no time at all, the musical entertainment was an hour delayed, simply because there was no end to the number of people who preferred to have a word with Major Blackpool rather than sit down for the performance.

"Major Blackpool, Major Blackpool," cooed a handful of debutantes, each elbowing the others out of the way to preen at Bartholomew. "Now that you're attending events again, shall I save a spot for you on my dance card at the next ball?"

Daphne's teeth clenched as she forced herself to look away from their rouged lips and fluttering lashes. 'Twas everything she had always imagined Bartholomew's life to be like. Rakish. Sparkling. Larger than life. Constantly surrounded by adoring eyes. She swallowed her jealousy. It wasn't as though she wished *she* were in the limelight. She was needed in her office, not onstage. Her best work was accomplished anonymously.

Yet, what must it be like to have so many friends? To have so many people *interested* in what one had to say?

Bartholomew pulled her closer, as if sensing her discomfort. Or her jealousy.

"I'm afraid we've gotten off on the wrong foot," he said to the coquettish young ladies, then winked at the gentlemen. "My *only* foot, that is." He turned to Daphne and smiled as if she had been sent down from the heavens. "May I present Miss Daphne Vaughan, who has done me the honor of agreeing to be my wife. She was dear to me when we were children playing on the hills of Kent and she is even more precious to me today. I am a man in love."

Daphne's breath caught. She had to grip his arm a little tighter to keep from swaying, and she *knew* it was utter poppycock. Yet she couldn't help but glance up at him from beneath her eyelashes and wonder how it would feel if he truly were a besotted swain.

Her cheeks flushed. Even thought he was acting a role, 'twas intoxicating to have a man who could choose anyone be focused on *her*. It was like sunlight to her soul. Rain to a flower. She had been starved for affection for so very long that even the pretense of it was heady and addictive.

If only it were as real as it looked.

A few of the debutantes stared daggers at Daphne. The others ignored her completely, as if the fight had only just begun. They made shameless calf eyes at Bartholomew whilst licking their lips and tugging coyly at their ringlets.

Daphne despised them all. Their lack of morals, their lack of sense. Why was it that *this* sort of woman could be confident in her ability to attract attention, whereas Daphne could dedicate her entire life to improving the world about them, and still not even earn a second glance?

She was irrelevant. An afterthought. No matter how hard she tried to be the best possible person she could be, 'twas never enough. She wasn't good enough to keep her father's attention, pretty enough to catch a gentleman's eye, intriguing enough to command anyone's attention.

Bartholomew would have forgotten her altogether, had circumstances not thrown them together. Even here, at his side, with her fingers curved about his elbow, the aristocrats and debutantes had dismissed Daphne without so much as a second glance. Even Bartholomew had been caught up in a conversation with several gentlemen on the merits and pitfalls of fox hunting.

Her throat tightened. What had she expected? All her life, she'd wanted to be noticed. To be loved. To be *worthy* of love. She had done everything she could to be an angel on earth and all it had earned her was a lifetime of loneliness. She'd had to learn to be strong. To define her own self-worth, rather than wait for someone else's approval.

As she gazed at the crowd, part of her wished she could be the sort of giggly, simpering debutante who never sat out a single dance. But it was too late for that. She hadn't been raised to giggle or simper. Now that she'd opened her eyes and her heart to the plight of the nation's poor, she could no more turn her back on them than she could have turned her back on her own father.

She rolled back her shoulders. As much as she might fantasize about being a giddy, feather-headed girl whose life revolved about little more than fashion and merrymaking, she had committed herself to a greater cause. A worthy cause. She might not interest others, but she would lose respect for herself if she gave society events more importance than human charity.

Even if it meant losing Bartholomew to one of these girls.

"You *rogue*," pouted one of the debutantes, edging closer to Bartholomew. "How cruel of you to tease us with your presence after all this time, when you're already taken."

An older gentleman raised an eyebrow at Daphne. "I imagine Major Blackpool considers himself quite fortunate."

"Fortunate?" Bartholomew turned to Daphne, eyes solemn. "I used to think the luckiest moment of my life was when I made it off the battlefield alive." He lifted her gloved fingers in his hands. "I now know it was the day I met you."

Her stomach dropped and her throat went dry. She stared back at him, speechless. He was everything she'd never dared to dream of.

His warm gaze never left hers as he pressed a kiss to her trembling fingers. She cursed the foolish weakness in her knees. The temptation to throw herself into his arms and beg for the betrothal to be real. For him to look at her and *mean* his incredibly romantic words.

When he turned away, she pressed her kissed fingers to her chest. Close to her heart.

"I don't know," laughed a freckled gentleman. "I'd still say the battlefield was your luckiest day. Let you come home to the lass, did it not?"

"What precisely happened? Carlisle wouldn't say a word," put in another. "Rescued two out of three of you, and you'd think it was just another promenade in the park. Did you see Boney?"

"Were you ambushed?" asked another.

"Tell us about Waterloo. Were you near Wellington at all times?"

"How many soldiers were on that field?"

The loud gaggle of gentlemen surrounded Bartholomew, separating him from Daphne with their thumps to his shoulders and their avalanche of questions. He sent several searching looks over his shoulder in Daphne's direction as he was enveloped into the tide.

She hugged herself. He would find her later. Probably. She sighed. If he remembered she was still here.

'Twas no surprise everyone found Bartholomew fascinating. Not only were he and his friends collectively referred to in the scandal sheets as the Dukes of War, Bartholomew was a major. A twin. A hero. A survivor. Despite a pulverized leg, he'd still tried to save his dying brother.

The whole thing was so gothic and heart-wrenching that the recital had been all but forgotten, and even Katherine resembled a wallflower for the first time in her life. It also meant she probably wouldn't see Bartholomew again until it was time to return home. She'd been left standing all alone. Adrift in an ocean of strangers.

Daphne sighed. If she'd but known she would be invisible this evening, she might have brought her work and a traveling desk with her and taken up office in one of the retiring rooms. And perhaps dedicated her time to someone who actually wanted it.

"Well?" murmured Katherine as she returned from the refreshment table with two cups of lemonade.

Daphne took a sip and winced at the criminal dearth of sugar. "Well, what?"

"The Blackpools are from Maidstone, so that's obviously how you met. But the major was off at war for three years and hasn't left London since he returned, so how the deuce did you get betrothed?"

"*Shh.*" Daphne flapped a suppressing hand in Katherine's direction. "You can't say *deuce*. Especially not in public."

"You may recall I never wished to attend this musicale in the first place."

"Don't say that either!" Daphne motioned Katherine over to the rows of chairs set up before the pianoforte. The audience section was currently the most private area of the entire Grenville estate. "I did see Major Blackpool recently. In Maidstone."

"And you fell instantly and deeply in love. Then forgot to tell me about it." Katherine squinted over Daphne's shoulder. "Hard to see him through the throngs of people. He cuts as dashing a figure as he ever did. Perhaps more so, now that he's a tragic hero as well. I believe it's safe to say your wedding will be well attended. Not that you've invited me to it."

"*Fine*." Daphne took a deep breath. "'Tis a lie. We're not getting married. He's only playacting to help me out of a scrape with my new guardian. After Papa died, I became ward to a man who would rather walk the plank than be responsible for me. He tried to force me into an unwanted betrothal."

"And Major Blackpool swept in to save you?" Katherine arched a brow. "This gets more romantic with every word. Do go on."

"It's not romantic, it's—" Daphne snapped her teeth together and briefly closed her eyes.

He *had* swept in to save her. It *was* romantic. She'd promised their scheme would be a secret, yet when their imaginary relationship fell under suspicion, Bartholomew hadn't hesitated to involve himself up to the ears just to keep her safe from her guardian's threats. To protect her.

"The look on your face tells me you've finally noticed your fiancé would be considered a fine catch." Katherine's eyebrows tilted toward the crowd. "Approximately every single female present appears willing to take your place, should anything untoward happen to your happy engagement. Such as a shocking termination, moments before the as-yet-unplanned ceremony."

"I can't marry him," Daphne burst out, her voice thick. "He doesn't even wish to. He's playacting."

"But are you?"

Daphne swallowed. She wasn't sure anymore. Not that she had a choice. The betrothal was a sham. Soon she would have the freedom she'd wanted. And the memory of what might have been. "You know how wholly my projects consume me. I don't have time for myself, much less a husband."

Katherine's expression was skeptical. "You wouldn't even marry for love?"

"*Especially* not for love." Daphne had thought it through. Repeatedly. Every time Bartholomew crossed her mind. "If I loved someone, I would want to spend every moment with him, which isn't remotely amenable to getting anything at all accomplished."

Katherine shrugged. "I'm sure a good husband could be counted upon to have interests outside the home."

"Yes, and I'm just as certain that a wife in love would spend *those* moments mooning over him or worrying about him or wondering what, precisely, he and his friends were up to and whether she oughtn't to go and investigate." Like right now. With a room full of unwed debutantes on the loose. She shook her head. "No, thank you. I'll stay unfettered and unencumbered." Life was simpler when her heart was only involved from afar. "There are thousands of people whose lives are affected by whether or not I act to protect them. I cannot jeopardize that over something as foolish as love."

Katherine's head tilted. "What projects are you working on now?"

Daphne gave her a shaky smile, relieved at the conversational reprieve. Charity work was a far safer topic than Bartholomew. "I'm terribly worried about the worsening situation with the weavers. There's scarcely any work and the people are starting to get desperate. And then the miners… The Davy lamp seemed like a miracle—who wouldn't wish to see what lurked in the shadows?—but the increased visibility makes workers feel safer in areas that are anything but, and the accident rate—"

"The what lamp? Why isn't there any work for the weavers?" Katherine clasped her hands together and leaned closer. "If I can't help you plan a wedding, at least let me lend a hand with your projects. I'm frightfully good at planning things. Last year I became patroness of an antiquities museum, did I not? Just look at how successful it is."

"An antiquities museum is nothing at all like—" Daphne stilled her tongue. Katherine meant well, but she didn't understand. "I wish you could help. If there were some way for you to know everything I know overnight, perhaps. But I don't have weeks to spend explaining the history or what's been done about it. I might not have weeks at all, if my guardian gets his way. I need to focus now more than ever."

"On being the most enamored fiancée in all of Christendom?"

Daphne pressed her lips together. So much for the conversational reprieve. Of course Katherine wasn't interested in charity. "No, on—"

"Wrong answer." Katherine motioned behind her.

Daphne turned. Bartholomew was heading toward them, leading the rest of the guests toward their seats as though he were the commander of an army.

Or the Pied Piper of Hamelin.

She narrowed her eyes. Whether the frivolous aristocrats were children or rats was hard to say. She was so frustrated with the upper class. They were the ones with the money and power to improve employment, safety, orphanages. Perhaps the ladies embroidered for charity now and again, but it didn't do much toward enacting *change*.

The men were even worse. Egotistic. Dismissive. She frowned at a sudden realization. What did it say about Bartholomew that they looked up to him so? Was he just as superficial? Just as narcissistic? The price of the waistcoat he was wearing could likely feed an orphanage for a week. He either didn't realize, or didn't care. The proof was right before her eyes. He *wasn't* the perfect romantic hero her heart had wished he could be. He was just like the others.

She let out a shaky breath. No matter. He had never been hers for the taking. She had promised herself to a greater calling. A purpose. The people she helped thought she hung the moon. They sometimes sent letters, signed by the whole family. They told her she *mattered*.

Here in London, she patently did not matter. She was of no interest to Polite Society. She intermittently commanded the temporary attention of her faux fiancé. When obligated to do so. It wasn't love. It was an old childhood friendship. Bartholomew didn't think of her as a woman, with hopes and dreams and desires. She doubted he thought of her much at all.

She wished it didn't hurt so much.

Her heart clenched at the pain. Once she no longer saw him every day, his indifference would cease to hurt her. She straightened her spine. As soon as their false betrothal was over, she would spend the rest of her days with people who looked forward to her presence. She would travel wherever her aid was needed most, providing support however she could. She would *force* herself to be happy.

The life she was given would have to be enough.

"There you are, darling." Bartholomew gave her a slow, devastating smile as his fingers brushed the small of her back. "I missed you."

Her breath caught. She had to fight not to shiver at his words. Or melt beneath the warmth of his gaze and the sensation of being the sole object of his complete attention.

He was playacting, just like her.

He was also better at it. He'd been a rake for most of his life, whereas she'd spent all of hers as a vicar's daughter. She would never be part of his world.

Yet she couldn't help but long for him to look at her like that and mean it.

She smiled back at him, hesitantly.

His gaze lowered to her lips. Her heart quickened. She licked her lips in anticipation. His eyelashes lowered, and for a single, soul-stopping moment she truly thought he might kiss her, right there in front of everyone.

And she stood there, waiting for it. Like the goose she was.

He lifted his gaze and gestured toward the seats. "Shall we?"

She swallowed hard and nodded. Her legs shook. She couldn't care less about the musicale, or even the crowd. All she could think about was how it might have felt if he'd kissed her. *Foolishness*. She pressed a hand to her chest. Her heart still pounded.

Katherine entered the row first, followed by Daphne and then Bartholomew.

As soon as Daphne sat down, Katherine leaned toward Daphne's ear. "I could have sworn he was about to—"

"He was not," Daphne whispered back, her face heating.

"Well, you certainly looked like you—"

"I did not," she hissed and shooed away any further comments. "Eyes on the stage."

A couple Daphne didn't recognize sat in the row in front of them. The man instantly turned around to cast a wide smile at Bartholomew. "Never thought I'd see you at a place like this, Blackpool. Didn't you always say you'd never set foot in a musicale?"

"Still haven't." Bartholomew lifted his false leg. "I couldn't even find my foot."

The man guffawed and half-turned to his wife. "You see this? Wouldn't believe it if I weren't witnessing it with my own eyes. Blackpool in love. I'll be damned." He grinned at Daphne. "Caught yourself a good one, miss. One of the very best."

"Thank you," she stammered. No. No stammering. *Be in love*. That's why they had come. She brushed her fingers against Bartholomew's chest and peered up at him through her lashes. "He's…"

Conscious thought failed her. He was playacting, she *knew* he was playacting, and yet the passion in his eyes was nothing short of smoldering. She could lose herself in eyes that blue. She yearned to brush her fingers against his chest again, to flatten her palm over his heart and feel it thunder beneath her hand. He seemed larger than before. Closer. As if she was leaning too far into him, offering herself into his embrace.

"Ladies and gentlemen," boomed a voice from the stage. "Heath, Camellia, and Bryony Grenville!"

Daphne flattened her spine against her seatback and prayed no one noticed the heat coloring her cheeks. *Playact*, she reminded herself fiercely. No actual kissing. The last thing she needed was to get compromised and have to marry him in truth. Not when he had to pretend to like her.

She breathed out slowly and kept her eyes locked on the stage.

Katherine leaned over. "That certainly didn't *look* like faux—"

"Kindly refrain from speaking during the musicale," Daphne muttered back. "It's considered rude."

Katherine laughed softly. "It's your show."

If only it were.

Daphne slid another glance toward Bartholomew. If she were a different kind of woman, his eyes would be fixed on her instead of on the stage. If she were only carefree and gay, coquettish and elegant, mysterious and irresistible. She could be his.

If she weren't Daphne.

Chapter Fourteen

Any victory Bartholomew had felt at having survived a musicale without falling on his face or punching everyone who asked how he was coping without his brother vanished the day he picked up Daphne to go riding in Hyde Park. He wanted it to look like a romantic afternoon ride. He wanted it to *be* a romantic afternoon ride.

The problem was his curricle.

Never mind that it was old. He'd bought it long before he'd joined the army and had spent a solid year testing its limits and its speed.

Never mind that it was *cold*. An open carriage was quite possibly the most ridiculous conveyance for February weather, but it was paramount that he and Daphne be seen together. That he and Daphne appear positively smitten.

The curricle was wrong because *Bartholomew* was wrong.

He'd been at sixes and sevens since leaving the house. Scratch that. He'd been at sixes and sevens since almost kissing Daphne in the middle of a musicale. Or perhaps since the moment Crabtree had saved her letter from the fire and her plea had sent his solitary existence down a whirlwind path.

A month ago, his biggest adventure was deciding whether to do his afternoon exercises before or after a spot of tea. This month, he had a beautiful faux fiancée. A pirate threatening her with Bedlam—and Bartholomew with Newgate. An entire city of curious onlookers pinning him and Daphne both under their watchful eyes. And three weeks to convince them all he was eagerly awaiting a wedding that was never going to happen.

Unfortunately for him, he *did* eagerly await the stolen moments he shared with Daphne. She had turned his life upside down, but he dreaded the day she was no longer in it. From the moment she'd taken his hand to present a united front before his parents, part of him had begun to want her in his life for good.

Impossible, of course. Not only was Daphne's refusal to wed abundantly clear, Bartholomew would make a poor husband for any woman. He'd left for war far from perfect. He'd returned home incomplete. After losing his brother, he no longer believed he *deserved* happiness.

Much less a woman like Daphne.

She was resourceful and clever. Gave freely of her heart and expected nothing in return. She was selfless where he had been selfish. Open to the world, whilst he had closed himself off from it. Fought for strangers to thrive, whereas he had left his own brother to die.

No, he certainly didn't deserve her. But, *oh,* how he wanted her anyway.

He pulled up in front of the Ross townhouse and banged the knocker. Within moments of being shown into the parlor, she was already descending the stairs, bonnet and gloves in place. As if she'd been looking forward to this outing as eagerly as he was.

"My lady." He offered his arm. "Ready for a spot of sunshine?"

She laid her fingers in the crook of his elbow and gave him a shy smile. "I've never seen Hyde Park before."

"Then I am honored to be your guide." He just hoped he didn't make a fool of himself doing so. He didn't want her to have to pretend to enjoy his company even when they were alone.

He handed her up into the curricle, then crossed around back to swing himself up from the other side. The air was brisk as they trotted west toward the park. Daphne edged closer. He wished he could believe she was drawn to him due to a physical attraction, not simply to seek relief from the winter chill.

Then again, perhaps the open carriage was a blessing in

disguise. Even if it were mutual, he had no business acting on his physical attraction. He was meant to protect her from an unwanted marriage, not compromise her into one as Carlisle had done. The earl and his new wife were happy with their fates. With each other. Daphne would not be.

Bartholomew would have to respect her wishes and keep his interest hidden. He was a pretend beau, nothing more. 'Twas what he had promised. And what he must deliver.

Navigating Hyde Park was its own gauntlet. His muscles tensed as his carriage joined the queue leading into the park. Today was his first time driving since returning from war. Everything about it felt awkward and out of place.

For one, this was his *racing* curricle. He'd never before had a woman in it. He'd never promenaded through city parks at all. He'd been too busy hurtling down Rotten Row with the wind in his face and his wheels tipping precariously as he took curves far too sharply.

He felt out of balance with both wheels on the ground. With his hat staying put. With Daphne in the carriage.

His gloved fingers tightened on the reins. Could she tell how discomfited he was to be here, to be doing this? Was his countenance a touch pallid? His clammy hands unsteady? His dark looks at the young bucks rocketing by in flying phaetons too obviously borne of envy for their easy, careless lives? Any one of the eligible bachelors buzzing about in search of a pretty face would be a better choice than a man with no leg.

He ground his teeth. How would they convince *anyone* that she had chosen him above all others, when there was no reason that she should?

Any other gentleman could stay seated on a saddle. Waltz without falling. Disrobe without humiliation. He glanced at Daphne and sighed. 'Twas impossible to convince anyone they were a love match. She was too perfect. He was too flawed. Even he could see it. Soon, she would, too. If she hadn't already.

Once she got rid of Bartholomew and enjoyed a year or two of independence, she'd start to wonder what it might be like to have a husband or a family. Bartholomew well knew the loneliness of self-imposed solitude. The nights would grow long. Whether she planned to or not, she would someday fall in love. It was inevitable.

The man she chose would be nothing like Bartholomew. He'd be some damnably happy fellow from a happy family, and have many happy memories of never having been to war or lost someone he cherished. He'd enjoy racing and dancing, make love like a stallion, and be the proud owner of both of his legs. In short, he'd be perfect, too.

Daphne deserved nothing less.

He slid another glance in her direction. She gripped the side of the curricle, staring out at the sprawling park and endless carriages with cautious green eyes. He rubbed the back of his neck. He'd thought she would love Hyde Park. Instead, she looked half terrified. As though instead of finding the serpentine throng invigorating, as he did, she found the crowd nerve-wracking. She looked like she might throw herself bodily from the curricle rather than spend another moment promenading in the park.

His jaw tightened. Not only did they fail to resemble a besotted couple, Daphne's current expression wouldn't look like she enjoyed his company at all. His cheeks burned. Perhaps she didn't. He ought to distract her with more pleasant topics.

He cleared his throat. "How have you been enjoying London?"

"I haven't." She made a frustrated sound and turned to meet his eyes. "Katherine is lovely, and her house of course is magnificent, but it isn't home. Not for me. I've done my best to turn my chamber into a study, but the wallpaper is too pretty to affix documents to it and the noise from the balcony is incredibly distracting while I'm attending to my correspondence. There's a park just outside, with any number of horses and children and pie vendors causing ruckus at all hours. How can anyone work in such conditions?"

He stared at her, nonplussed. Everything he loved about London, she hated. The finery, the food, the fun. His stomach clenched. 'Twas yet another reason no one in their right mind would believe them slated for marriage. Even he couldn't believe they were that incompatible. The attraction between them had been too palpable. For a moment, he had even thought... He shook his head.

"Never say you've spent every moment you're not with me focused on nothing but your projects."

Her eyes flashed. "Of course I have. *Someone* needs to champion these people's rights. 'Tis who I am and what I do."

He raised his brows and turned his gaze back to the road in silence. She found his sense of charity lacking. The implication was clear. His fingers tightened on the reins in annoyance. And envy. Until Waterloo, he, too, had known who and what he was. Now he had no idea. And he'd managed to offend her in the process.

No doubt she believed he thought her silly for choosing to fight iniquity instead of taking a husband. She was wrong. He did not consider her ideals silly at all.

He thought them futile.

One woman couldn't save everyone. An entire army hadn't even been able to save everyone. Some wars just couldn't be won.

She arched a brow. "How have you spent your valuable time since last I saw you? Drinking champagne and frequenting gentlemen's clubs? What is it that *you* do?"

He smiled tightly. "Absolutely nothing."

He knew his answer would infuriate her as much as if he'd said "rutting with whores" or "designing a new waistcoat." Her belief in the potential goodness of others was too entrenched. By nature, she interpreted any fun-seeking activity as willfully ignoring orphans or worker safety or rookery famine. No doubt she judged him just as frivolous and useless as the rest of London. And she was right. There *were* better uses for his time.

But he wasn't her. He wasn't even *him* anymore. No longer a rake, no longer a soldier, no longer a twin. He was nothing. As dull and lifeless as the wooden prosthesis strapped to his knee. A heartless man carved to look like the real thing, but empty inside. Too tired to be a martyr.

"Let's not argue." He leaned over. "When there are

witnesses about, you should at least pretend to tolerate me."

She tossed him a saucy smile. "I *do* like you. Very much. You were my hero before you ever left for war. I just thought you of all people would understand." Her shoulders eased. "But you're right It's not even necessary that we agree. By next month, it won't matter."

True. The warmth of her remarks faded. By next month, he would be back in his townhouse. Alone with his thoughts and his regrets. "Will you be returning to Maidstone?"

Her nose wrinkled. "I can't. Cousin Steele owns the cottage and I cannot live under the same roof. Not after deceiving him. Besides, that's not where I can do my best work."

He straightened, his heart suddenly light. Perhaps there was hope. "You'll be staying here in London?"

"Hardly." She shook her head. "I will go wherever I'm needed most. South Tyneside first, then Leicester. I'm unlikely to see London again for a long time."

Or him, in other words. Bartholomew's fingers tightened around the reins. What had he expected? That a few weeks with him would trap her in London's web? Leave her hopelessly addicted to his company? Make her fall in love with a man who wasn't even certain he deserved the emotion?

"I'll miss *you*, though." Her soft words pierced his armor. "Even more than I did when you first left Maidstone. I didn't even think such a feat possible." She laughed sadly. "It seems the jest is on me."

"The jest is on both of us," he admitted gruffly. "I wish you well, but I do not look forward to your departure."

Several minutes passed in silence.

He wished he hadn't spoken. Hadn't admitted that he cared. Every other relationship he'd ever cared about ended in shambles. He didn't wish to add Daphne to that list.

She tilted her head, her green eyes curious. "And you? How will you spend your time?"

He pretended to think it over. "Perhaps I'll take up coal mining or fabric weaving so that we'll meet again."

She stuck out her tongue. "Rubbish. You'd get your

cravat dirty."

He shuddered. "Thank God you warned me in time. Fitz would have my head on a silver platter."

Her eyes laughed at him. "One can always trust Bartholomew to be Bartholomew. You'll stay here in the city, I presume?"

His jaw tightened. Did she truly think him as featherbrained as that? Perhaps it was for the best. He couldn't disappoint her if she didn't hold any expectations.

"London is where the best tailors are. I wouldn't dream of living anywhere else."

Her expression grew pensive. "And your parents?"

"Should stay as far away from me as possible." As should Daphne, if she wished to escape the inevitable hurt he caused everyone he loved. The visit with his parents should have illustrated how badly he'd disappointed them. "What did you think when you saw them?"

Her gaze softened. "That they love you very much."

He scoffed and returned his gaze to the road, unable to meet her eyes. "They did. Before I lost Edmund."

"They *still* do. You cannot possibly have failed to notice that your mother—"

"Lives in a state of constant hysteria? I noticed. It's my fault." He hated that his tight knit family had shattered in the space of a single moment. He scraped a hand through his hair. If only there was some way he and his mother could be closer without leading to madness for them both. "My presence in Maidstone wouldn't be beneficial to either of us. I do not require a nursemaid."

"She misses you."

"She misses Edmund. She thinks I can replace him by being *both* of us. By filling the hole and being me, too." He took a deep breath. "I *cannot*."

Daphne's voice lowered. "Your father?"

"Is empty now. I disappointed him, and Edmund broke his heart. I cannot fix that." His smile was mirthless. "I can't fix anything."

She frowned. "It wasn't your fault—"

"*Don't*," he snapped. "You weren't there, and you aren't

me. Don't presume to tell me how I should feel."

She fell silent.

He set his jaw and fixed his gaze on the horizon.

Shite. He hadn't meant to snarl at her, but it wasn't her brother that had been talked into fighting someone else's war and then left on a battlefield to die. It wasn't her family who was too broken to speak to each other. If Bartholomew could undo the past, he would.

His shoulders slumped. None of it was worth it.

So little ever was.

Her miners and weavers would be no exception, unfortunately. But 'twas not his duty to crush her dreams. She'd learn soon enough how the world truly worked. Her dogged idealism and precious causes were all well and good, but if three years in the army had taught him anything, it was that one cannot save everyone, no matter how hard one tries.

"Blackpool!" called a voice alongside the carriage.

A distraction. *Thank God.*

"Who goes there?" Bartholomew leaned his head out of the curricle and faked a shudder. "Good Lord. Not even a mother could love a mug that ugly."

The Marquess of Sainsbury's handsome face split into a grin. "Good to see you back, old man. A few of us are off to race phaetons here in a few moments. I see you've better company this time, but we'll meet again next week if you think your ancient nag can manage Rotten Row. I've twenty pounds that says it can't."

"A snail could outpace you," Bartholomew shot back. "But I'd hate for you to lose your money. 'Tis the only way you'll ever attract a bride."

The marquess laughed. "How on earth did you get yours? Congratulations to both of you. I never thought I'd see the day!"

Bartholomew kept his smile pasted on as the marquess snapped his reins and rode away. Pensive, he turned to look at Daphne. The sunlight caught her golden curls, softening the no-nonsense exterior she liked to project. Her lips were rosy and her cheeks flushed pink from the winter wind. Her warm green eyes were intelligent and discerning, and looked back at him with the same intensity that he gazed at her.

"You *are* one of the good ones," he said softly. "You could have a real husband if you wished."

She shook her head and glanced away. "It doesn't matter what I wish. I wouldn't fit into a husband's life. Nor would he fit into mine."

He nodded. Perhaps. And perhaps not. Someone out there had to be a match.

She was right that it would be difficult to reconcile a wife's duties with her current obsessions, but he couldn't imagine her *never* finding love. There was passion hidden within her. Passion for more than displaced weavers and children's rights. Passion waiting to be explored by the right man.

His heart beat faster. The other night at the musicale, there had been several moments where it had taken all his self-control not to tilt her face up to his and kiss her. Even now, her arms looked soft and inviting. She smelled like heaven. And her lush pink mouth was simply begging to be tasted.

But she was not to be his.

The two of them were beyond incompatible as a married couple. On that, they could agree. But he imagined they might have quite a bit in common when it came to matters of the flesh. He swallowed hard.

How different things might have been if they'd only been thrown together back when he was a whole man.

Chapter Fifteen

A few days later, Bartholomew found himself calling upon the Ross house once again.

This time, it wasn't to whisk Daphne off to a musicale or for a drive in Hyde Park. They wouldn't be leaving the town house. This was the night of the soirée Lambley had referred to weeks ago, when he'd asked Daphne if she would be in town visiting his cousin.

Everyone, it seemed, was visiting Lambley's cousin.

Carriages had queued from around the next block. Hackney carriages, private coaches, even a donkey cart. Bartholomew couldn't imagine what all these people had in common, much less why they'd all be under one roof. He was intrigued by the mix.

For once, perhaps he wouldn't be the oddity.

The butler motioned him in the door without questioning whether Bartholomew had an invitation. Fortunate, that. Given that he didn't have one.

On the other hand, it didn't look like any of the guests were being questioned too closely, or even at all. They were simply welcomed in, relieved of their coats or bonnets, and motioned to join the others in the parlor.

The amount of people crammed into one spacious, but clearly inadequate room put even the annual Sheffield Christmastide ball to shame. In fact, Bartholomew could have sworn he'd glimpsed Lord Sheffield himself on the other side of the teeming horde. Perhaps he and his wife were taking notes on how to outdo themselves next year.

"You came," said a surprised voice from just behind him.

Daphne. He tucked her hand around his upper arm and

lowered his lips to her hair to breathe in her scent. "Of course."

Was it scandalous to feather a light kiss against those sweet-smelling red-gold ringlets? Perhaps.

Was he going to do it anyway? Absolutely.

He lifted his head to survey the motley crowd in wonder. Even Vauxhall wasn't this diverse. "Who *are* these people?"

Daphne lifted a shoulder in sympathy. "The only people I know in London are you, Katherine, and Lambley."

"But what kind of party is this?"

"A Katherine party," Daphne answered with a little smile. "Katherine is... eccentric. She doesn't think there is any reason why earls and poets and solicitors can't mingle." Her eyes softened. "It's why I love her."

An elderly woman with white powdered hair caught his attention. She made a beeline straight toward them. "Daphne, is that you, dear? Introduce me to this fine gentleman at once. Hoarding the handsome ones is strictly verboten."

"And have you steal him from me?" Daphne's smile widened indulgently. "Mrs. Havens, this is my fiancé, Major Bartholomew Blackpool. Major Blackpool, this dear lady is Katherine's great-aunt and the widow of the previous Maidstone vicar. Mrs. Havens is a legend."

The name clicked in Bartholomew's brain. "Of course! Mrs. Havens, how wonderful to meet you. Daphne's father was vicar in my earliest memories, but I cannot recall a time when you and your husband weren't spoken of with great admiration. It is an honor to meet you."

Mrs. Havens beamed at him, then stage-whispered to Daphne, "Handsome *and* charming. Hold tight to this one."

Daphne's hand tightened reflexively about Bartholomew's arm. "Of course, ma'am. I wouldn't dream otherwise."

One of the footmen passed by with a tray of champagne flutes. Mrs. Havens stopped him to make certain both Bartholomew and Daphne took a glass.

"Moderation, not libation," she cautioned with a wag of her finger. "Especially you, Daphne. Don't let London go to your head."

"No, ma'am." Daphne shook her head gravely. "I certainly won't."

Emptiness filled Bartholomew's chest. He doubted Daphne would stay in London a day more than necessary after she inherited her portion. She was too eager to leave. To seek out a better life than what she could find here.

"Blackpool!" The Duke of Lambley emerged from the sea of faces. He nodded in the direction of Daphne's fingers curled about Bartholomew's arm. "Cupid knock you off your cloud, did he?"

Bartholomew paused, unsure whether this was meant as a gibe for having "stolen" Daphne away from the others, but the last thing he wished was to cause a scene. He gave his best careless smile. "Cupid's arrow was true. I fell hard, but as you see, I always land on my feet. Or foot, as the case may be."

Lambley chuckled and clapped him on the shoulder. "Losing a leg would slow anyone down. Of course you couldn't dodge the arrow. Well, they say reformed rakes make the best husbands. Good to see you cheerful again. Congratulations to both of you. You make a lovely couple."

Daphne's smile didn't reach her eyes. "Thank you."

As Lambley glided away, Daphne frowned at his retreating back. "He should not have made a teasing comment about your leg."

Bartholomew placed his untouched champagne glass on the tray of a passing footman. "*I* made a teasing comment about my wounded leg."

"You should not have, either."

He shrugged. Jokes were all he had. "Ignoring it won't grow it back."

Before Daphne could respond, her friend Miss Ross slipped from the crowd to join them.

Her cheeks were flushed, her eyes bright. "Good evening, Major. I do so love a party. How are you enjoying your evening so far?"

"It's… overwhelming," he admitted. "And impressive. Do you actually know all these people?"

"Of course!" She moved closer so that she could gesture

without others noticing. "You see the older gentleman with dark hair and a cleft chin?"

Bartholomew scanned the crowd, then nodded. "The one who looks like John Kemble, the actor?"

"That *is* Mr. Kemble. He manages the Theatre Royal in Covent Garden. Which is why he's at the opposite end of the room as that young gentleman with the foppish hair, the one sneaking all the biscuits from the refreshment table."

"Is he another actor?"

"Heavens, no. Mr. Wyatt is too serious by far, when there are no biscuits about. He designed the other Theatre Royal, in Drury Lane. He and Mr. Kemble have already exchanged several heated words about parquet and acoustics." Miss Ross grinned as if this were a hallmark of a successful party. "Can I help with any introductions? If neither the business nor the performance aspect of theatre pique your interest, surely the wonders of Egypt catch your fancy?"

Bartholomew arched an eyebrow. "Are there mummies or a misplaced pharaoh somewhere amongst all those people?"

"Close." Miss Ross leaned closer. "Look for a portly gentleman by the piano. Balding, with tufts of gray hair over his ears? Mr. Bullock is a naturalist, the antiquarian behind the Egyptian Hall in Piccadilly." She lowered her voice toward Daphne. "I tried to get him to let me help manage the exhibit when it first opened. The knave categorically refused."

Daphne's eyes twinkled. "Is that why you sponsored a completely different antiquities museum?"

"Did I?" Miss Ross blinked back at her innocently. "Egyptian artifacts aren't the *only* interesting relics in history."

"You would have been the best thing to happen to the Egyptian Hall," Daphne said staunchly. "It is his loss."

"Yes, well, there are no hard feelings." Miss Ross lifted her chin. "All of these people are very special to me or to this city, and I'd be delighted to introduce you to any one of them. Just say the word."

Bartholomew kept mum. He was happy to stay in the shadows. The less attention, the better.

"Kate!" Mrs. Havens all but bounded over, her clear blue eyes sparkling against the pale of her skin and the powdered white of her hair. "What a lovely gathering." She glanced at Bartholomew and Daphne. "Are you two enjoying yourselves?"

He smiled back at her. "How could we not, in company as delightful as yours?"

"I see you don't have any champagne, young man." Mrs. Havens flagged down a footman. "Champagne for the gentleman, please. But just one. Moderation, not libation!"

Bartholomew frowned and lifted a hand to forestall the footman. "None, actually. I no longer imbibe spirits. I thank you for your consideration, ma'am."

Mrs. Havens' eyes widened in pleasure. "I'm very impressed. So many young men these days have little restraint. Oh, is that Lady Grenville? If you'll excuse me, I must greet an old friend."

She was gone before anyone could reply.

Miss Ross shook her head, laughing. "That was Aunt Havens. She's three times my age and has twice the energy. I'll introduce you when she flutters back by."

"I believe I did meet her." Bartholomew darted a questioning glance toward Daphne. "A half hour ago, perhaps."

"Ah, well." Miss Ross's grin didn't falter. "Don't be offended if you meet her a few more times tonight. She has good days and forgetful days, but she's the best aunt anyone could possibly—is that Mr. *Godfrey?* I'll be back, darlings. He owns a shipping conglomerate I've an interest in, and I must speak with him about his experiences contracting with the East India Company."

In a blink, she was gone.

"She's going to be just like her aunt," Daphne lamented, lifting the back of her hand to her forehead in mock dismay. "Two whirlwinds under one roof. Be prepared to turn down a lot of champagne this Season."

Bartholomew grinned before her words sank in. Her

prediction was well meant, but flawed. He wouldn't be around to turn down much more champagne. In a few weeks' time, their fake betrothal would be over and Daphne would be gone. He would no longer have a reason to leave his home.

"Major Blackpool?"

A happy, smiling couple stepped out from the crowd. He smiled. It *had* been Lord and Lady Sheffield that Bartholomew had spotted across the room. Until her recent marriage, he'd known Lady Sheffield as Lady Amelia, sister to the Duke of Ravenwood, one of Bartholomew's closest friends.

"If only my brother were here," Lady Amelia said now, clasping her hands in delight. "He was so pleased to hear you were out in Society again. You really should pay him a visit. Both of you."

Bartholomew shook his head fondly. The introductions hadn't even been made, and already Ravenwood's sister was organizing Daphne's schedules. "Lord and Lady Sheffield, let me present my fiancée, Miss Daphne Vaughan. Daphne, Lord Sheffield is a very respectable viscount who wed the extremely managing elder sister of my friend, the Duke of Ravenwood."

Lady Amelia whacked him on the shoulder with a painted fan. "Lies! And if not, then they're secrets. Miss Vaughan, I'll have you know I'm not the least bit..." She trailed off, frowning up toward the chandeliers.

"Now you've done it," Lord Sheffield groaned. "That's the expression she makes when she's accessing her memory pantry."

Bartholomew blinked. "Her what?"

"Vaughan of the Maidstone Vaughans," Lady Amelia breathed. "Your father was vicar there for many years. I'm so sorry for your loss."

Daphne's eyes widened. "How did you..."

"She just does." Lord Sheffield lifted his wife's fingers to his lips. "I don't think I'm exaggerating when I say she has the greatest mind in all of England."

"And she's not afraid to use it," Bartholomew put in with

a smile. "There was the time when Ravenwood—"

"Now, now, we don't want to bore Miss Vaughan with stories from the past." Lady Amelia pointed her fan toward Daphne. "Drop by for tea anytime you please."

"She'll probably have it ready and waiting when you do." Lord Sheffield cast his wife a sly grin. "She has a way of… anticipating needs. Don't you, my dear?"

Lady Amelia flushed scarlet and tugged him toward the crowd. "Benedict, if you'd still like me to—"

"Have you ever seen such a happy couple?" Bartholomew shook his head. "And to think, just last year, Sheffield was infamous for his rigid schedule. From eight in the morning until eight at night, he locked himself in his office and forbade all visitors. Then from eight at night until eight in the morning…" Bartholomew coughed into his hand. "He, er, attended to other matters."

Daphne's lip curled. "He wasted twelve hours a day on pleasuring?"

"Not… every day." Bartholomew should have known she wouldn't find the humor. "I'm sure he slept. Occasionally."

Her eyes rolled heavenward. "I cannot stand the frivolousness of the *ton*."

"Sheffield's not frivolous," he protested. Just because Daphne spent every waking moment with her charity work didn't mean everyone else was idle. She didn't even know the man. "Didn't you just hear me say he worked for twelve straight hours, every day without fail? How many men do you know that do that?"

"I allow that taking infrequent breaks is important for one's well-being, but you cannot expect me to condone the behavior or the character of a man who dedicates half of every day to self-serving debauchery."

"Perhaps you should keep your prejudices to yourself." His tone hardened despite himself. "If you don't want your hallowed peasants to be dismissed unfairly, you shouldn't make sweeping judgments against upper crust friends who might have helped you."

Her mouth turned downward. "Shouldn't I? How many

of your friends will be at the demonstration next weekend?"

"At the… what?"

"Precisely. I doubt they know or care about merchants gathering on Gracechurch Street to discuss overthrowing the income tax laws. There have only been hundreds of pamphlets posted up and down Cheapside."

"Let me guess." He rubbed his temples. "I suppose you plan to attend?"

Her nose lifted. "Of course I will. I'm circulating a petition."

He sighed. She was so focused on others, she was blind to her own needs.

"This is why you're not married," he muttered.

Daphne's cheeks flushed. "Even if I were the most sought-after debutante in England, I couldn't marry. There are too many people counting on my help. My personal desires are irrelevant."

Before he could reply, loud clapping drew their attention toward the pianoforte.

"I've had another request for dancing," Miss Ross called out. "With a room so full of talent, there must be dozens of accomplished ladies who can wring music out of this ancient thing."

Several young ladies giggled and stepped forward.

"That, for example." Daphne leaned toward Bartholomew. "Do you consider competency at the pianoforte a legitimate female accomplishment?"

He shrugged. "I see your point. Why should the achievement be limited only to females?"

Daphne's lips pursed. "Don't be obtuse on purpose."

"Why not?" he demanded. "You're being obtuse on accident, so I figure we both might as well get angry enough to make it a good fight."

Lambley stepped out of the crowd and bowed toward Daphne. "I promised you the first dance. Is it still open?"

She arched a brow at Bartholomew as if to say, *What was that about no one wishing to marry me?* Her chin lifted defiantly as she placed her hand into Lambley's and allowed the duke to twirl her into the crowd.

Bartholomew's fists clenched. He wasn't jealous, of course. He couldn't be. Daphne was his fiancée, not Lambley's... for the next few weeks, anyway.

Besides, Bartholomew couldn't dance. Probably. He might be able to if he worked at it hard enough, but it wasn't worth the risk of public humiliation if he fell.

He missed it, though. Not just dancing. *Music*.

That's why he'd ordered the pianoforte in his parlor. He'd never entertained in his town house—well, not more than one person at a time—so there'd been no reason to invest in such an instrument before his confinement.

After the accident, banging at the keys had given him something to do in the early days when he wasn't weeping or looking for things to break. When he'd given up whisky, he'd discovered he actually had some talent. Deciphering sheet music and memorizing foreign melodies had been a welcome respite from the agony of his endless stretches and exercises.

To him, skill at the pianoforte wasn't a *female* accomplishment. It was an *accomplishment*. Full stop.

Particularly for an ex-soldier who'd had to drag himself out of the darkness note by painstaking note.

But he'd be damned if he plunked out a waltz in front of all and sundry, just so Lambley could hold Bartholomew's fiancée and swirl her about the dance floor in ways Bartholomew would never be able to do again.

He forced himself to look away from Daphne. Away from the crowd. Now everyone was dancing, save for a few young bucks here or there who couldn't tear themselves away from their champagne glasses or the biscuits on the refreshment table.

And him, of course. He was still in the corner, in the shadows. All of the other men were strong enough, *whole* enough, to sweep Daphne into their arms waltz after waltz, and dance until the sun rose.

Bartholomew was just broken enough to let her go.

Chapter Sixteen

Daphne twirled about the crowded parlor in the arms of a duke, but Bartholomew was the only man she could think about. Her chest tightened with self-recrimination. She should not have left him like that. She should not have left him at all.

He wasn't likely to understand her passion for championing the invisible class of people High Society never even thought about, but had she truly expected to change his priorities and his worldview overnight? Why should anyone? But their useless argument wasn't why she was so disappointed in herself.

She couldn't help wishing she was in Bartholomew's arms instead of Lambley's.

Foolish, of course. Bartholomew didn't want her. She was a temporary fiancée who would be out of his life in less than a month. She had intended to be distant with him in order to make parting easier. If they found each other vexing, it would be easier to say goodbye.

Except it wasn't working. The only reason she found him vexing was because she could not quit him from her mind. She had even begun to dream about him at night. Every night. In her dreams, they didn't have to say goodbye. They were too busy kissing to say anything at all.

The unbidden image sent a shiver down her spine. She missed a step and inadvertently trod upon the Duke of Lambley's toes. Her cheeks flushed.

The duke's quick blue eyes flashed with chagrin. "It only now occurs to me that I've never seen you dance. Forgive me for not inquiring if you had permission to waltz, or even knew how."

Permission? Daphne smiled weakly. Wonderful. Something else she hadn't considered. Katherine had first butted against the various rules of Almack's patronesses and Polite Society so long ago, Daphne had forgotten them completely. She probably embarrassed Bartholomew every time he escorted her in public.

Unlike Katherine, Daphne hadn't had a formal come-out. This was her first visit to the city. There was much she didn't know. Would never know. She couldn't fit into London life even if she wanted to. She was precisely the green rustic they likely all thought she was.

That she knew how to dance at all was also Katherine's doing. Whenever she'd visited Maidstone, Katherine had always dropped by the vicarage with amusing anecdotes about some exploit or another. That she'd taught Daphne to waltz was less surprising than the idea of boisterous Katherine paying attention to a dancing master in the first place.

"'Twas kind of you to stand up with me," she murmured to the duke. Her response didn't address his implied question, but then again, it was too late to worry about permission. "I don't often attend dinner parties or soirées."

His smile was droll. "I noticed. Eligible gentlemen might despair of catching your eye, much less your heart."

Daphne swallowed. Eligible gentlemen, like him? Or did he mean gentlemen of her acquaintance in general?

It was true that she didn't often attend events of any kind. It was further true that if she *had* attended said parties, she had done so under duress and likely bore a countenance so vexed it would have frightened away even a duke.

If someone had warned her at the time that her obvious disdain for the interests of those around her would give her a reputation for being cold and impossible to please, she wouldn't have cared a button. Those weren't the opinions that mattered. Then or now.

Except… She couldn't stop herself from seeking out glimpses of Bartholomew. Or notice all the other young ladies who were doing the same. Even the gentlemen couldn't help from going out of their way to have a word with him, and they all laughed heartily at whatever witticisms he said in reply.

He was handsome and popular and charming and competitive and everything that she'd never wanted, all wrapped into one gorgeous package.

There was nothing he hadn't done. No horse he hadn't raced, no pugilist he hadn't boxed, and no heart he hadn't won. The men wanted to dress like him and the women wished he'd take their dresses off. He knew everyone there was to know, and they all considered themselves the richer for it. He was *made* for London.

And the only reason he was here today was because of her.

The moment she cried off, he'd go back to the shadows, back to his town house. Back to his memories.

This time, with scandal attached to his name. Because of her. Her throat tightened with guilt.

"You've gone awfully serious," Lambley said as the music came to an end. "Is everything all right?"

"Everything is splendid. Thank you for the lovely dance. I must get back to my fiancé." She curtseyed and hurried away, eager to return to Bartholomew. If they both had to be at this party, she wished to spend it at his side.

Or in his arms.

The more she tried not to think about how it might feel to be held, to be kissed, to be *wanted*, the harder it was to resist the temptation to find out firsthand. Their betrothal might be false, but that didn't mean they couldn't share a true embrace.

No reason except that if she dared to let her heart get involved, she'd be tempted to stay. To burrow in his arms, in his bed, and beg him never to let her go. To be the first person who chose to stay. Who chose *her*.

She came up behind him as he was speaking to a ruddy-faced gentleman.

"—as smart as she is beautiful," Bartholomew was saying. "I am the happiest of men."

A wave of pleasure flushed her cheeks. Until she remembered he was only acting a part. Then again, their scheme only required him to act betrothed, not besotted. If Bartholomew was saying nice things about her, it was because he wished to. Because *he* was nice. Not because she deserved it.

He'd gone so far above and beyond the initial favor she'd asked of him that she would never be able to repay this debt. She had been so desperate to deflect her guardian's nefarious plans, she hadn't given much thought to the false betrothal's effect on Bartholomew at all.

Worse, whenever he was within sight, she was finding it harder and harder to remember the betrothal *was* false. She wanted him to see all the good works she was trying to do and conclude that she, too, was a good person. She wanted him to *like* her. More than that, she wanted him to miss her when she was gone. She would certainly miss him.

"I doubt a dandified rake would make anyone the happiest of women," the man chuckled. "I've got fifty quid down at White's that says even a peg-leg like you will be on to greener pastures by spring."

Daphne's jaw fell open. Outrage flooded her system, electrifying her nerves and freezing her in place.

"On the contrary," Bartholomew replied evenly, as if he deflected these sort of comments every day.

She swallowed. Perhaps he did.

"A man in love spends extra blunt on a prosthesis, not a pegged leg. That way, the leg-shackle won't slide off." Bartholomew gestured toward his false leg, his tone light. "I'm afraid this rake is a reformed man."

"More like a deformed one," the man said with a laugh. "Maybe she's the one in search of greener pastures. Even a vicar's daughter can do better than—"

Daphne darted forward and slid her hand around Bartholomew's upper arm. His muscles were tight, as if he were poised to fight. If he wished to plant this knave a facer, she wouldn't stop him. She lifted her chin. "There *is* no better man than Bartholomew."

"Darling." Bartholomew pressed his lips to the top of her head. "I'd introduce you, but this 'gentleman' was just leaving."

The man's eyes widened at the obvious cut. A sneer curved his lips. "Have it your way, Blackpool. You'll be tripling my fifty quid."

He stalked away before anyone could reply further.

Daphne's mouth tightened. She clutched Bartholomew's arm a little tighter. "Who *was* that odious blackguard?"

"Phineas Mapleton." Bartholomew's hands were curved into fists. He visibly tried to calm himself down. "The worst part about this whole charade is knowing it *will* line his pockets the moment you cry off."

No, Daphne realized, her stomach sinking. For Bartholomew, the worst part of this whole charade was every single moment of it. She just hadn't seen it until now.

He'd closed himself off from society for a reason. Soulless cretins like Phineas Mapleton were perhaps the bottom of the barrel, but she had no doubt Bartholomew withstood countless questions and implied insults about his injury and his ability to still be a man, even if he laughed them off.

Worse, she suspected, were the people who felt sorry for him. Who thought they were being kind when they showered him with pity or treated him like an invalid incapable of caring for himself.

As a woman, she'd long been familiar with a world that dismissed her concerns, opinions and aspirations, simply because she was female. As a champion for the poor and the marginalized, she well knew the maddening, soul-consuming frustration of being discounted for something over which there was no hope to change.

She had never thought it could apply to Bartholomew.

The back of her throat tightened. 'Twasn't right. One could not change one's gender, or one's parentage, or grow back a leg. But that didn't make one any less important, any less worthy. And she certainly couldn't do anything that would make his situation even worse.

"About that…" she began, her voice unsteady.

Bartholomew's brow furrowed. "About what?"

"About me crying off." She bit her lip as she considered how to proceed.

If she was the one to cry off, she would make him a laughingstock. Perhaps make it impossible for him ever to find a real bride.

Bartholomew deserved better. He deserved to find love.

"You want to do it now?" He darted a glance about the crowded room. "Don't you need to wait until your birthday?"

"Not here," she said quickly, caressing his arm with her thumb. "And not until my birthday. But when I inherit my portion, I need *you* to cry off."

"Out of the question," he said without hesitation. "It would ruin your chances of ever getting married."

Precisely why she couldn't do the same thing to him. Not after all he'd been through. What she was still putting him through.

"I don't ever want to get married," she reminded him. "You'll be doing me a favor."

He shrugged. "I won't do it at all."

"You must," she said firmly. "Because I won't do it, and we're not getting married. You *must* cry off."

He laughed. "You cannot truly expect me to jilt you. It would be disastrous to your reputation under the best of circumstances. In our case, even worse. The gossip will already be horrendous. No man will ever play suitor to a woman even a peg-leg wouldn't marry."

"Don't *say* that about yourself," she said fiercely. "My goals hinge on me remaining single, but your dreams do not. Your injuries won't preclude you from finding a wife. Not if you're the one who jilts me. I'll make it known that you're the greatest catch this town has ever seen. By the time I'm done, there won't be a marriageable young lady in the entire country who wouldn't give her last penny for a chance to catch your eye. I'll—"

Bartholomew spun her in front of him and grasped her wrists so hard she winced at the sudden pain. A mottled flush crept up the sides of his neck.

"Wrong," he snarled, nostrils flaring. "Don't you *dare* turn me into one of your causes. I don't want your charity."

He tossed her hands aside and turned and stalked away.

Chapter Seventeen

Furious, Bartholomew flung open the tavern door and stormed inside.

A few short days ago, he had walked out of the Ross town house because he could not, *could not*, listen to the woman he was protecting act as though he were the one in need of *her* protection. His mother's lack of confidence in him was bad enough. He bloody well didn't need it from Daphne.

She was the one who had called upon *him* for help. He'd agreed to help her out of a scrape. Not to help her plot her next crusade for poor, peg-legged Major Blackpool. He didn't need her to do him any favors. To throw away her future, just to improve his.

She *would* cry off. He would ensure it.

He'd be the largest thorn in her side, a constant nettle on her nerves, until she'd rather pull out her beautiful hair than spend another moment with her name linked to his. The morning of her birthday, she'd have retractions in every newspaper and scandal sheet in all of England.

If he didn't throttle her first.

He spotted her red-gold ringlets across the tavern. Dratted woman. His ears pounded in exasperation. He shoved through the swarm of shopkeepers and drunkards until he was finally close enough to grab her by the upper arm and haul her away from buzzing voices and spilt ale.

"What the *devil* do you think you're doing?"

"You came!" She had the gall to look delighted at his presence. "I didn't think you'd remember."

"I didn't think *you'd* be foolish enough to show," he snapped.

"This is Cheapside," she admonished him. "Whitechapel is several blocks away. And what if it weren't? The rookeries have as much right to self-improvement as anyone else."

"What right might that be?" He motioned toward the cracked, pungent tables. "The right to ruin your reputation beyond repair by traipsing unchaperoned through back alley pubs?"

"Of course not." She pointed over the heads of the men seated on the benches to a petite brown-haired maid cowering in the far corner. "You recognize Esther, don't you? I'm perfectly respectable. Wouldn't go anywhere without at least a lady's maid. Especially since Katherine was too busy to join us today."

He couldn't believe his ears. "You invited the Duke of Lambley's cousin to accompany you to a Cheapside tavern?"

Of course she did. He should have known. Given the motley guest list at Miss Ross's soirée, the greater miracle was that the woman had passed on the opportunity.

"'Tis better that you're here, of course." Daphne winked conspiratorially. "We can be a young couple in love, presenting a united front against the injustice of the government's greed."

"What I would *love* to do," he ground out, "is throw you over my shoulder and march you straight home."

"Don't be ridiculous." She pointed behind him. "How would Esther get home?"

He ran a hand through his hair to keep from making good on his threat. "How indeed. I suppose we should just stay here then, and hope no one notices us?"

"I hope *everyone* notices us. The laboring class is counting on it." She held up a sheet of parchment half-covered with scrawled signatures. "This petition is going to join dozens of others and be presented to the House of Commons."

He squinted at the paper. "What makes you think they'll listen to you?"

"Not to me." She gestured over her shoulder. "*Them.* When thousands of righteous voices ally against a common injustice—"

"Income tax isn't an evil plot. How else do you expect the government to manage the National Debt? It's at seven hundred million pounds and rising."

She blinked in surprise.

He could've kicked himself. Now she'd suspect the truth. He hadn't just perused newspapers during his convalescence. He read them assiduously, and paid as close attention to the details as she did. That didn't mean he agreed with her methods. Such as an utter disregard to her name and her safety.

Daphne lifted her chin. "I expect the government to manage its own finances, and to allow the rest of us to do the same." She shook out the petition. "I'm not the only one who thinks so."

He plucked the parchment from her grasp. Name after name covered most of the front side. "Who are these people?"

"Merchants, manufacturers, tradesmen. Landowners. Bankers. A better question is, who *aren't* they?"

He snorted. "Easy to answer. They're not anyone with any influence. I don't recognize a single name on that paper."

"Yes, well." She bit her lip. "If you could ask a few friends in high places to—"

"I will not have anything to do with this or any other of your well-meant but ill-conceived notions. Nor will I presume to beg my friends to do so." He rolled up the parchment. "Not that they would."

Her eyes narrowed. "Just because you don't agree with a cause doesn't mean that the people shouldn't have a voice before the representatives who govern them. Wasn't the war you just fought in response to a tyrannical emperor who—"

"Point made. Everyone's voice deserves to be heard." He glanced about the loud, boisterous room. "Can we leave now?"

She shook her head. "Not until everyone has had an opportunity to sign the petition."

His jaw clenched in exasperation. "Where is the pen and ink?"

"At each end of the room. I brought two sets. What are

you…?"

He scanned the tables for the closest inkwell and marched straight into the fray. When he got within reach of the first table, he slapped the petition onto its scarred surface, dipped the idle pen into the pot of ink, and handed it to the closest shopkeeper. "Stop talking. Sign."

Startled, the shopkeeper accepted the pen and scrawled his name below the others without more than a cursory glance at the heading across the top.

"Excellent." Bartholomew pushed the petition in front of the next one. "Sign."

The shopkeeper stared up at him in befuddlement. "What do you think you're—"

"Changing the future," Bartholomew interrupted in an exaggeratedly pleasant voice. "Isn't that why we're all here? Income tax is high. Employment is low. Here's a petition. Do you prefer to be compliant or triumphant?"

The man quickly signed his name. Bartholomew moved on to the next one. Perhaps Daphne's plan wasn't as daft as it had first sounded. These men *had* given their time to join forces to try to have a voice before Parliament. Perhaps it would even work. If they set down their ale long enough to truly take action.

He took another look at the long list of signatures covering the petition and grudgingly admitted that the strange sensation inside his chest was pride. His faux fiancée's methods were unconventional, but he now saw how fortunate all her charities were to have her on their side. If anyone could save the miners and the weavers and the orphans and the Cheapside shopkeepers, it was Daphne.

He headed to the next table of laborers feeling lighter than he had before.

Daphne hurried to keep up. "You *knew* employment was low and there was unrest in the streets?"

"I told you. I spent seven months with nothing else to do but read the papers."

"Then why didn't you—"

"—become an insurrectionist and try to spark a revolution? I don't know. Perhaps because I'm an ex-

Corinthian without a title or a leg to stand on. Literally." He touched a finger to his chin and peered down at her. "Or perhaps because I'm not *mad*."

Her eyes flashed. "I'm not mad!"

He grinned at her. "How do you know? All the best revolutionaries had a few bats in the belfry. How else did they get the courage to try and change the unchangeable?"

She blinked in confusion. "You don't... disagree with the idea?"

"I disagree with you traipsing about taverns with no more chaperonage than that terrified chit hiding in the corner. Make-believe betrothal or not, I forbid you from taking unnecessary risks with your life or your safety. You won't help anyone if you're in a hospital or Bedlam or dead."

He collected the pen and ink and made his way to the next table.

She gestured at the petition in his hands. "Are you just humoring me to keep me safe?"

When he'd first found out about her charity work, that answer might have been yes. Four weeks ago, he would have dragged her out of the door and turned her over his knee if he had to in order to wake her up to the world around her.

But somewhere along the line, she'd begun to wake *him* up to the realities around them.

Did he think she and her shopkeepers would overthrow income taxation? Not a chance in hell. But he couldn't help but admire her drive, her heart, and her courage. The passion she brought to everything she did, no matter how unlikely it was to succeed or how unworthy the recipient of her attention.

If he pulled her onto his lap today, it wouldn't be to scold her.

It would be to kiss her senseless.

Chapter Eighteen

No kissing, Bartholomew promised himself a few days later as he escorted Daphne to a dinner party at the Willoughby town house. No kissing, no matter how desperately he longed to taste her lips. He needed her to break off the engagement, not to compromise her into marriage.

He'd devised a plan of attack. As long as he concentrated on rubbing her the wrong way, her wrongheaded campaign to salvage his image at the expense of her own should dissolve on its own. Fortuitously, they were seated right across the table from each other. There would be no escaping his onslaught of annoyances.

He started by engaging the young bucks in his vicinity in conversation. The only topics of interest to them were phaetons, pugilism, and the proper folds of a neckcloth. Not only would Daphne consider all of these subjects to be typical *ton* frivolousness, they also happened to be areas in which Bartholomew had a great deal of expertise. Nothing would repulse her more.

"The first time I was invited to Brummell's toilette," he began as pompously as possible, "'twas because he sought my opinion on whether the knot of his cravat should contain an asymmetrical cascade of folds."

The aspiring dandies were, as expected, utterly enthralled. Even a few of the young ladies stared in open fascination, their interest as likely due to the questionable propriety of mentioning one's toilette in public as to the wonder of having been one of the select few Beau Brummell had invited into his dressing room to witness his infamous five-hour morning ritual.

Bartholomew had done no such thing, of course, but since Brummell had recently fled to France to escape debtor's prison, 'twas unlikely he'd walk up behind Bartholomew and spoil the Banbury story he was inventing as he went along.

"Oh, yes," he answered one of the young bucks with as much earnestness as he could muster. "Brummell always said that if it took less than an hour to fold one's cravat, one was obviously doing it wrong. Each fold should be an expression of one's inner passion."

Daphne cut him a look of utter disbelief. Not because she doubted his ability to overcomplicate a neckcloth—if Captain Xavier Grey were here, he might enquire whether Bartholomew was wearing a bed sheet *and* the four-poster canopy—but because he'd helped her during the demonstration. She now believed he had more rattling about his head than waistcoats and racing curricles. She imagined he might become a crusader.

He intended to correct that misconception once and for all.

"A gentleman must endeavor to put his best leg forward, Brummell always said." Bartholomew leaned forward to wink at his crowd. "In my case... my *only* leg. He and I did get off on the right foot."

Daphne covered her face with her hand.

He smiled. *Good.* One did not delay parting ways with someone one found dreadfully embarrassing.

As he kept up a lively, nonsensical conversation about the proper temperature of pomade to style one's hair and whether a gentleman ought to alter the color palette of his waistcoat before or after the vernal equinox, a curious thing began to happen. So curious, in fact, that it took him a prodigious amount of time to even determine what it was.

He was having fun.

It had been years since he'd discussed fashion—three and a half years, to be precise—and it was amusing to discover that he still *could*, despite a complete lack of knowledge about whatever intricacies of vogue and tailoring had transpired since then.

He'd missed the latest technological advances in virtually every style of carriage. He hadn't played faro or polo since before purchasing his commission. And if he visited Gentleman Jackson's today, he doubted he'd recognize half the faces.

Yet he was having *fun*.

It struck him as so unlikely, so impossible a circumstance, that he froze with his serviette halfway to his lips in consternation. And guilt. Did he *deserve* to have fun?

Enjoying life again despite being crippled would be nothing short of a miracle. But enjoying life again without Edmund seemed nothing short of a betrayal.

He'd led his brother into danger and left him to die. There. He wasn't *worthy* of happiness. Of fun and laughter. Question answered. He'd better not get too used to being on center stage. As soon as he'd completed his favor for Daphne, he'd shutter himself back in his shadowed town house where he belonged. No curricle rides. No dinner parties. No Daphne.

This time, he'd finally let his valet go. It was cruel to keep someone of that talent tethered to a man who fully intended to live out the rest of his days as a recluse.

Perhaps Captain Grey was in want of a valet who knew how to tie a proper bed sheet.

"*Almack's*," Daphne breathed in response to some unheard question. Her eyes met his only briefly from across the table, but their glittering contempt was enough to chill his blood. "Why, no, I *don't* have a voucher to attend a pretentious weekly showcase run by judgmental dragons who can think of no better use for their money or influence. Why do you ask?"

He barely refrained from dropping his glass into his lap. Either Daphne recognized his game, or she'd come up with the same plan on her own. And was winning.

"Gowns are *very* important," she was saying earnestly to some poor bastard on her right. "Textiles have an unparalleled impact on the economic balance and living conditions of manual laborers in Lancashire and other areas. One needn't be a Luddite to see the increase in displaced weavers makes entire families more susceptible to famine and disease."

This time, Bartholomew covered his face with his hands. No one was looking at him anyway. Every eye was trained on Daphne in horror.

"Well, then." Lady Willoughby rose to her feet. "I think its time for dancing. Are we all in agreement?"

The debutantes certainly were. If the men retreated into another room for their customary after-supper glass of port, the girls would all be stuck in the side parlor with Daphne and her displaced weavers. Once the carpets were rolled up, one of the Willoughby chits took a seat at the pianoforte and began playing a country-dance. Partners took to the floor with unprecedented alacrity.

Nonetheless, he couldn't get her words out of his mind. He made a mental note to investigate whether the textile industry in Lancashire were half as bad as she claimed.

Daphne walked up to him wearing a pained expression.

He slanted her a look. "You didn't have to be rude. There is no sense alienating the very people who could help you effect change."

"They're the very people who won't." She rubbed her temples, dislodging red-gold tendrils from their matronly twist. "Aristocrats won't listen to me. I'm nobody. This isn't my world."

He raised a brow. "Where should you be? In a Cheapside tavern?"

"At my escritoire, concentrating on the textile situation." As she stared at the dancers, her shoulders slumped. "If I toadeated the way I'd need to in order to get these people to accept me, I wouldn't have time to champion causes at all."

His gaze flicked across the crowd. Daphne was right. These families were unlikely to listen to her. But that didn't mean they were heartless. Many of the women had charities of their own. They simply also took time to have fun. He wished Daphne could, too. She could use some happiness. "Your 'causes' are all commendable projects, but must you make them your entire life?"

"My causes *are* my entire life." Her eyes glistened and

she looked away. "It's the one way I can make a difference in the world. No one will remember me when I'm gone, but my efforts will have improved lives. That has to count for something."

He frowned at her. "What do you mean, you won't be remembered? Everyone will miss you when you're gone."

"Everyone who? My dead grandparents? My dead mother? My dead father? Katherine, of course, but she doesn't need me, and her aunt has no doubt already forgotten me." Daphne's fingers curled into fists. "I want my life to matter. The weavers, the miners, the farmers... they desperately need *someone*. Why shouldn't it be me?"

He shook his head. "Because you can't do it by yourself. No one can. You would need an army of volunteers, contacts with direct governmental influence—"

"So I should sit back and do nothing? Beg Lady Jersey for permission to waltz?"

He coughed into his fist. "You don't have permission to waltz?"

"Are you even listening to me?" she demanded, cheeks pink. "Or to yourself? Who cares about Almack's patronesses when there are a hundred more important matters right outside our doors? I know it doesn't bother *them*"—she motioned toward the laughing, dancing partygoers—"but doesn't it matter at least a tiny bit to you? You used to care about what happened to others. You went to *war* to defend the defenseless."

"And look how splendidly that turned out," he said through clenched teeth. "It ruined my life and stole my brother's."

"*Never* stop fighting." Her clear green eyes pierced him. "Many people are desperate for aid. Are you truly the sort of person who would let them die without lending a hand?"

Anger raced through his blood at her presumption. She had no idea what the war had cost him. What he was no longer willing to give up. His jaw worked.

He was saved from answering by the arrival of one of the young bucks from the dinner table.

The boy blushed. "If you don't mind, I've more

questions about when it's better to wear trousers versus knee breeches."

The fire in Daphne's eyes indicated her head might combust.

"I'm afraid your life-or-death trouser questions will have to wait." She reached for Bartholomew's arm. "I quite adore a country-dance, and I believe my fiancé was just about to invite me."

"Doubtful," he responded. "I'm afraid I don't dance."

Her fingers dropped from his arm as her cheeks flushed scarlet. "You can't... I'm so sorry. I didn't even think."

"I *can*." His voice had gone brittle the moment he registered the horror on her face was due to his missing leg. "I choose not to."

"Then I shan't either." She reached out her hand, her eyes pleading. "Bartholomew, forgive me. I—"

He blasted his most charming smile in the direction of the young dandy. "I would consider it a personal favor if you were to stand up with my fiancée this set. It seems she quite adores a country-dance."

"Of course," the boy stammered, his wide-eyed gaze darting between them. "Right away."

He hurried Daphne onto the dance floor to join the other couples.

Bartholomew crossed his arms and wondered whether she really did enjoy country-dances. He certainly hated watching her perform them with other men.

He'd realized partway through supper that half the reason he was furious with her for burning bridges with abandon was because if she was no longer welcome in London—once she was no longer *in* London—he was unlikely to ever see her again.

He was no longer doing an old friend a favor. He was enjoying spending time with someone whose presence would be missed when she was no longer part of his life.

Mrs. Epworth, a recent widow, sidled up to him while he was staring daggers at the lad dancing with Daphne.

"It's so good to see you back in society, Major Blackpool," she cooed. "You're as handsome as ever."

He grunted noncommittally.

"Is there any chance I can talk you into wearing your regimentals for me?" She fluttered her eyelashes. "Or better yet, talk you out of them?"

Never! shot through his head like a bullet. Not with her. Not with anyone. His casual rakish encounters weren't just over; his days of physical intimacy were through. Even *he* could no longer bear to look at himself naked.

Mrs. Epworth gave a slow, suggestive wink.

He turned and walked away.

His jaw worked. The widow Epworth was known for taking her dalliances with men who allayed her ennui. Actors, foreign dignitaries, the occasional marquess. That she was speaking to him at all meant she considered him a novelty. His hands shook.

He had no intention of being her next novelty. Of being chosen because the thought of lying with a one-legged soldier amused her.

Being a curiosity was even worse than being pitied. He was no longer a whole man, but nor was he a freak exhibition at a penny circus.

He never should've come back out into Society.

The music changed. A waltz. Daphne was in the arms of Willoughby's eldest son. Bartholomew despised all of them. All of the young bucks and bachelors and married men with their perfect legs and happy lives.

There was nothing wrong with Willoughby's eldest son, of course. He was a year or two younger than Bartholomew, of fine stock and gentle humor, and heir apparent to a coronet. His obvious lack of offense to Daphne's gaucheness at dinner spoke to his empathy and good breeding. Perhaps he was even now capturing Daphne's heart.

Bartholomew wished the idea didn't make him feel like planting that fine young man a facer.

After the waltz ended, Daphne returned to his side. "If you're not going to dance, can we go? I believe we've made our mark."

Gladly.

Pausing only to thank their hosts for their hospitality, he

had a footman summon the carriage and sent another to fetch their outerwear. By the time the landau appeared, they were both bundled against the wretched winter weather.

Heads down, they hurried out the door and into the carriage.

As soon as the door locked tight against the wind, she tossed her muff to the squab in disgust. "Thank heavens *that's* over. If you think for one second that I enjoyed anything at all within those walls—"

He cupped her chin with his hand and kissed her.

She didn't rear back or slap his face. She curled her fingers about the lapels of his greatcoat and pulled him close. *Good*. The last thing he wished to do was let her go. He pushed the pad of his thumb against her chin, encouraging her to open her mouth to him.

Her mouth yielded to his immediately. Sweetly. She tasted of berries and honey. Ambrosia in his arms.

He deepened the kiss and she met him with equal urgency. Tasting. Taking. She was everything he wanted and knew he couldn't have. He pulled away, gasping for air. Straining for self-control. He could not kiss her again.

If he did, he might never stop.

Chapter Nineteen

Daphne stared blankly into the looking glass as her lady's maid plucked a few artful tendrils free of the elegant chignon the girl had managed to twist from Daphne's stubborn hair. She didn't register any of it. Her mind was still replaying the last few moments of the previous night.

A small stack of correspondence rested on her escritoire. Unread. Katherine had no doubt already summoned a carriage meant to whisk them to the new exhibition at the antiquities museum. And yet the only thought Daphne's muddled brain was capable of forming was:

He'd finally kissed her.

And regretted it almost instantly—there was no misinterpreting his vociferous self-reproach—but before he had practically shoved her into the town house, before they had spent an awkward half hour in stony silence, he had lifted her face to his and kissed her senseless.

Worse, she hadn't just *let* him take such a liberty. She'd *liked* it. Welcomed it. Wished he'd done so sooner. Wished he'd *keep* doing it. Charity work be damned.

Impossible.

Upon realizing that the attraction she'd tried so hard to deny was just as reluctantly reciprocated, Daphne's second reaction was horror. She *couldn't* wed. And absolutely not *Bartholomew*. He was her opposite in every way and would clearly never condone the rootless, monkish life she intended to live, traveling wherever help was most needed, immersing herself in every walk of life.

But wasn't that putting the cart before the horse? All they'd shared was a kiss. A single, beautiful, utterly addicting kiss.

Mutual attraction didn't have to mean marriage. Bartholomew had left a trail of broken hearts and happy sighs before leaving for war. He hadn't felt compelled to wed any of those women. None were debutantes; they knew precisely what they were and weren't getting: a chance to indulge mutual attraction for a few hours.

Perhaps a woman destined to a scandalous life of lonesome crusading could spare a night or two before setting out on her journey. Indulge in something utterly and completely for herself.

The question was, could *she?*

A year ago, Daphne would have been wholly against the idea. Today—or, rather, the moment that he'd kissed her— the desire coursing through her traitorous body strongly felt that a carriage was as good a place as any to do something scandalous, and Bartholomew was precisely the right man to do it with.

As maddening as he could be, she'd wondered what it would feel like to have his lips on hers ever since the faux engagement began. Now that she knew the answer, keeping a safe distance would be that much harder.

She bit her lip. Was restraint necessary, if the man in question was as disinterested in marriage as she was?

Not only could he be trusted with her best-kept secrets, he was actively campaigning for her to jilt him first. If there was ever going to be a man with whom a crusader for the unfortunate could exchange the occasional bone-melting kiss, that man was Bartholomew Blackpool.

The better question was, how would she feel about it once they parted ways? Would he be a pleasant memory of stolen moments and passionate kisses? Or would she turn into a rabid harpy and long to claw the eyes out of all the other women that would replace her in his arms?

There would undoubtedly be many. Daphne's hands curled into fists. She wasn't blind. Neither were the glamorous, worldly women who cast heavy-lidded gazes at him across the room.

She hadn't missed the obvious intent in Mrs. Epworth's sashay up to Bartholomew's side, and the lewd invitation she'd no doubt whispered into his ear. The widow believed him to be betrothed and still hadn't wished to let an opportunity slip away. Once he was single again, there'd be no end to the buffet of eager, elegant ladies lined up to help fill the void.

Not that she'd be there to see it, Daphne reminded herself sternly. She'd be in Manchester or South Tyneside or wherever help was needed. And she absolutely wouldn't be stupid enough to scan the scandal sheets for mention of his name.

Probably.

"There." Esther slid the last of the pins into Daphne's hair and stood back to admire her handiwork. "Perfect."

Daphne blinked at the looking glass.

The woman reflected back at her was a calm, coiffed, elegant stranger. The kind of woman who would be completely unconcerned about her faux fiancé's many admirers because she, quite frankly, wasn't one of them, and looked forward to dissolving the temporary alliance and never crossing paths again.

Daphne averted her gaze. She didn't wonder when she'd ceased being that cold, disinterested woman. She wondered if she'd ever truly been her to begin with.

She thanked Esther and rose to her feet, determined to make it through the evening with some semblance of self-control. No more pining for Bartholomew. Katherine was thrilled about her antiquities museum's new exhibition. Daphne would smile and applaud and be thrilled for her. That's what friends did.

Even if it meant going to an antiquities museum.

When their carriage arrived, the bounce in Katherine's step and the nervous excitement in her eyes made Daphne rethink her initial reluctance to attend. Her escritoire contained a mountain of correspondence pertaining to dozens of worthy causes, but did that truly make Daphne the better person? She now recognized that one reason she cared so deeply about charity work was because she wanted people to care about *her*.

In contrast, Katherine cared about her antiquities

museum because she wanted people to care about... antiquities.

Put like that, whose motives were purer?

Daphne's cheeks heated in shame. Bartholomew was right. She'd let her prejudices alienate the very people she ought to have been befriending. She reached over and gave Katherine's hand a squeeze. "Everyone will love your new exhibition. The party will be splendid."

Katherine's face lit up. "I hope so. Thank you so much for coming with me. I hated to tear you away from more important work, but it wouldn't feel like celebrating without you here, too."

Daphne swallowed a lump in her throat. "It's my pleasure. You've worked just as hard as I do, and you deserve to succeed."

Katherine pulled her into a quick hug. "You're the best. Promise me you'll try to have fun tonight?"

Daphne nodded wordlessly. She didn't regret the path she'd chosen in life, but for the first time she wondered if there could be more than one right option. The choice between pleasure and charity work had always been clear. She now wished there was a way to have both. To travel to all the families who needed her, fight for justice and employment and safety, and have someone to come home to when the day was done.

Her chest felt oddly hollow, despite the steady stream of excited guests flooding into the museum. At least she wouldn't be required to speak coherently with anyone. Antiquities were Katherine's expertise. Daphne was just there for support. She could fade into the shadows and try to imagine a life where she not only got everything she'd been working toward, but also something extra. Something even better.

Love.

She grabbed Katherine's arm when the very object of her thoughts strolled through the main doors on the other side of the room.

"What's *he* doing here?" she whispered, simultaneously delighted and despondent to spend the next hour under the same roof. *He* was the reason her easy decisions were suddenly so hard. Charity work was a sure thing. Love was a risk.

And Daphne wasn't much of a gambler.

Katherine flashed her a smile. "Major Blackpool? I invited him. The more the merrier, and he's a treasure with crowds."

Daphne wished she'd worn a prettier gown.

Her best friend was right, of course. The more attention Katherine could bring to the new exhibition, the better. And Bartholomew *was* incredible with crowds.

Daphne wasn't the only one who found him charismatic. Even when every word falling from his silver tongue was unadulterated balderdash, people listened to him. Gobbled it up. Sought him out for more. He appeared more energized with every such encounter.

She, on the other hand, hated to be on display. She went wherever people needed help because it was the right thing to do, not because she had any particular fondness for crowds. She much preferred the distance and anonymity of letter writing and a good pseudonym. The only reason she and Katherine had become friends was because Katherine had never not made a friend in her life.

Much like Bartholomew.

He was currently regaling a group of preening fops with an anecdote so sidesplittingly hilarious, several dandies looked dangerously close to soiling their buckskin breeches.

What must it be like to be universally admired? Exhausting, she supposed. Daphne sighed. She would never be effortlessly popular like Bartholomew or Katherine. She was made of different stuff.

No matter. While her name would never appear in scandal sheets or history tomes, her life still had meaning. She would be the woman who made the world a better place.

Just as soon as she quit gazing across the room at Bartholomew.

If she hadn't been watching him with as much focus as a lioness stalks her prey, she might not have noticed the slight wince in his smile every time he was forced to move a few inches in one direction or another.

The wince didn't appear to be borne of pain. Nor did he even have a limp. With or without the handsome swordstick he occasionally carried, the man was more graceful now than Daphne had ever been. So why the wince?

She studied him even more minutely. The barely perceptible tic was more a grimace than a wince, and only occurred when he moved his right leg.

His *missing* right leg.

She tilted her head as she considered his prosthesis. Its wooden calf was just as shapely and equally concealed behind stockings and shiny leather footwear. She'd been told the ankle joint even boasted catgut tendons for greater flexibility and aesthetics.

The craftsmanship was a mix of artistry and the latest in modern technology. It certainly wasn't anything to be ashamed of. Just by glancing at him, one would never guess that everything below the knee was false.

By *listening* to him, however… Daphne frowned. Now that she thought upon it, there was a distinctive *snick* as the articulated foot section clicked into place. Her eyes widened.

Up until now, she'd assumed his disinclination to rejoin society—much less to dance—was due to the very understandable concern that his false limb might not support his weight or activities, and he might injure himself even further in a fall.

She now suspected what he suffered was a visceral fear of humiliation.

He'd been a rake, a dandy, and a soldier. All three aspects had garnered him nothing but admiration from his peers. He no longer fit those roles because he no longer felt the part. Instead of being proud of his body, he was shamed by it. He'd obviously been mortified that morning in the vicarage when his leg had collapsed in front of witnesses. But it hadn't been his fault.

Daphne doubted *she* could've withstood the force of Mrs. Blackpool launching herself deadweight into Daphne's arms. Anyone would have fallen. Not everyone would have leapt back up. Bartholomew's impairment hadn't made him weaker. It had made him *stronger*.

He was still achieving victories that would have destroyed another man. The only person who thought him lesser for his injury was Bartholomew himself.

She edged closer to where he conversed with the other dandies.

His blue eyes sparkled when he saw her and he held out a hand to pull her closer to the group. "Have you all met my ravishing fiancée? This delightful young lady is Miss Daphne Vaughan. Darling, these ruffians are Mr. Dunham, Mr. Bost, and Mr. Underhill. Pay them no mind."

"Betrothed!" teased one of the men. "Don't you know wives are expensive?"

"They cost an arm and a leg," Bartholomew agreed innocently, then winked as he gestured toward his prosthesis. "I've already paid the first installment."

The gentlemen roared with laughter.

Daphne heroically refrained from throwing a slipper at her betrothed's head.

His constant self-deprecation finally made sense. Bartholomew didn't make light of his loss because he didn't care what people thought, but because he very much did. He tried to belittle himself before others could do so, in order to save his pride the blow of public humiliation.

She wished she could shake some sense into him. Such efforts were misguided and unnecessary. The only people who didn't flat out adore him were the ones who were jealous of him, like that horrid Phineas Mapleton.

As soon as Bartholomew realized that, he'd regain the only thing he was truly missing: his confidence. When would he realize he needn't poke fun at himself?

She frowned at the dandies. Was she the first one to understand it took just as much courage to face his peers with gregariousness and wit on their own battleground as it did to purchase a commission to sail off to war?

That he could do so with charm and a swagger made him seem even more of a legend, even larger than life, than when he'd been at the height of his popularity three and a half years earlier. His determination was awe-inspiring. If he'd been irresistibly arrogant before... once he regained his confidence, he'd be nigh on unstoppable.

Already there were a gaggle of interested ladies making eyes at him from the other side of the exhibition hall. Daphne's fingernails bit into her palms. Perhaps she should encourage him to make his leg-shackle jokes a little louder.

No. She needed to cry off, not stake her claim. In fact, she needed *him* to cry off. Realizing he could return to his previous unencumbered rakish life might help him do that.

She swallowed her jealousy as a pair of giggling young ladies wiggled up to him to present their fingers for a kiss. Who cared if they ignored her? Daphne wouldn't be around much longer.

Once she and Bartholomew went their separate ways, they would both be free to do as they pleased, to be whatever kind of person they wished. Separating was the only way to ensure happiness for both of them.

She bared her teeth at the simpering young ladies. They were too enthralled with Bartholomew to notice the mousy woman on his arm.

It didn't matter. Soon she wouldn't have to witness such blatant flirtation. Soon she would be halfway across the country, crusading for better causes. She was *winning*. She'd gammoned her heartless guardian and would soon have her independence. Freedom was within reach.

She just wished it didn't feel like the only one she'd tricked was herself.

Chapter Twenty

Just as Bartholomew finished the last of his strengthening exercises, his butler entered the parlor bearing a platter of afternoon mail.

Crabtree dangled it toward the fire. "Shall I torch the post at once?"

Bartholomew held out his hand in silence.

"As you wish, sir." His face carefully devoid of smugness, Crabtree placed the stack into Bartholomew's hand and quit the parlor without a backward glance.

Bartholomew hauled himself up from the floor and into a chair to read. He hadn't burnt correspondence without opening it since the day he'd left for Kent to rescue Daphne.

Nonetheless, Crabtree never missed an opportunity to point out his master's previous obstinacy by politely enquiring whether he ought to set fire to every missive that crossed the threshold.

Ignoring his butler, Bartholomew flipped through the pile. The topmost items were invitations to upcoming events. Another musicale, a few dinner parties… the Caxton ball. The corner of his mouth tilted as an idea formed.

He ought to take Daphne. A woman ought to experience at least one ball.

There was nothing so grand back in Maidstone. If Daphne followed through on her goal to become a nomadic crusader for England's voiceless poor, she was unlikely to have another opportunity to attend such a rout. Much as she denied it, he suspected she *did* adore a country-dance.

If he'd thought he could do it justice without embarrassing himself—or her—he would certainly have tried. He already regretted turning down an opportunity to have her in his arms while he still could. No London in her future meant no Bartholomew in her future.

His jaw tightened. He was finding himself ever more disinclined to accept such a fate.

Less obvious was what to do about it.

Daphne wanted her independence. The right to marry when and if she found someone worthy of her love. The freedom to determine what to do with her life and where to live it. Even if that meant never seeing her again.

London was his home. He belonged here. He would never have the sort of life he'd imagined for himself when he'd been younger, but that didn't mean he could no longer enjoy the city. Hope unfurled in his chest. Dinner parties, card games, friends... He was still welcome.

Not at Almack's, of course. The marriage mart would be as disinterested in him as he was in it. A broken soldier wasn't meant for the altar, but he now realized that didn't mean he needed to close himself off completely. London had something for everyone.

He broke the seal on the next letter and bolted upright. *The report.* A fortnight ago, he'd hired a man to investigate the facts behind Daphne's pet causes. He read through the front in dismay. His jaw dropped when he turned the page. The reality was even worse than Daphne had claimed.

The issues she championed were more than real. They were positively hopeless. He flipped to the next page and winced at the numbers. At the suffering. *Someone* needed to help these people.

His stomach twisted. He should never have discounted her fervent charity work as a foolish obsession. Daphne deserved his respect, not his indulgence. She was right about everything.

Horrified, he scanned the pages even faster. Every paragraph was more appalling than the last. There was no possible way that one young woman, no matter how intrepid, might save the orphans, protect the miners, employ the weavers, curb wheat inflation, calm the Luddites, improve workhouses... It would take an army of Daphnes to even make a dent.

He closed the report with a shudder. He could no longer stand between her and her goals. *His* idle, self-pitying life was scarcely a nobler cause. He slipped the document into his waistcoat pocket. There had to be some way he could help.

If so, he might not need a pretext to stay in contact with Daphne after all. If they were both crusaders, perhaps they wouldn't have to say goodbye.

Quickly, he sifted through the rest of the post. The last letter in the pile bore a seal from the Duke of Ravenwood's estate. Eyebrows rising, Bartholomew broke the wax.

He hadn't seen the Duke of Ravenwood since Oliver's wedding. Not unusual, in and of itself. Of their core circle of friends, Ravenwood had always been the most serious. He'd inherited the dukedom at a young age and rarely attended frivolous Society entertainments.

Ravenwood did, however, cherish his friends. He, Xavier, Oliver, Edmund, and Bartholomew had once been inseparable.

Perhaps the duke's sister had mentioned running into Bartholomew at Katherine Ross's crush the other night. The soirée had been so well attended, Bartholomew almost wondered that Ravenwood hadn't made room in his schedule. Miss Ross had apparently managed to wrangle every other Londoner into accepting the invitation.

Smiling, Bartholomew unfolded the letter.

> *Blackpool,*
> *Come to Ravenwood House at your earliest*
> *convenience. We need to talk about S.*
> *Ravenwood*

Sarah. Bartholomew's flesh chilled. He had failed her completely. Heart sinking, he leaned his head against the back of his chair and closed his eyes.

There was nothing to talk about. He'd broken his promise to bring Edmund home alive.

When he'd learned she was pregnant, he did not offer himself as a means to save her reputation and give her baby a name. He couldn't.

And now her life was over. Bartholomew's niece or nephew would be born a bastard. His parents would lose their minds. Her friends would abandon her. All because Edmund had followed his brother to the ends of the earth.

Bartholomew tossed the note aside and rubbed his face. What was left to say?

He pushed to his feet. He was no coward. Whatever the situation, he had to face it head on. It was his fault Edmund had joined the army and his fault Edmund hadn't left the battlefield alive. Sarah's predicament wasn't going to get any better. Bartholomew would do whatever he could to help. He owed her that much.

He owed it to Edmund.

Within the hour, Bartholomew was seated in the duke's private study.

Ravenwood dismissed his servants and shut the door before taking a seat across from Bartholomew. His face was drawn, his cheeks pallid.

None of which was helping to calm Bartholomew's growing trepidation.

The duke steepled his fingers. "When my sister married Lord Sheffield last month, she left Ravenwood House in clockwork condition."

Bartholomew furrowed his brow. Ravenwood wanted to waste time with small talk before discussing the matter at hand? 'Twas so unlike the duke, it took a moment for Bartholomew to gather the wits to respond. "I believe we can all agree that Lady Amelia whips everything she touches into clockwork precision."

"Just so." Ravenwood nodded slowly, then drew up straight. "My home is now without a mistress. Sarah and her unborn baby need a name. I have decided to give them one."

Bartholomew's mouth fell open. "You're making Sarah your *duchess?*"

"Do you think her unworthy of the position?"

"Of course not." Bartholomew sputtered. "She's been one of us since we were children. My brother was going to *marry* her."

Ravenwood's voice was grave. "You think I should refrain out of respect for your brother?"

"No, I…" Bartholomew shoved a hand through his hair. "Every single day, I ask myself what Edmund would want. The answer, of course, is the safety and happiness of his intended and their child."

Ravenwood inclined his head. "But?"

Bartholomew hesitated. "I've thought of marrying her myself, for the reasons you state. I've denounced my own selfishness for failing to do so. Edmund was my brother. The child in Sarah's womb is part of my family. Why should *you* be the one to sacrifice your future happiness?"

"Who said I…" But even Ravenwood couldn't complete the thought. Of the four friends, he was the romantic who had always sworn to only marry for love. Thus far, it hadn't happened. Now it never would.

"Do you love her?" Bartholomew asked quietly.

Ravenwood looked away. "We're all fond of Sarah."

"Don't play cute," Bartholomew chided him. "Do you *love* her?"

Ravenwood arched a brow. "Since when do you care about love?"

"Since recently," Bartholomew admitted. "But you've searched for it your whole life. Are you prepared to throw your dreams away to help a friend?"

"Isn't that what friendship is?"

Was it? Bartholomew tapped his fingers against the armrest and tried to think of a situation that would work out for everybody. He failed to come up with one. "I'm not trying to talk you out of marrying. I can't think of anything better that could happen to Sarah or her baby. I just hate to see you miserable."

"That is a trade we were both willing to make," came the duke's clipped reply.

Bartholomew straightened. "You've already spoken with her?"

Ravenwood laughed humorlessly. "She was harder to convince than you were. We have never thought of each other as more than friends, and she fears the union will necessarily result in me resenting her or the child for taking away my opportunity to marry for love."

Bartholomew winced. Those were very good points. "In the end, you prevailed?"

"The *babe* prevailed." The duke's smile was grim. "She won't get a better offer. Or any offer. The midwife believes Sarah is just a few weeks away from giving birth. I am their only hope." He lifted a shoulder. "What choice do we have?"

Bartholomew's heart twisted. When he and the others had purchased their commissions into the army, they had pitied Ravenwood for having to stay home and mind a dukedom rather than rush headlong into adventure.

The war hadn't brought any of them glory. Nor had a dukedom let Ravenwood escape unscathed, evidently. It turned out there were plenty of consequences to go around.

Ravenwood brushed invisible dust from his breeches. "Can I count on you to be a witness? You may say no, if you feel your loyalties are too divided."

"My loyalty is to you and Sarah." Bartholomew shifted uncomfortably. Of course he would stand up as witness to two of his dearest friends giving up their dreams for love in order to rescue the future of an unborn child.

He swallowed. Who was to say they wouldn't find love?

As the duke had pointed out, they were all fond of her. She would make any man a good wife.

And as for Ravenwood, what was not to love? He was one of the finest men of Bartholomew's acquaintance. A touch solemn, perhaps. Attentive to duty, certainly. But also clever, kindhearted, honest...

Certainly a better choice than if Bartholomew had offered himself in the duke's place. Ravenwood was a whole man in every sense, not a patchwork monster missing half his leg and half his heart.

Bartholomew's chest tightened. He could never marry. A daughter would need a father to dance with, to swing her up on a pony or teach her to swim. A son would need a father to spar with, to toss him into the air as a baby and to race across the countryside astride new stallions. And a wife...

He swallowed hard. Years before, he hadn't been worth

considering for marriage because he was too self-centered, too much of a rake. Now he wasn't worth considering because he wasn't much of anything at all.

"Thank you," the duke said quietly. "Your support means everything."

Bartholomew exhaled. "As does yours."

"Come." Ravenwood rose to his feet. "I'll see you out."

Bartholomew pushed up from the chair and followed him down the corridor.

The front door opened just as they reached the entryway. Ravenwood's butler helped Lady Amelia inside. Her eyes sparkled to see the two of them together.

"Brother dear. Major Blackpool." She bussed Ravenwood on the cheek before turning to Bartholomew. "How bad of you to be leaving just as I arrive!"

He bowed. "Perhaps we will see each other again the next time Miss Ross sponsors a fete."

Lady Amelia laughed. "Perhaps so. It was certainly lovely to meet your fiancée. Where will you be getting married?"

Nowhere, of course. But he would wait until Daphne officially cried off before letting anyone know.

"My parents would disown me if I wed outside of Maidstone," he said instead. That much was true. "It was all I could do to talk them out of begging Ravenwood to help me procure a special license so we can have the wedding in my parents' rear garden."

Ravenwood's eyes widened in surprise. "If you had but mentioned—"

"The banns and a church are perfectly fine," Bartholomew assured him. *And also perfectly unnecessary.* He turned back to Amelia. "How are you adapting to married life? Do you miss lording over Ravenwood House with your iron fist?"

"I miss having something productive to do with my time," she admitted with a smile. "My husband's estate is shockingly efficient."

An idea began to form in the back of Bartholomew's mind. "It sounds like you could use a project or two. Have you ever heard of a Davy lamp?"

"I have not." Lady Amelia tugged a small journal and the nub of a pencil from her reticule. "Tell me everything."

Ravenwood chuckled. "Mind your step, Blackpool. Whatever plot you're brewing, Amelia is bound to overtake it entirely."

"Perhaps that's just the thing." Bartholomew considered the viscountess in silence. She would be a formidable ally. "Daphne is passionate about charity work. She has more projects than any one woman could reasonably hope to accomplish. I was thinking to myself that what she needed was an army—"

"—when you realized all she needs is a *lieutenant*," Lady Amelia finished with a sharp nod. "Say no more. *I* shall assemble the army."

"Told you," Ravenwood murmured. "She'll have everything sorted by suppertime."

"I wish I thought it were possible for things to be sorted within our lifetimes," Bartholomew said. "But if we get enough people working together toward a common goal…"

His blood pulsed faster. If Lady Amelia *could* amass an army, perhaps Daphne wouldn't have to travel the country, immersing herself in potentially dangerous situations. With London as a command center, perhaps she could stay right here.

With him.

Hope flooded him for the first time. What if he could give Daphne a reason to stay? A reason not to break the betrothal after all? Perhaps even a reason to love him?

"No need to take notes." He yanked his investigator's report from his waistcoat pocket and presented the roll of papers to Lady Amelia. "That should give you a fair idea of what Daphne's hoping to accomplish. Take a look, think it over, and perhaps the three of us can meet to discuss your ideas in a week or two?"

"In a week or two, we'll have an army of charity soldiers at your fiancée's disposal." Amelia tucked her journal and the report into her reticule. "May I just say how refreshing it is that you intend to help, rather than hinder, a wife who knows what she wants? The world could use more men like you, Major Blackpool."

Ravenwood grinned. "Lord help us. London's going to be awash in strong-willed, opinionated ladies when the fashionable Major Blackpool starts a new trend."

"I, for one, think he chose wisely." Lady Amelia dipped a curtsey. "I shall be honored to do charity work with your wife. And I do hope it starts a trend."

Bartholomew's smile faltered. If only he could start such a trend. But he hadn't chosen Daphne any more than she'd chosen him. Yet he could no longer hide the truth. If he *could* choose a wife…

It could only be Daphne.

Chapter Twenty-One

Daphne wished she could drum up the proper level of enthusiasm about the Caxton ball. That it would be a sumptuous gala, more magical than anything she'd previously experienced, she had no doubt.

She also knew it would be her last.

Her birthday loomed around the corner. She had an appointment with the bank and a solicitor set up for that same afternoon.

All that was left was packing her trunk and purchasing passage on the first mail coach heading toward Lancashire. She'd already prioritized her list and mapped out the best route to visit the most urgent cases personally. By this time next week, she'd be gone.

All that was good news. *Wonderful* news. There was no reason at all for the great yawning emptiness inside at the thought of finally realizing her hard-won dreams.

No reason except Bartholomew.

He was escorting her to tonight's ball. Escorting her, Katherine, and Mrs. Havens, to be precise. He'd scowled at her as though it were *her* fault they required extra chaperonage because he no longer believed the presence of a mere maid could stop him from kissing her.

She hoped the chaperones would fail.

She was tired of being proper. Tired of pretending she didn't want Bartholomew. Tired of him protecting her from his passions when what she truly wished was to be swept away by them. To have a few moments in his embrace. Moments where all else fell away and all that was left was each other.

Bartholomew, on the other hand, thought the Caxton ball

would be a fine place for her to publicly jilt him.

As if she would. As if she *could*. He had become too important to her. It was taking every ounce of her will and courage to leave him behind in order to devote her life to improving the lives of others. She rubbed her arms, chilled at the thought. He *had* to cry off. Her first act as a free woman couldn't be to ruin him. Not when he was finally coming back to life.

She took a deep breath and made her way toward the stairs.

Bubbling voices indicated he had already arrived, and that Katherine and her great-aunt were conversing with him in the front parlor.

Daphne hurried down the stairs, but pulled up short when she reached the open doorway.

Bartholomew was breathtaking. His eyes were the same crystalline blue, his brown hair the same soft mane, his cravat and clothing as tailored and impeccable as ever. What had changed was *him*. He no longer carried himself like a cautious, grief-stricken ex-soldier. He carried himself like the popular, self-assured rake he'd once been. The powerful, captivating man he still was.

His confidence had returned. His arrogant swagger. His irresistible charm.

The effect was devastatingly attractive.

A flutter unfurled in her belly. *This* was how he'd earned his reputation. Not because he consciously set out to charm and seduce women, but because they couldn't help but insert themselves in his path, hoping he might notice them even a fraction as intensely as they were enthralled by him.

Elderly Mrs. Havens all but preened before him, her infectious giggles a trifle too loud, her unwavering gaze a trifle too melting.

Even Katherine—she who needed no man!—was toying unconsciously with a tendril of hair, her eyes on Bartholomew. Katherine had licked her lips no less than three times in the scant minutes since Daphne had appeared in the doorway.

Heaven help her. Every woman at the Caxton crush

would be drawn to him tonight.

She wasn't jealous, she reminded herself firmly. He was *hers*. If only for another week.

Her stomach twisted at the thought.

He glanced up toward the doorway. His blue eyes softened when he caught sight of her. "Daphne. You've always been pretty, but tonight you look stunning. I'll be the envy of every gentleman when I escort you to the ball."

Her cheeks warmed, and her voice came out breathier than she'd intended. "Th-thank you."

He then proceeded to take Mrs. Havens' arm, not Daphne's.

She forced her tense facial muscles to relax. He was escorting all three of them, so of course Katherine's aunt took precedence. What Daphne hadn't expected was that their brief exchange of pleasantries would be the only thought he spared for her. Not when she couldn't stop thinking about him.

She hadn't even cared about balls until the opportunity for Bartholomew to escort her arose. Then her mind bubbled over with gowns and curling tongs and long, slow dances. She'd wanted to impress him. She'd wanted tonight to be special. She'd wanted to feel like a real fiancée.

Instead, Bartholomew sat next to Mrs. Havens in the carriage. He set about charming her with amusing anecdotes during the entire ride, delighting Katherine and annoying Daphne, though she tried valiantly not to show her hurt at being forgotten.

Her fingernails bit into her palms. She'd been ignored and insignificant her entire life. She should have known better than to let herself believe she mattered to him. He hadn't even bothered pretending.

If he intended to spend their last evening out without so much as light conversation, much less illicit kisses, perhaps that was for the best. It was high time she got used to living without him.

When they arrived at the Caxtons', he all but vanished the moment their names were read. Other than catching the occasional glimpse of the back of his head as he talked with this marchioness or that countess, Daphne might not have realized they were under the same roof at all.

He certainly seemed to have more interest in flattering crafty-eyed widows than he did in the woman he was allegedly courting.

Katherine, for her part, didn't notice or care. She knew every person who crossed her path, and effortlessly amused the sillier chits and fops, and then held the investors and collectors captive with more serious talk before she was whisked off to dance with a seemingly endless stream of eligible gentlemen.

Daphne's dance card was nowhere near that full, but whenever she did get a nibble, Katherine cheerfully took Daphne's place watching over her great-aunt, so that Daphne could enjoy a set or two swirling about the Caxtons' magnificent ballroom.

Except she couldn't enjoy it. Not when the one man who interested her was too interested in everyone else.

He was currently surrounded by a flock of fawning debutantes, each with more feathers protruding from her hair than the last. Daphne clenched her teeth. Every one of those girls was precisely the sort of mindless, adoring sycophant that she had long suspected men tended to marry. The kind of woman Daphne wasn't.

She forced herself to look away. If that was the sort of young lady Bartholomew preferred, then he was welcome to them.

No matter how wonderful her husband, no matter how deeply she fell in love, she would never be the sort of person who could spend the rest of her life worshipping a man. She couldn't devote herself to one person when she could be devoting herself to many.

Then again, she supposed a fair number of rakes shared that same thought process before (and after) they took a wife. Society marriages were strategic alliances, not love matches. Rare was the man who preferred his wife's bed to that of his mistress.

That kind of husband would certainly be much less demanding on a wife's time. Cocksure and arrogant, he'd flit from one bed to another, swaggering home only when it was time to beget an heir.

She used to think she'd prefer a husband like that.

She now knew she'd kill him.

That was her problem, she realized. She wasn't just being forced to accept his divided attentions. He wasn't hers at all. And he didn't seem the least bothered.

How much worse would it be if their betrothal was real, but his affection was not? She was right to walk away. The worst kind of marriage wasn't a husband who wished to spend too much time with her. It would be a husband that didn't care about her at all. Spending the rest of her days with someone who was indifferent toward her would be a loneliness more empty and endless than any she'd ever known.

Her focus should remain on the people who *did* need her. Not tangle up her heart fantasizing about what could never be. She wasn't fated for romance. Her fate was to be left behind. Forgotten.

Bartholomew had kissed her and swaggered away, with no more thought to it than that. Why should she expect any different? He was a rake. A temporary pleasure. The flirtatious women hanging on his arms knew precisely what they were—and weren't—getting.

So did Daphne. Their relationship was in name only. Bartholomew wanted her chaperoned in order to keep his mouth at a safe distance, but that didn't mean his lips weren't busy elsewhere.

They had every right to be. Daphne held no true claim on the gentleman or his kisses. No right to his time after their betrothal had come to an end.

But, oh, she wished she did.

What's more, she wished *he* were the one wondering what she was thinking and doing. She wished he were less confident about her interest. Uncertain he could steal a kiss even if there were no chaperonage for thirty miles. She wanted him to want *her*.

But she knew she couldn't keep him.

When the music ended, she pasted a smile on her face

before returning to Katherine and Mrs. Havens. She would pretend she was enjoying the evening, not yearning for a man she shouldn't desire.

Katherine frowned. "What's amiss? Have you the indigestion?"

Daphne stopped trying to smile. She gestured at the crowded ballroom. "I think I'm just over warm."

"Care to take a turn in the garden?" came a low, warm voice from behind her.

Bartholomew. She spun to face him, not at all sure whether she were more likely to strike him for his flirtations or throw herself into his arms and beg to be kissed. Either way, she shouldn't be trusted alone with him.

"Why, yes." Mrs. Havens beamed at him. "I would love a turn in the garden."

"Not you, Aunt. He means Daphne." Katherine motioned for them to go on ahead. "Come, Aunt. Let's find the ratafia."

Daphne scowled at their backs. Traitors.

Bartholomew's brow creased. "Are you all right?"

"*Splendid*," she bit out in a tone that probably indicated she was anything but.

He was wise enough not to question her further.

Instead, he escorted her toward the folding screens separating the garden entrance from the rear of the ballroom. He bid a footman to fetch her pelisse. Once she'd donned it, he allowed her to take no more than a few steps onto the stone path before coming to a halt.

She squeezed his arm. "What is it?"

He frowned. "We're the only ones out here."

"It's February," she reminded him with a smile.

"It's foolish. I wish to speak with you, but…" He tried to pivot her toward the ballroom. "We must return to the party."

She refused to budge. "Speak with me about what?"

He glanced over his shoulder.

The folding screen blocked most of the light from the chandeliers, but the music from the orchestra wafted past as if carried on the wind. The garden was vacant and devoid of flowers, but its very emptiness gave them privacy. A thin sliver of moon was the only light they needed.

He took her hands. "I spoke to Lady Sheffield about your projects."

Daphne's stomach tightened. She supposed it was inevitable that her life's work would become gossip fodder at tea parties. She just wished it didn't make her feel so alone. "You spoke to whom?"

"The Duke of Ravenwood's sister." He rubbed his thumb over her knuckles. "You might recall her from Miss Ross's party. She's Lord Sheffield's new viscountess. She more commonly can be found managing households and holiday fêtes, so when I mentioned your concerns for the miners and the weavers—"

She jerked her fingers out of his grasp. "I don't need you or anyone else mocking my beliefs or thinking me mad for trying to help. Many of these people will die without outside aid. The working conditions are deplorable and their *living* conditions horrid."

"She wants to help."

Daphne's body froze. "What?"

"Lady Amelia is formidably efficient. She dubbed herself lieutenant of *your* army. Your people definitely want her on their side."

"My people?" Daphne echoed faintly, her mind spinning. She had an army on her side? And a viscountess?

He took her hands again, his expression earnest. "The other women I've spoken to seem divided in ways one might anticipate. The debutantes probably won't be interested in helping other people until they have secured their own futures. Ladies married to titled husbands already have more than enough tasks to keep them occupied. But there are quite a few dowagers and even a handful of widows who—"

"*That's* what you've been doing?" she blurted. Her cheeks heated. "All those women you were speaking to…"

"I presumed ladies would be more easily persuaded to charity work than their husbands, but I intend to convince the men next. I'm still a member of several gentlemen's clubs and, believe what you like, they are not *solely* dens of iniquity and vice."

She gazed up at him, speechless. Guilt flooded her. Despite their past weeks together, she hadn't hesitated to discount Bartholomew as a rake and a ne'er-do-well, when in fact he'd been crusading for *her*.

"Men may be less likely to dedicate their spare time toward volunteer work, but the more affluent might be free with their pocketbooks." His eyes sparkled as he outlined his scheme. "With Lady Amelia's organizational talent and a reasonable amount of initial funding, *all* of your projects can be priorities."

He hadn't forgotten her. Quite the opposite. He had aligned himself with her causes publicly and personally, in front of all the people whose opinions he valued. She stared at her feet. Bartholomew wasn't the shallow one.

She was.

Who cared if it was her project or her ideas? Wasn't forward progress the important part? Making a change in people's lives? Was there any reason she *shouldn't* allow others to help, if they were so inclined? Like Katherine always said, the more the merrier…

Daphne's throat grew thick. Her best friend had offered to help in any way. Perhaps she could! Being patroness of an antiquities museum didn't mean Katherine *wouldn't* be just as valuable of an asset when it came to Daphne's many causes. Katherine knew everyone and they all loved her back. She'd be an exceptional lieutenant to add to the army. New recruits would flock to her flame.

Then Lady Amelia Sheffield could organize the troops, and Daphne would pick the battles.

Bartholomew was already their major… and Daphne's saving grace.

"Thank you." She threw her arms around his neck and pressed a kiss to his cheek. "Thank you for helping me when I was too blind to help myself."

"Your servant," he said gruffly. But he didn't let her go.

She rested the side of her face against his chest. His strong arms wrapped tightly about her, enveloping her in the heat of his embrace.

Contentment flooded her. As long as she was in his

arms, nothing else mattered. He'd keep her warm. He'd keep her safe. He'd do everything within his power to keep her happy. She snuggled closer, listening for the beat of his heart. He was perfect. No wonder she couldn't bear to let him go.

Her stomach dropped as she realized the truth. She wasn't just attracted to him. She was in *love* with him.

And she was going to have to walk away.

She lifted her cheek from his chest. Rather than release her, he shifted his stance so that her right hand tucked into his and the fingers of his other hand splayed above the small of her back.

Slowly, he began to lead her in time with the music. Her breath caught. They were *waltzing*.

He gazed down at her. "I have wanted you in my arms since the moment you first mentioned you might come to London. I would have danced with you every day, if I could." He met her eyes then glanced away. "It's just so… humiliating. You'd already seen me fall. To add the clacking of my leg…"

She didn't hear any clacking. She could barely even hear the music over the thundering of her heart at what this moment meant to him. He wasn't just dancing with her. He was risking all the rejection and humiliation he'd had to cloister himself into his town house to avoid.

He was confronting his deepest fears just for the chance to waltz in the garden with her.

She touched the side of his face. "You don't have to do this if you're afraid someone might see."

"I don't care about anyone's opinion but yours. If I fall…" His lips curved wryly as he met her eyes. "I think I've already fallen."

Her heart thudded. "Then it's fortunate we find ourselves in each other's arms."

"Indeed." He lowered his mouth. Slowly. Giving her plenty of time to turn away.

She slid her fingers into his hair and lifted her lips to his. *He* was what she wanted.

His kisses were gentle. Tender. She didn't want

gentleness. Her heart yearned for him too sharply to be content with mere tenderness.

Her kisses were hungry, demanding. She wanted every taste, every sensation to be seared upon her soul. If she couldn't keep him in her arms, she would keep moments like these in her memory. Cleave them to her heart.

His feet stilled and, slowly, he broke their kiss. Their private waltz had come to an end.

She couldn't repress the small sound of disappointment that escaped her throat... until she realized how far they now were from the ballroom. Although still and bare, the gardens' trees and fountains provided a dark, secluded nook, sheltering them from prying eyes and the winter wind.

They were alone. Scandalously, deliciously, alone.

She didn't think for a moment that it meant he was finally willing to introduce her to hedonistic pleasure—no matter how many nights she dreamt of just such a liaison—but she was greedy for any part of himself he was willing to share.

He led her to a stone bench and pulled her onto his lap.

Eagerly, she wrapped her arms about his neck, thrilling at the warmth of his embrace. He could have forced her to go back inside. Yet he cradled her in his arms instead. She wished she could be there forever. Her heart beat so rapidly, pressed against his.

He kissed the top of her head, the side of her temple, the shell of her ear. Letting her know he wanted more. Letting her know it was her choice.

Of course she would choose him.

She lifted her parted lips to his. He took her mouth. Her soul. His arms were heaven. She devoured him, her tongue dancing with his. He held her closer. The heat and passion of his kisses proved the intensity of his desire matched that of her own.

Her skin grew hot. Her clothes, restrictive. She wished she could tear his greatcoat from his beautiful shoulders. Feel her mouth on his warm neck, his muscled arms, his bare chest. To taste him on her tongue and know that he was hers.

The fantasy was so intoxicating, it stole her breath. If she could have had him, she might never have become a crusader. Might never have *had* to make do with clandestine kisses on a garden bench. She would have been able to give herself to him every night and cherish him every day.

His kisses heated her flesh. Robbed her ability to think. All she could do was lose herself in the moment. Surrender to his mouth, his touch. Pray he never let her go.

He splayed his hands against her ribs, just beneath her spencer. Taking possession. She arched closer. He suckled her tongue, nipped her lower lip. Branded her. This was Bartholomew. *Her* Bartholomew. As desperate for her as she was for him.

She slid her hands in his hair and kissed him back. Only a foolish woman would ruin the moment with unnecessary words. He was right where she wanted him: in her arms. He would not be there forever. A smart woman would take advantage while she still could.

The pad of his thumb traced the lower curve of her breast. She gasped as a sudden yearning shot through her to twist into his touch until he was forced to cup her breast in his hand. She gripped his shoulders, his hair. How could he have so much control whilst she had none? She could be his, if only he would take her. Her body had surrendered completely.

Her nipples were taut with desire. The shiver racing down her spine had nothing to do with the chill of winter and everything to do with the man whose mouth fed so hungrily on hers, whose thumb was rising toward her nipple with deliberate, torturous slowness.

Did he think he might shock her with his touch? Too late. She had already shocked herself with how completely she desired him. With the nights she had awoken, drenched in sweat, her pulse pounding in her ears at the taste of his name still hot on her tongue.

Here he was, in her arms at last. Hers for the moment. She gasped in pleasure, in *need*, as his fingers teased her aching nipples. He was everything she wanted. Her body burned to have his bare flesh against hers.

If the wind were not so bitter... If they were not a

stone's throw from discovery…

His fingers dropped as if she had spoken the words aloud. He broke the kiss, but rested his forehead against hers. Both of them panting, their hearts racing, their swollen lips only a breath away.

The wind had vanished, the music forgotten. He cradled her to him as if he, too, struggled to resist the temptation to indulge in a single passionate moment. Here, now, they could not do more than kiss. But they did not yet need to stop.

She opened her mouth to his once more, confessing her desire, her love, with every lick, every gasping breath.

The future would wait. All that mattered now was the heat of his embrace, the matching hunger in his kisses. Soon enough, they would resume their separate lives. Until then, she was his. She would love him with her mouth, her tongue, her hands in his hair, her body yielding completely in his arms for as long as he wished to hold her.

Laughter spilled from the other side of the garden. She froze with her lips on his, her heart pounding in alarm.

"'Tis perhaps fortunate that our interlude cannot continue." He rubbed her cheek with the pad of his thumb then took her mouth in one last kiss. "It seems even the chill of winter cannot cool my ardor whilst in your presence."

She did not feel fortunate. She rose from his lap only because footsteps approached. She'd forgotten the weather altogether until she no longer had his warm arms and heated kisses to shield her from the wind. An involuntary shiver wracked her. As soon as he rose from the bench, she clutched his arm and pulled him as close as she dared. But not as close as she wished.

For that, there would need to be no barriers between them. No curious partygoers. No icy wind. No clothing. Just her and Bartholomew, united at last.

She swallowed hard and glanced away.

'Twas an impossible dream. She could not have him. Her presence was temporary. She bit her lip. Her presence had always been temporary, for everyone in her life. Her loved ones left, or they forgot her. Bartholomew was no different. He had done so before and would do so again. A year from now, she'd be nothing more than a memory.

Yet her heart would break when it was time to walk away.

Chapter Twenty-Two

The evening of her birthday, Daphne descended from a hackney carriage as though she were pushing through molasses.

She should be happy.

She clutched her documents to her chest and stared up at Katherine's elegant town house. At the second story room Daphne no longer required. It was over. She could leave right now if she wanted and never return to London again. She should be *thrilled*.

Her lady's maid alighted from the hack. "Everything all right, ma'am?"

Esther. Daphne shot a despairing glance at her maid. What was she meant to do about Esther?

With simple living and an eye on her budget, Daphne's small portion was enough to provide for her and perhaps a maid-of-all-work as a companion.

No lady's maid—not even a kind, unpretentious lady's maid accustomed to no more fine living than what might be found in a simple vicarage—would wish to trade the slow, pleasant country life for the wretched, grueling drudgery of an overburdened, underpaid maid-of-all-work.

Even less likely was the idea any maid would wish to be dragged through the poorest, most far-flung corners of England. Daphne's itinerary was not for the faint of heart. Failing farms. Teeming rookeries. Dangerous mines. It was not for Esther.

Once Daphne became an independent, unchaperoned crusader, she would no longer have the option of avoiding high society. She'd be *obligated* to avoid them. With a reputation that tattered, the only lord or lady who wouldn't give her the cut direct without a second thought was Katherine.

And, perhaps… Bartholomew.

Daphne let out a slow breath. The silver lining to losing one's reputation was that there was no longer any need to go to heroic measures to protect it. In fact, she rather appreciated the freedom her classlessness brought. If Bartholomew wished to kiss her, here she was.

For now.

"Everything's fine," she assured her maid, before forcing her feet up the walk to Katherine's front door.

Whether or not everything was fine remained to be seen. The only certainty was that everything was changing.

Daphne handed off her coat and gloves to the butler and started up the stairs. Perhaps she should stay a few days before leaving. One couldn't sack a cherished servant out of the blue.

She would also love to put her head together with Lady Amelia Sheffield one last time before the viscountess could no longer associate with Daphne publicly.

She frowned. There were plenty of black clouds to go with the silver lining of freedom.

Now that she finally had an army—and a lieutenant— she could do battle with more than her pen and writing desk. Lady Amelia didn't seem the sort to require in-person instruction. She had already shouldered a fair chunk of Daphne's letter writing, and had created teams of volunteers and detailed journals for each of her campaigns.

When Daphne reached her guest chamber, she rang for a tea tray and a hot bath. This might be one of the last times in her life to have such luxuries at her fingertips, and it was difficult not to wish to make the most of them while she still could.

The butler had informed her that Katherine had taken her aunt to the theatre and left instructions for Daphne to join them, but after the stress of so many weeks spent agonizing over whether she'd celebrate her birthday a free woman, Daphne wanted little more than to relax in the hot water and enjoy an evening away from crowds. Away from pretending.

An evening of being herself, without need to impress or playact or mind her tongue sounded just like heaven.

Once she was clean and dressed, she gave Esther the rest of the evening off. Daphne needed to sit down at her escritoire and decide what could be done for her maid. A task much easier without the maid in question staring at her from across the room.

Daphne affixed her reading spectacles to her nose and began to create a list of what Esther might need.

Passage back to Maidstone, of course. If Esther wished to return to Kent. London might well offer more and better opportunities for an experienced maid. Daphne nodded. She'd write several letters of recommendation. It might be difficult for the post to locate her as she traveled, so the best thing to do was provide Esther with a good quantity up front, as well as a month's wages in case there was any delay securing employment.

The vicarage servants had been few in number, but they were loyal and kind, and in most cases had been with the family since before Daphne was born. Now that Captain Steele had inherited the cottage, heaven only knew what would become of them. Perhaps she should send letters of recommendation for the entire staff, just in case they found themselves in need of a way out.

Presuming Captain Steele didn't intercept her recommendations and toss them straight into the fire.

A knock sounded upon her chamber door.

Daphne rose and discovered one of the footmen in the corridor with the afternoon post. She thanked him and carried the small pile to her escritoire. As expected, the mail was addressed to various aliases, in response to one cause or another.

All except one.

Frowning, she broke the drop of wax. A folded document tumbled onto the desk.

A document she recognized.

With shaking fingers, she unfolded the parchment. *Her betrothal contract*. She gasped and hugged the cursed document to her pounding heart. One of the servants must have managed to smuggle it from her father's study.

A laugh burbled in Daphne's throat. It would never have occurred to a pirate who trusted no one that most of the household knew the combination to her father's safe!

For a servant to have risked discovery, however, meant that Captain Steele must have already left on his next pirating adventure after all. Which meant Daphne could happily send off multiple letters of recommendation to everyone on staff. They had taken care of her since she was a child, and they hadn't stopped doing so just because her father was no longer their employer.

But first—!

She leapt up from the escritoire and strode toward the hearth, intent on ripping the contract into shreds and feeding each scrap to the crackling fire.

No. She paused just as her fingers made the first tear. This was a moment that deserved to be shared.

And it wasn't the only copy of the contract.

She hurried back to the escritoire and dashed off a quick summons for Bartholomew, telling him everything was fine—better than fine!—and to please present himself and his copy of the contract at his earliest convenience. She rang for a footman to deliver the letter.

As soon as the note was gone, a thought occurred to her. Captain Steele hadn't just lost his hold over Daphne. She'd lost hers over Bartholomew. As soon as they destroyed both copies of the contract, he would no longer need to fear Captain Steele dragging him into prison. Bartholomew would be free to walk away.

Unless she gave him a reason to stay the night.

Now that she was an independent woman, what did she intend to do with her newfound freedom? Even if marriage wasn't in her future, there was only one way she wanted to spend the present evening: in Bartholomew's arms.

She turned to the closest looking-glass. Her cheeks were flushed with excitement, her eyes bright and shining. Her simple day dress wasn't precisely the sort of gown one wore when plotting a seduction, but she'd already let Esther go for the evening and…   .

Daphne's blush deepened. *Yes*. This was absolutely a seduction. She was free from the machinations of Captain Steele, free from Society's prim dictates, free to live her life where and how she chose. She couldn't think of anything more fitting than for her first act as a free woman to be making love to a man she cherished.

And would likely never see again.

She glanced down at the journal she used to plan her schedule. By this time next week, she planned to be in South Tyneside. From there to Leeds, then on to Shrewsbury.

Daphne doubted she'd soon return to Mayfair or Hyde Park. There were too many people who needed too much help elsewhere in the country. There were plenty of worthy causes in the London rookeries as well. However, those dirty streets weren't where one stumbled across rakish childhood friends. Once she embarked on this adventure, she'd never be welcomed back.

She inhaled a slow, shaky breath. Whatever was going to happen, needed to happen tonight. The stars were aligned as well as they would ever be. If Bartholomew didn't get her message, or was tied up with other engagements until later in the week… then it wasn't meant to be.

Of course, now that she'd *sent* the invitation, her stomach was tangled in knots. She removed her spectacles and rubbed her face. So much could still go wrong. What if he didn't receive it until the morrow? What if he did receive it—along with a more salacious offer from that beautiful widow with the long, seductive glances? What if he arrived, only to chuckle in amusement when she revealed her intent to seduce him?

What if he didn't want her, not in that way?

Her heart skittered in trepidation. He'd been a rake for the past decade, while she'd remained good old *Laughy Daffy*, the forgettable vicar's daughter from the country. He'd kissed her, but that was all. Rakes were scarcely renowned for their restraint. If he'd had any inclination to seduce her, surely he would have already done so. Wasn't that omission clear enough? Did she really need to force him to reject her to her face?

Panic coursed through her. Heaven help her, she should never have sent that letter. With any luck, Bartholomew wouldn't be at home to receive it. Or perhaps he'd send a note of apology, and come round some other time, when they wouldn't be so *alone*, and the circumstances so ripe for—

"Miss?" Outside Daphne's open door, a footman consulted a pristine calling card. "Major Bartholomew Blackpool is here. Are you receiving callers, or shall I send him away?"

"*No*," she said, too quickly. Her cheeks flushed. "I should like to see him. Is he in the parlor?"

The footman bowed. "He is indeed. Shall I order tea?"

She hesitated for only a moment. "No, thank you. I've important matters to discuss with Major Blackpool, and it will be best if we are not disturbed."

The footman nodded crisply and took his leave.

Daphne snatched the stolen copy of the betrothal contract from atop her escritoire and strode out of her chamber.

At least she had a pretext. Regardless of Bartholomew's interest in her physically, he would be just as relieved as she was that she no longer required a guardian's care or a fake fiancé. She swallowed. In fact, he might be delighted to learn he could now resume his previous habits and need not concern himself with vagabond crusader Daphne Vaughan again once he left these premises.

The thought of Bartholomew returning to the infamous rake he'd once been...

Parchment crinkled as Daphne's trembling fingers curled into a fist.

She halted outside the parlor to try and regulate her breathing. They were independent souls. If he wished to lie with every debutante from Exeter to Newcastle, that was his business. Just as choosing to devote herself to improving the lives of the less fortunate was hers. She held no claim to his time or his heart. He wasn't here to sign a contract, but to burn one.

There could be no future beyond tonight. No sense ruining it with jealousy over liaisons he hadn't yet had. She took a deep breath and stepped into the parlor.

At the sound of her footsteps, he spun to face her. His brow was knit with concern, but his warm blue eyes were filled with something deeper. Not the cool perusal of a disinterested rake, but the hungry fire of a wolf that had just been hand-delivered a succulent lamb.

Her heart thundered as she latched the door behind her, but she could not keep a self-satisfied smile from curving her lips.

The heat in his gaze indicated tonight's seduction would be decidedly mutual.

"I received your note." His fingertips touched his chest as if her letter were inside his waistcoat pocket, tucked safely against his heart. "You said to come at once."

"And so you did." There was a knowing edge to her voice that she barely recognized, a deliberate swing to her hips as she closed the distance between them. Being the object of his undivided attention emboldened her.

Without taking her eyes from his, she flattened her hand against his chest and slid her fingers beneath the lapel of his tailcoat. His heart thundered against her palm as her fingertips brushed the telltale edge of folded parchment.

"I missed you." He clapped his hand over his chest, trapping her fingers between layers of silk and linen that she held no right to touch.

Layers she intended to remove, piece by piece.

He lifted her chin with his free hand, then slid his fingers into her hair to cup the back of her head as he crushed his lips to hers.

She gasped, and he swept his tongue inside her mouth, teasing her in such a way that her entire body trembled with desire and want. She clutched the hard muscle of his upper arm and met him kiss for kiss.

When he finally lifted his mouth from hers, the corner of his beautiful mouth twitched with arrogant satisfaction. He well knew how potently he affected her. She might have felt powerful before, but she was powerless in his arms. There was no hiding the fact that she was his for the taking. He suckled her lower lip into his mouth.

Breathless, she pressed herself even closer.

He bit her lower lip gently before releasing it and licking the spot his teeth had grazed.

"Is this why you summoned me?" he asked, without lifting his mouth from hers.

She suckled his lower lip the way he'd suckled hers, then bit it slightly harder before touching her tongue to his. "Not the *only* reason."

The wicked promise in his eyes nearly melted her chemise right off her body. "I watched you lock the door. If there is anything you wish to discuss, tell me now before we have no more use for words."

As tempting as it was to forgo words completely, 'twas even more important that he know he no longer ran the risk of having to marry her.

"Whatever happens between us..." she began, whilst fervently hoping everything that could happen, *did*. "You are officially a free man."

He stepped back, frowning. "What do you mean?"

She bit her lip. "Did you bring the betrothal contract, as I requested?"

He gestured toward one of the tea tables. "I brought you more than that."

Her heart warmed. The table he'd indicated was laden with roses and Queen Anne's lace.

She peered up at him shyly. "You brought flowers?"

He lifted a shoulder. "It's your birthday. All those roses were cluttering up my garden rather awfully, so I thought—"

She narrowed her eyes in suspicion. "Do you even have a garden?"

He widened his eyes, the very picture of innocence. "Not anymore. Everything I had is over there on your tea table."

Her lips quirked. "That was very thoughtful. The flowers are lovely. I do thank you for digging up your garden for me."

"It'll grow back." He waved a careless hand. "Try not to have another birthday until next year."

Until next year.

Daphne's smile fell. No more teasing. Next year, the

months they'd shared together would only be a memory. It was past time to let him know.

"The bank finalized my inheritance." Her voice was low and surprisingly calm, given the turbulence she felt inside. Once Bartholomew realized he need not playact any longer, there would be no reason to stay... except for her.

"Your finances are in order?" His eyes were shuttered, his face unreadable. "Then it is a very happy birthday, indeed."

She nodded. Or meant to. She'd achieved precisely what she'd hoped for. So why did she feel torn in two directions at once?

"I am much relieved," she said. "My portion is what I thought it would be. Not enough to rub shoulders with high society, of course, but more than enough to meet my simple needs."

"Congratulations. You can finally tell that pirate cousin of yours to shove off." He reached inside the breast of his tailcoat and removed a tightly rolled document. "I presume that's why you asked me to bring this?"

"Yes. This morning, I received..." Suddenly realizing her hands were empty, her gaze darted about the parlor until she spied a corner of parchment protruding from beneath one of the chairs. The betrothal contract must have fluttered from her fingers during their heated kiss. She knelt to retrieve the fallen document and handed it to Bartholomew. "My father's servants managed to liberate Captain Steele's copy. I thought we might toss them into the fire together."

Bartholomew didn't exhale with relief at the end of their charade, nor did he laugh merrily at the servants' ingenuity or the arrogant pirate's certain disgruntlement once he discovered he hadn't been as clever as he'd thought. Instead, Bartholomew simply handed back the captain's copy and motioned toward the hearth. "After you."

She gave a determined smile and strode up to the low iron grate. Lazy orange flames licked upward from a jumble of charred logs, warming her cheeks and fingers with their heat. She held the corner of the contract up over the grate, where it would be sure to fall into the flames. The lowest corner of the parchment instantly began to brown from the heat.

"Ready?"

In a single breath, Bartholomew was next to her, holding his own copy of the contract above the flames. Because it had been rolled, the edges curved inward, but it too would tumble directly into the fire.

He gave a sharp nod. "Ready."

"To freedom," she whispered, and released the parchment.

Bartholomew met her eyes as he let go of his copy. "To Daphne."

The fire crackled and snapped as it hungrily consumed the new offerings. In seconds, both documents had browned, burned, and scattered as ash.

"It's truly over. All of it." She turned to smile up at him. "Thank you for coming to my rescue."

He sketched a bow. "I am ever your servant."

"If there is ever anything I can do for you…" Her voice trailed off. She cursed her awkwardness. That was not what she'd meant. She'd invited him in the hopes he would stay for a seduction and instead, she'd made it sound like good-bye. "The worst part about ending our sham relationship is that we no longer have any reason to—"

"No," he interrupted, his blue eyes intense. "The *best* part about ending a sham relationship is that you'll know for certain that what I'm about to do is because I wish to, and not for any other motive."

Hope filled her. "What are you about to do?"

"This." He hauled her against him and covered her mouth with his.

Elated, she wrapped her arms about his neck as she kissed him back, letting him feel with every lick, every nibble, every kiss just how much she wanted him, too.

She loved him even more for this, although she knew better than to say so and risk him walking away. They'd made each other no promises. Their betrothal contract was nothing more than a smudge of ash.

But even though their paths would diverge on the

morrow, this was no idle coupling. She would love him passionately with her heart, her mind, and her body, just as she would if he were her husband. Hers to have and to hold. Hers to keep. If only for tonight.

She ripped his cravat from his neck. He unbuttoned her gown without breaking their kiss. His fingers were tender, his mouth urgent. Cool air whispered down her spine as he unlaced her stays and tossed them aside.

When his fingertips grazed her hardened nipples through the thin layer of linen, she shivered at the delicious sensation.

His mouth broke from hers. "Daphne. Are you certain?"

"I want it all," she murmured against his lips, pushing her gown and chemise off her shoulders so that they puddled onto the floor, baring her body before him. "I want *you*."

He swung her into his arms and over to the chaise longue, where he lay down beside her and slanted his mouth over hers.

She drank him in greedily. The chill on her flesh from the exposed air evaporated the moment his warm hand splayed against her ribs. Her breasts seemed to swell in anticipation of his touch, every inch of her body alive and tingling with expectation. Her heart swelled. She hadn't been waiting to make love. She'd been waiting for *him*.

When at last he cupped her breast, she knew she was lost. As his fingers rolled across the peak of her nipple, toying, teasing, an answering tension surged between her legs, a sharp yearning unlike anything she had ever imagined.

He lowered his mouth to her breast and slid his fingers down her stomach to the cleft between her legs. Pleasure shot through her.

Her head fell back against the pillows, her eyelids fluttering in bliss at the twin sensations. She arched her breast into his mouth, let her thighs fall open to give him greater access. Longing stabbed through her as his fingertips stroked and dipped, teasing her with hints of the ecstasy to come.

As much as she wanted this—wanted *him*—a growing part of her desperately wished that it *could* be forever. That he could truly be hers.

"Bartholomew..." she whispered.

He slid two fingers inside her and conscious thought vanished. The pad of his thumb swirled against her slick nub as his fingers surged within her. She could barely breathe at the onslaught of sensation.

Her legs began to tremble as the pressure built to a crescendo, then burst in waves of pleasure. She grasped his hair with both hands, clutching his mouth to her breast as her inner muscles contracted around his fingers with delicious abandon.

When at last the tremors ceased, he slid his fingers from between her legs and covered her mouth with fevered kisses. Her heart warmed. This was only the beginning.

"Make love to me." She tugged impatiently at the shoulders of his tailcoat, suddenly cognizant that she was completely nude and he was completely clothed. She yearned to feel the heat of his flesh against hers. Two bodies, two souls, with nothing between them. She reached for the buttons of his tailcoat. "Bartholomew, make love to me."

He lifted his hips up off the chaise and slid his hand between their bodies. Rather than unbutton his waistcoat, however, he simply unfastened the fall of his breeches. As he settled his hips atop hers, the hard length of his shaft fell perfectly against the wet heat between her legs.

She frowned and tried to prop herself up on her elbows. "What are you doing?"

He tugged her lower lip between his teeth and smiled. "Making love to you. Just like you asked."

She shook her head with frustration. "*Not* like I asked. I want you to make *love* to me."

"Happily." He reached between them and guided his shaft toward her core.

This was it. This was all he was willing to share. As close as he was willing to get. Disappointment flooded her, erasing all the pleasure of the moments before and leaving her with nothing but a great, yawning emptiness.

This wasn't making love. This was him, fully clothed, already planning to leave her. Just like he left everyone. Just

like everyone always left her.
 Not anymore.

Chapter Twenty-Three

The sudden shove to his solar plexus caught Bartholomew off guard. He grabbed the back of the chaise in order to keep from tumbling arse-first onto the carpet.

Daphne no longer looked like she wanted to make love. She looked like she wanted to kill him.

He refastened his breeches for safety. "You said you wanted—"

"Not like *this*." Her voice broke.

The disillusionment in her eyes cut him to his soul. He realized she wasn't angry with him. He'd hurt her. He just wasn't sure how. "Daphne..."

"*Look* at you," she hissed, her eyes welling with tears.

Look at him? His smile felt brittle.

It had come to this. He didn't have to look at himself to know what a prize he wasn't.

The body he'd once taken for granted was now broken and scarred. Incomplete. Even if he'd had the foresight to put out the fire and extinguish every candle, there was no hiding the truth. He didn't deserve her.

And he'd never loved anyone more in his entire life.

He tried to put his arms around her, to show her with his embrace that he loved her with all of his heart, even if he no longer possessed all of his body.

She shoved him off the chaise.

The breath whooshed out of him as his head hit the floor. Heat raced up his neck. She'd taken advantage of his lack of balance and *pushed* him. As if he were of no substance at all. His fingers shook with embarrassment.

By the time he rolled to his knees, she was on her feet and snatching her chemise and gown from the floor. Their interlude was over. It had gone even worse than he'd feared.

Perhaps there was still a chance to save it.

He brushed off his breeches and faced her. "Are you going to tell me what the matter is?"

She swung her head to look at him, mouth open in disbelief. "Me? Are *you* going to tell me what the problem is? I am naked before you. *Naked.* Begging you to make love to me. And all you do is unbutton the fall of your breeches—"

"Actually a key step in the lovemaking process," he murmured.

"A *step*, not the entire journey." Her eyes flashed as she yanked her chemise over her trembling body. "Making love is something two people do together. Equally. I'm not going to bare myself to you and let you tup me like I'm a penny whore. I'd rather hoped we could tear each *other's* clothing off."

"I'm not disrobing in front of you. Now or ever," he snapped. "Even my valet doesn't see me naked. It's nothing personal."

A frown flickered across her forehead as if neither of those situations had ever occurred to her. She turned away and slipped her gown back on before facing him again.

"Making love *is* personal," she said stiffly. "At least to me. I'm not your valet, and I'm not some two-bit strumpet who doesn't care a button about intimacy or if she'll ever see you again. Either we both are naked, or no one shall be. And it appears I am no one."

He grabbed her hand and pressed her palm against his thudding heart. "When I first arrived, your fingers brushed against a folded paper in my breast pocket. Do you know what it is?"

She tugged at her fingers then glared at him when he didn't release his hold. "My letter, I suppose? Requesting you come burn that horrid contract?"

"No." He released his hold. This was not at all how he'd wanted the evening to go. "I've never wanted you to be temporary, Daphne. These weeks with you have been the happiest of my life. I *love* you. I was rather hoping you'd do me the honor of being my wife."

He handed her the folded document, his heart in his eyes.

She opened the parchment without looking at him.

From this angle, he couldn't read the scripted words. Not that it mattered. He already knew what each line said. He ought to. He'd rewritten them dozens of times.

The first draft had read:

BETROTHAL CONTRACT

I, Bartholomew Blackpool, enter willingly and joyfully into a betrothal with Miss Daphne Vaughan. What is mine, is hers.

I pledge to be faithful and loyal. Loving and kind. Joyful and tender. Smitten, until our dying day.

My money is hers to spend. My time is hers to command. My life is hers to share. My love is hers to keep. She already owns my heart.

Signed,
Bartholomew Blackpool

Obviously, it wouldn't do. It was too poetic. Too embarrassingly honest. It appealed to emotions he wasn't certain she shared, rather than to the intelligent mind she preferred over her heart. Daphne was too pragmatic for love. She needed to see how *practical* a union with him would be.

He had regained enough of his old confidence that risking the loss of the *ton*'s good opinion no longer concerned him. Losing Daphne, on the other hand, was the one rejection he wasn't willing to risk. The odds were already against him. She intended to remain unwed. He might only have one chance to change her logical, goal-oriented mind.

After hours of tossing crumpled drafts into the fire, he finally settled upon:

BETROTHAL CONTRACT

> *I, Bartholomew Blackpool, enter willingly into a betrothal with Miss Daphne Vaughan. I pledge to aid her in her endeavors and be an exemplary husband in all things.*
>
> *Anything she needs, she shall receive. Anything she desires, she shall have. Her money remains hers. Her time remains hers. Her freedom remains hers.*
>
> *She and her charity work shall have the full support of my staff, my acquaintances, and myself whenever she has need of us, and complete autonomy when she does not.*
> *Signed,*
> *Bartholomew Blackpool*

He held his breath while she finished reading.

She glanced up at him with empty eyes and tossed it directly into the fire.

His hopes plummeted.

"*Words*," she spat. "You obviously don't mean them."

He reached for her hands, desperation coursing through him. "They're not just words. They're true. We would make a formidable couple. It's an advantageous proposition."

"'Anything she desires, she shall have?'" she quoted, her tone mocking. "I hold nothing. You won't even make love to me properly."

"My love…" Bartholomew felt like his whole world was crumbling to ash. Just like the betrothal contracts in the fire. He had hoped to woo her with romance. With pragmatism. Anything but cold disdain. "Please listen to me. You hold my heart in your hands."

Her eyes were wild, her voice thick with unshed tears. "You were still wearing your boots and your tailcoat. Give me one good reason why anyone would 'make love' in the privacy of a home, wearing boots and a tailcoat."

"You can't possibly understand." His neck heated. "My leg—"

She shoved his chest. "Your leg isn't everything,

Bartholomew! Your leg isn't *anything*."

He shook his head. "You have no idea how unsightly—"

"You have no idea how much I don't *care*." She swept up his cravat and tossed it at his chest. "Your leg is not *you*. Do you know how often I think about your prosthesis? Never. That's how often. I don't worry about it, I don't think about it, I don't care one button." She grabbed her stays up off the floor. "How often do you think about my spectacles? Do you fret when I misplace them and cannot read a word?"

"What?" He blinked at the sudden change in topic. "I don't really notice when you're wearing them or not. Your spectacles have nothing to do with who you *are*."

"Neither does your prosthesis. The End." She made a disgusted expression and turned toward the exit. "There are people out there with real problems. You're no longer one of them."

He clenched his cravat in his fist. "Tip-top condition, am I? Take a closer look. I'm scarcely *fine*." He bounced his ruined knee to make the ankle joint clap. "If I keep myself hidden, it's for a reason."

Daphne unlocked the parlor door, then cast a long, pensive glance at him over her shoulder. "The only person who thinks you a lesser man is *you*." Her lips tightened into a line. "Until you can give a woman everything you still *are*... Well. I wouldn't sign any more betrothal contracts."

She quit the room without another word.

Chapter Twenty-Four

It was raining by the time Bartholomew pulled his landau up in front of his town house.

A footman ran over with an umbrella to walk him into the warm safety of his home, but Bartholomew waved him away. He didn't want to go back inside his dismal, lonely town house. He didn't want to leave his carriage, or come in out of the rain. The only thing he wanted was Daphne.

His fingers clenched. How could she dare compare a missing leg to something as trivial as a pair of spectacles?

He leaned his head against the wall of the landau and sighed. He knew precisely why Daphne would compare a prosthesis to reading spectacles. It wasn't that she considered the two to be of the same relative importance. It was that she didn't see either condition as particularly important in the first place.

It was more than important. It had destroyed his entire life.

Daphne might not find an amputated leg diminishing in any way, but the rest of Bartholomew's peers certainly did. He was a mockery. A cripple. A mere shadow of the man he'd once been. No one could look at him the same way. Even his servants…

He frowned. It was true that he hadn't allowed his valet to assist him since returning from war. His pride couldn't allow himself to be pitied or coddled. But *had* he prevented Fitz from pitying and coddling his disfigured master? Or had he simply prevented his talented valet from performing the normal duties for which any given valet was employed?

Captain Steele hadn't treated Bartholomew like an invalid, but rather, an adversary. He was given no special consideration for having lost a leg, nor treated any differently than the other suitors. When he'd chosen not to go riding with the others, the pirate had mocked Bartholomew's apparent lack of camaraderie, not his impaired horsemanship.

Chauncey Whitfield hadn't acted like Bartholomew was worthless. He'd asked for advice on sparring partners and fighting stances, and reminisced about the old legends. Fairfax, Lambley, Xavier, Sarah... None of them had treated Bartholomew any differently than they'd ever done.

His mother, of course, had made a dramatic fuss over her son's unfortunate condition. But when had she not? Even when Bartholomew and Edmund had been in the peak of youth and health, she'd been convinced her lads were one cough away from consumption and too delicate to withstand the tamest physical activities.

Before, it hadn't been true. And now?

He would never have his leg back, but the rest of his body was as strong or stronger than it had ever been. Whether or not that was enough, it was all he had. His half-leg was unsightly, the strapped-on prosthesis a poor substitute... But there was really only one opinion that mattered.

Daphne's.

She might *say* his disability never so much as crossed her mind—it might even be true!—but there was a wide gulf between the theoretical and the practical. It was easy enough to discount his false leg when it was out of sight beneath layers of clothing. It was another thing entirely to expect Daphne to wish to make love to a man whose leg ended just below the knee.

It was worse than unsightly. It would extinguish her ardor completely.

His prosthesis was the best money could buy, but the leather straps affixing it in place and the hand-carved toes at the end of its foot wouldn't fool a woman looking at him from less than an arm's length away.

Even without her spectacles.

If Daphne truly didn't care... then neither should he. Not if it was keeping them apart.

He *loved* her. If there was still a chance, however slight, that he could convince her to let him at least try to win her heart. He couldn't allow the opportunity to pass him by. He *had* to talk to her.

Bartholomew collected the reins and set his landau on the path back to the Ross town house. The rain slowed his progress. By the time he arrived, his gut churned with more nerves than the first time he'd stepped foot onto a live battlefield.

What could he possibly say that would prove his sincerity? What would he do if she tossed him out, again? If he was unable to change her mind?

He hesitated before alighting from the carriage, torn between racing through the rain and risking a fall, or taking it slow and arriving upon her doorstep a bedraggled mess. Ruining what little was left of his looks wouldn't do much to endear her to his cause.

Hurrying as fast as he dared, he exited the landau and made his way to the front door, where he made good use of the knocker, just as he had done a few hours earlier.

This time, however, the butler was less keen to allow him entry.

Rain trickled down Bartholomew's neck. "I'm here to see Miss Vaughan, please."

The butler stared back at him impassively.

Perhaps the downpour had left him all but unrecognizable. He searched his waistcoat pocket for a dry calling card and came up empty. "I'm—"

"Please wait here, Major Blackpool." The butler turned and disappeared around the corner.

"Thank you," Bartholomew said to the empty entryway.

He checked the floor to see if his clothes were leaking rainwater all over the entryway, but aside from his bootprints, all was clear. He was not as wet as he'd feared, based on the butler's obvious displeasure at his presence.

He consulted his pocket watch and grimaced at the hour. Of course. It was much too late to pay a social call. But the damage was done, and now that he was here—

"Major Blackpool." The female voice that greeted him

belonged not to Daphne, but to her friend, Miss Ross…
whose always-merry face was unnervingly devoid of both
smiles and laughter. "What brings you here?"

"Miss Ross." He bowed with as much grace as he could.
"I was hoping to have a word with Miss Vaughan."

She pursed her lips. "You cannot. Good night."

"Wait," he stammered. "Will you tell her I'll call
tomorrow? What time do you recommend I stop by?"

"I don't. She's leaving at dawn and must keep to a tight
schedule."

He gaped at her. "Leaving? Where is she going?"

Miss Ross shrugged. "If Daphne wished for you to
know, you already would."

True. He tried not to lose heart. "It's imperative that I see
her."

"And she has said that it is imperative that you do not."
Miss Ross's brown eyes filled with pity.

Not for his missing leg, he realized, but for his missing
heart. Somehow that hurt even worse.

"I'm sorry, Major Blackpool. Whatever has occurred
between you and Daphne… She's asleep now, and I shan't
wake her."

He nodded and bowed, for there was nothing else to do
and nothing else to say, and stepped back out into the rain.
The door closed smartly behind him.

Halfway down the front walk, however, he wondered if
all was truly lost. *Was* Daphne asleep? Or might there still be
a few moments to convince her to stay? He squinted at the
upper story.

During their drive in Hyde Park, she'd mentioned that
her guest chamber was the one with a balcony overlooking
the park. Perhaps he could walk that direction, try to see if
any candles still flickered in her windows. If not, he would
have to go home. But if she were still awake… He couldn't
risk losing her.

Ducking his face to the wind and rain, he followed the
street to the corner and crossed over to the park. At this
hour—and in this weather—the park was deserted. More
than one balcony faced this direction, but the room Daphne

was in was obvious.

She was just now rising from what was likely some sort of desk and crossing over to the window. He cupped a hand over his eyes to watch. She closed the curtains without so much as pausing.

He let out his breath. Of course she hadn't seen him. It was so dark outside that the only image she would've seen in the window was the reflection of the fire in the hearth and the flames of her candles. Which were disappearing one by one before his eyes.

His fingers curled in determination. If he waited any longer, she *would* be asleep. But how was he supposed to get to her?

He scanned the facade. If rain weren't sleeting down, turning Mayfair into a slick, mud-splattered danger zone, even more so for someone with a false leg, he'd dash across the street and toss pebbles at her window until she was forced to acknowledge him.

If the trees were perhaps slightly closer to the wrought iron balconies—or if he had worn climbing shoes, and was possessed of two working ankles and two sturdy feet—he'd scale the slippery looking tree closest to her window and vault onto her balcony with acrobatic grace and romantic charm.

Unfortunately, he possessed none of those elements. And he was going to have to do it anyway.

He shoved his sodden hair out of his eyes and marched through the biting rain, across the street and over the lawn to the base of the most adjacent tree. Bless London for being overrun with tall, slender, multi-branched trees perfectly suited for climbing.

Presuming that the climber was not a one-legged ex-rake whose first and only marriage proposal had been burnt on sight by a frustrating, maddening, impossible-not-to-love woman who expected more of him than he believed himself capable of giving.

He reached the base of the tree and shook the rain from his face. The moon was dim. Winter still stalked the city. The spidery branches held few leaves to block dirt and rain from falling into his eyes. He would have to keep them shut. His hands would be occupied with the critical task of not tumbling to the hard, wet ground.

"You can do this," he muttered beneath his breath. "You're a soldier. It's just a tree."

It might as well have been a mountain.

He closed his eyes against the onslaught of rain and stretched for the tallest branch he could close his fingers around.

The bark was familiar beneath his palms, its overlapping patches slick and smooth. He'd climbed thousands of these trees in his youth. He and Edmund had been monkeys, competing to see who could reach the highest peak or lying in wait to leap upon one's unsuspecting twin as he chanced to pass beneath.

In those days, the sensation of the thin sheets of bark crumbling beneath his palms had been no cause for concern. Just part of the adventure.

Tonight, the slightest misstep would prove disastrous.

Not misstep, Bartholomew reminded himself dryly. Since his footing could not be trusted, the trick would be not stepping at all. He would have to pull himself up on the strength of his arms alone.

He gripped the branches as firmly as he could and hoisted his body up off the ground. What would happen if he fell? What would he do if he climbed so high and landed so hard that he knocked his false leg clean off? He would die, that's what he'd do.

But he had no choice. Daphne was worth it.

At home, his strengthening exercises had included half an hour of using his arms to pull his chin level with a horizontal iron bar. Unlike branches, the iron bar was sturdy and dry, with neither nettles nor peeling scraps of bark slipping beneath his palms. The bedchamber floor was never more than a mere foot away.

Without allowing time to second-guess himself, he wrapped his thighs around the trunk of the tree and reached for the next highest branches. This hoist required more maneuvering, as he needed to work his leg up and over the previous branches in order to slowly rise to the next. And the next.

And the next.

Breathing hard, he pulled himself higher, bit by bit. The branches grew thinner and closer together, making each hard-won inch harder and harder to achieve.

He squinted to check his progress. Close. And yet too far. His heart sank. He was high enough in the tree that he could now look down onto the balcony. Sort of. Leaping onto its slick, narrow tile *would* have been straightforward.

If he could release his stranglehold on the branches and trust his feet to launch him in the correct direction. He couldn't. But he hadn't come this far just to slink home without trying. He wouldn't forgive himself if Daphne left London without ever knowing how much she meant to him.

He took a deep breath and jumped.

He even almost made it.

His fingers grappled for the vertical iron bars of the balustrade. The weight of his body and the momentum from springing through the air made it impossible to hold tight. His fists slid down with lightning speed, burning his palms. He pulled up short when the base of his hands slammed against the sharp edge of the tiles. His body swung forward from the momentum, weakening his grip.

He dangled there for a moment, to catch his breath. If he let himself fall now, he would almost certainly catch one of his legs beneath him at a truly unpleasant angle.

The only direction to go was up.

He bent an elbow, shifting his balance to one side and then swung his weight toward the other. He released his free hand briefly in order to grasp the iron bar a few inches higher up. Using his body like a pendulum, he repeated the process, letting each alternating fist move a few inches higher.

At last, the edge of his hand brushed the top of the railing. With a grunt, he hauled himself up and over, and landed on his good foot in an awkward crouch.

He was half tempted to lay flat upon the tile, rain and all, until his heart stopped pounding and his icy fingers regained feeling.

No such luck. The curtain swung open.

Daphne stared out at him from the other side of the glass with her lips parted and her eyes wide with shock.

He lifted his aching arm and waved.

She unlatched the window and pushed it open wide. "Are you *mad?* What on earth... *How* on earth?"

He gripped the sill and hiked himself into her bedchamber. "Hullo, Daphne. Did I wake you?"

She pushed at his chest, her hands shaking. "What were you thinking?"

"That I wanted to see you. I did attempt more traditional methods first, but Miss Ross implied you would never again receive my call, and since you were leaving at first light, I figured—"

"—that you would scale a *town house* in the middle of the night and pop in via my balcony?" She shoved her head out the window and paled. Her breath was ragged. She closed the glass violently and sagged against it. Her eyes flashed. "It's *raining*, you daft man. What if the railing had given way? What if you'd *fallen?"*

"I've already fallen," he said quietly. "I'm in love with you, Daphne. You're my first thought every morning and my last thought every night. Marry me. Please."

She pushed away from the window, away from him. "I told you—"

He stepped in her path. "You think I haven't given myself to you, not completely. That I'm afraid to bare my body. Look at me, darling. I'm baring my soul. I give you everything I have."

She peered up at him warily. It was all he could do not to pull her into his arms and kiss her. But he needed more than her kisses. He needed her trust. Her love.

Desperate, he stepped over beside the fire, to place himself fully in its light. "What do you see before you? A rakehell who cares naught for your feelings? Or do you see the man who once fancied himself more fashionable than Brummell, standing before you a sodden mess, just to speak with you? Just to beg you for your hand?"

She crossed her arms beneath the bodice of her nightrail,

but her gaze tracked down his tattered finery, then back up to his eyes.

He yanked off his ruined cravat and tossed it to the floor. "Marry me."

Wordlessly, she shook her head.

He shucked off his wet greatcoat, its tailored seams irreparably split and ragged. "Marry me."

She shook her head.

As he unbuttoned his waistcoat, his fingers shook as much with nervousness as with fatigue from the strain he'd put them through. If only she could see what she was doing to him. What he was doing for her. He tossed the waistcoat aside. "Marry me."

She shook her head.

He crossed his arms at his waist and peeled his white linen undershirt up and over his head, the once-billowing material wet from rain and exertion. His chest was bare, the muscle flecked with scars. "Marry me."

She stared at him in determined silence.

He yanked the chair out from her escritoire and sank down onto it to tug off his boots and stockings. First, the good foot. Then the false one. He steeled himself for her reaction. "Marry me."

Her expression didn't change.

He unfastened his breeches, shoving them down over his bare arse, over his ruined knee, over the leather-strapped prosthesis he hated with every thunderous beat of his heart. Shaking, he hurled the breeches across the room and rose to his feet. Completely naked. Bared to the soul. "Marry me."

Her gaze heated. She reached behind her neck and untied her nightrail. It fluttered to the floor.

Every inch of his body was instantly alive, the cold and fear forgotten. He stepped forward. She hadn't said yes. But she hadn't said no. There was still hope. He pulled her into his arms and crushed his lips to hers. "Marry me."

She wrapped her arms tight about his neck and kissed him. Her tongue was warm honey, her body heaven against his. Soft. Beautiful.

He lifted her up and set her bottom on the edge of the

four-poster bed. Her hips now perfectly aligned with his. He couldn't get enough of her mouth, her taste. He kissed her as though he were starving, and her love the only thing that could sustain him. She made him live again.

Gently, he slid his hands up over her hips, past the curve of her waist, to the edge of her breasts. She leaned into his touch. His shaft pulsed between them as he teased her already hard nipples and his tongue mated with hers. Without her, he was nothing. With her, she made him whole.

"Marry me," he whispered between kisses.

He slipped one of his hands between her legs and slid two fingers into her slick heat. *She wanted him.* Even after seeing him naked. She didn't think him broken at all. He lowered his mouth to her breast, suckling as he drove his fingers inside her. She clutched his hair, trapping him to her.

She needn't have worried. He was hers, forever.

He slid his slick fingers from her, and she whimpered. He gently pushed her backward, then sank to his knees to lave with his tongue and bring her to pleasure. He would love her until she loved him back. He would love her into eternity.

She gasped, and arched into his mouth. As he licked and suckled, her legs began to tremble, holding him in place. He joined his fingers to his tongue, licking, invading, loving. She cried out, legs shaking, her muscles tightening about his fingers.

Before her contractions had even ceased, she struggled upright and tugged his hair so that he would rise to his feet. Her skin was flushed, her eyes glassy with pleasure. His heart flipped. He hoped to bring her to ecstasy for the rest of their lives.

She widened her legs and reached for his shaft. At first, hesitant. Then bolder. Squeezing. Stroking. He closed his eyes and tried to keep breathing. Each touch, each stroke, sent shivers of desire through his body. *This* was the woman he wanted beside him for the rest of eternity.

When she began to rub his shaft against her cleft, his heart jumped. She was ready to make love. This time, so was he.

He slid a hand into her hair, cradling her head to devour

her with passionate kisses. With his other hand, he guided his shaft to her opening. Before entering, he paused to get her attention. "I'm sorry… This may sting."

She licked his lower lip and smiled. "You'll make it feel better."

Or die trying.

He swept his tongue into her mouth and grasped her by the hips. Slowly, gently, he rocked into her inch by careful inch.

She gasped once, but held him even tighter until his shaft was fully seated within her. Her kisses became more heated. He hesitated, wanting to give her body time to get accustomed to being stretched like this. She wiggled against him, indicating she had no wish to keep waiting.

Thank God.

Still gripping her hips, he drew almost completely out, then drove himself back inside. She dug her fingernails into his shoulders. His heartbeat doubled. She was perfect for him. He wanted to be the same for her.

He slid a hand down so that his thumb could tease her nub as his shaft pistoned within her. Spine arching, her head lolled backward and her eyelids fluttered in pleasure. His body tightened in response, longing for release.

He lowered his mouth to her neck and touched his tongue to her throat. Her pulse raced as rapidly as his own. The proof of her desire was everywhere. The passion blurring her eyes. The slick wetness at her core. The spice of lovemaking in the air. But the proof of her love was still locked in her heart.

His muscles tightened as something unfurled in his chest. He *wasn't* an incomplete man. Not any longer. He kissed her deeply. Thanks to Daphne, he had finally found himself again. Was able to *give* himself fully. Her legs tightened about his hips, their softness only making him harder. His blood pounded as he took her mouth with kisses. He had never felt so alive.

"Here I am," he said as his shaft surged within her. "I bare myself before you. I give myself to you completely. What you see is what I am. This is all that I have to offer."

Her eyes met his, stormy and passionate. She slid her fingers deeper into his hair.

"I *love* what I see. I love what I feel." Her inner muscles clenched against him as she rocked against him. "You've always been enough, Bartholomew. There is no one I want more."

"Then marry me," he begged desperately as his hips slammed into hers. He wouldn't be able to hold out much longer. "*Please.*"

Her fingers tightened in his hair and she gasped into his mouth. "Only if you promise to do this every night."

Victory shot through him. *She'd said yes.* "With pleasure."

The moment she arched and her inner muscles contracted about him, he welcomed his own climax at last, releasing himself into her with every thrust of his hips, every beat of his heart. Spent, he cradled her in his arms and held her close.

He had always been hers.

And now, finally, she was his.

Chapter Twenty-Five

The next afternoon, Bartholomew and his very real fiancée made the trek to Maidstone to visit his parents. With Daphne at his side, he was finally ready to face his brother's empty grave.

His parents met them at the small gravesite at the far end of the garden.

His mother held flowers. His father held his hat to his chest. Bartholomew held tight to Daphne's hand.

A few months earlier, he hadn't thought himself strong enough to face this moment. To face his devastated parents, or the accusing letters carved into his brother's tombstone.

It wasn't easy.

He would never forgive himself for failing to save his twin. Nor did he deserve his parents' forgiveness, or Sarah's. He had failed to keep Edmund safe. Failed to bring him home at all. There was no need for a false grave to remind him of what he'd lost. He lived with that failure every single day.

Daphne handed him a clutch of flowers they'd clipped together that morning.

He accepted them with cold fingers, and went to join his mother and father before the chiseled stone. Before laying the flowers on the undisturbed ground, he turned to his parents. Daphne was right. They *did* love him. Even though Edmund's death was on his shoulders.

"I'm sorry," he said brokenly. "I'm sorry I failed you. I'm sorry I couldn't save him. I'm sorry I ever suggested we give up our foolish rakish lives and purchase a commission to go fight that godforsaken army. I'm sorry I—"

"Son." His father's brow creased as he laid a hand on

Bartholomew's arm. "We never blamed you. Edmund was his own person. His death is not your fault."

Bartholomew felt as if the world had ceased spinning.

"My darling boy." His mother wrung her pale hands. "We *all* lost Edmund that day. Not just your father and me. You lost your *twin*. And I... we... I'm your mother, and I couldn't *fix* it. I couldn't make anything better. I put up this stone to at least give us *something*, a symbolic way to unite our family again. But I made it worse. We were still broken. You stopped speaking to me. Your father stopped eating. We were lost. A mother is supposed to keep her family together, and I failed all of you."

Bartholomew's heart cracked. He reached for his mother and hugged her tight. "You never did, Mama. You never did."

"I was no better," his father said gruffly. "I didn't know what to say or what to do. Everything I tried came out wrong. I couldn't console my wife. I couldn't even console myself. We weren't avoiding you, son. I thought you'd heal faster without us."

"No one can heal without their family," Bartholomew said quietly. It had taken him a long time to figure it out. "Healing *is* family. It's letting other people in, even when you're angry or frightened."

His father's arms wrapped around them both. "Forgive me, son."

Bartholomew held them close. "There is nothing to forgive. We're a family again. From now on, we'll miss him together."

Epilogue

They had the wedding in Maidstone, in the nave of her father's church.

Daphne couldn't have imagined a better location. Her only regret was that neither her father nor Bartholomew's brother were still alive to share the moment with them. Her husband's parents were thrilled, however, and their happy excitement made the ceremony just as joyful.

Afterward, with her hand tucked inside her husband's, they made their way to his carriage. Bartholomew had managed to politely decline his mother's repeated invitation to move in with them, but settled on having the wedding breakfast at his parents' house instead.

Daphne begged him to swing by the vicarage before continuing on to the Blackpool estate, in order to thank the servants who had risked their employment to mail her the stolen betrothal contract. They had valued her happiness above their own, and deserved to know that she was absolutely, positively, euphoric. She was in love with a man who was in love with her. They would forge their future together.

Nothing could have made her happier.

As the landau approached the old vicarage, Bartholomew turned to her with a nostalgic smile. "The last time I directed my carriage to this address, I hadn't anticipated pitting myself against three men and a pirate for the chance to win your hand."

She licked the lobe of his ear. "You won then, and you won now. There was never any contest."

"Of course not. You were destined to be mine." His grin was all arrogance. "Did you ever see Fairfax or Whitfield again, after that?"

She frowned and shook her head. "They were obviously not as ardent of admirers as they might've had me believe. The only gentleman I saw again was the Duke of Lambley, and that's only because he's Katherine's cousin."

"He waltzed with you," Bartholomew reminded her, pulling a jealous face. "Very badly done of you. You'll note *I* manage to refrain from waltzing with *my* cousins' affianced friends."

She leaned against his side. "It was just dancing. If you must know, Lambley didn't act particularly disappointed not to have been able to press his suit. He never even mentioned it."

"It would've been bad form to have done so." Bartholomew cast her a look of angelic innocence. "Only the most lovesick of swains would have pursued you up a tree and over a balcony in the rain."

She kissed his cheek and whispered, "If you ever do anything that foolish again, I'll kill you."

Within moments, they pulled up before the vicarage. Bartholomew leaped out of the carriage to circle around and hand her down. They had scarcely reached the front door when it swung open from within.

Captain Steele stood there to greet them, wine glass in hand. "Good morning, lovebirds. Lost, are we? Now that my ward is married, this is no longer her direction."

Daphne blinked up at him. "How did you know—"

"How wouldn't I know?" Captain Steele wiggled his brows. "I sent you the betrothal contract, didn't I?"

Her mouth fell open. "*You* sent the contract?"

"No one else could have done. The first thing I did when I inherited this old place was change the combination to the safe." He swirled his glass of port. "Besides, 'twas your birthday. What with that pittance you call an inheritance, I figured either you'd marry the man you'd rushed into a betrothal with, or you wouldn't't."

She nearly choked in outrage. "*Rushed* into a betrothal? You were the one who invited a random assortment of completely unsuitable men in order to pack me off to the first bidder—"

"Not precisely." Captain Steele cleared his throat and flashed a mischievous smile. "I may have implied that was the case to *you*, my dear, but Mr. Whitfield and Mr. Fairfax hadn't the least idea of your existence before they arrived on these premises."

"Then why—"

"Believe it or not, a man can have business with another man that does not involve marrying one of the lads off to his termagant cousin." He sipped his port. "I *did* invite Lambley for you, though not as a suitor. I told him you had become quite despondent when your father died. After that heart-wrenching rejection you'd sent in response to that Ross chit's soirée invitation—"

"You read my letter to Katherine?" she sputtered.

He arched his eyebrows. "I read all your letters, *Mr. Caldwell*. Or are we Mr. Smith today?"

Her cheeks heated. Of course he had read her letters.

"At all events," Captain Steele continued. "I told Lambley what a wet blanket it was to have you mope around all maudlin, locking yourself in your chamber for days on end, pretending to be bourgeois gentlemen and whatnot. Didn't seem healthy. I thought the duke might be able to cheer you up, or at least talk you into going somewhere else. Your depression was beginning to wear on my nerves."

"Then why did you tell me you intended to give me to one of those men?" she demanded. "You threatened me with *Bedlam* if I didn't comply."

"I knew you'd have none of it, of course." He drained the last of his port. "As inventive and stubborn as you are in fighting for your 'causes', I knew my best hope for marrying you off was tricking you into doing it yourself. You sent for Major Blackpool here within minutes of my little fib, and you brought him up to scratch quite nicely, I daresay. Well done."

Her mouth fell open. She slanted a disbelieving gaze toward her husband. "I cannot credit that he lied about forcing me into an unwanted betrothal just so I'd pick someone I *did* want."

"That *is* devious," Bartholomew admitted. He swung her into his arms and spun them toward the carriage. "But I can't say I'm displeased with the outcome."

"What are you doing?" she hissed into his shoulder. "You can't just pick me up and turn our backs on the captain without so much as a by-your-leave."

"Why not? I'm sure he does that sort of thing all the time," Bartholomew answered drolly as they reached the landau. "'Tis our wedding day, my love. If you'll recall, you had me make you a certain… promise?"

Her neck flushed as she remembered the feel of him driving into her as he begged her to marry him. How she'd wanted him to make love to her again and again. She settled herself into the carriage and curved her lips into a seductive smile. "I believe you vowed quite convincingly that you'd be interested in repeating the act?"

"Quite interested," he agreed. He swung onto the seat beside her and stole her breath with a heated kiss. "Every day for the rest of our lives."

She spread her fingers over his chest. "And every night?"

"And every minute." He wrapped his fingers about the reins and glanced over his shoulder at the empty road. "I can park this carriage around the next corner if you'd prefer not to wait for a proper bed."

She grinned wickedly and slid her hand into her husband's lap. "Perhaps you'd better."

They arrived forty-five minutes late to their own wedding breakfast, and quite suspiciously disheveled.

But they couldn't have looked happier.

The End

Thank You For Reading

I hope you enjoyed this story!

Sign up at EricaRidley.com/club99
for members-only freebies
and new releases for 99 cents!

Reviews help other readers like you.

Reviews help readers find books that are right for them.
Please consider leaving a review wherever you purchased
this book, or on your favorite review site.

Let's be friends! Find Erica on:

www.EricaRidley.com
facebook.com/EricaRidley
twitter.com/EricaRidley
pinterest.com/Erica_Ridley

**Did you know there are more
books in this series?**

This romance is part of
the Dukes of War
regency-set historical series.

Join the Dukes of War facebook group for
giveaways and exclusive content:
http://facebook.com/groups/DukesOfWar

In order, the Dukes of War books are:

The Viscount's Christmas Temptation
The Earl's Defiant Wallflower
The Captain's Bluestocking Mistress
The Major's Faux Fiancée
The Brigadier's Runaway Bride
The Pirate's Tempting Stowaway
The Duke's Accidental Wife

**Other Romance Novels
by Erica Ridley:**

Too Wicked To Kiss
Too Sinful To Deny
Let It Snow
Dark Surrender

About the Author

Erica Ridley learned to read when she was three, which was about the same time she decided to be an author when she grew up.

Now, she's a *USA Today* bestselling author of historical romance novels. Her latest series, The Dukes of War, features roguish peers and dashing war heroes who return from battle only to be thrust into the splendor and madness of Regency England.

When not reading or writing romances, Erica can be found riding camels in Africa, zip-lining through rainforests in Central America, or getting hopelessly lost in the middle of Budapest.

For more information, please visit her website at www.EricaRidley.com.

Acknowledgments

As always, I could not have written this book without the invaluable support of my critique partners. Huge thanks go out to Darcy Burke, Emma Locke, Jackie Barbosa, and Morgan Sneed for their advice and encouragement.

I also want to thank my incredible street team (the Light-Skirts Brigade rocks!!) and all the readers in the Dukes of War facebook group. Your enthusiasm makes the romance happen.

Thank you so much!

9 781517 070816